VIOLET SKIES

BRENDA POPPY

First published by Glass Fish Publishing 2024

First edition
ISBN: 978-1-7356181-9-7

Cover artwork by Wes Cathon.

www.glassfishpublishing.com

For the outsiders, the weirdos, and the misfits.

For all those who dream in Technicolor.

Prologue

Violet stood above the body, her hands dripping with blood. Splashes of red dotted her chest, disappearing into the matte black of her gown. She could smell it in the air, feel it drying on her skin. She could even taste it on her lips, the harsh metallic flavor staining her tongue with guilt.

What had she done?

The man lay unmoving at her feet, face up, with a dagger plunged straight through his heart. Violet's own heart was shrieking beneath her chest, pumping panic through her veins. In contrast, the room around her was quiet and still, with nary a soul to be seen.

In the distance, sirens screamed to life, fracturing the deathly silence. The mournful melody called out across the ship, echoing Violet's distress.

She froze, waiting for the song to fade and the spell to break, but destiny had other plans. The cry strengthened and sharpened until certainty rang through Violet's bones. The

Guards were coming for her.

How did they know?

Violet's gaze flicked from the body to the locked door and back. It was only a matter of time before they burst in, thrusting their weapons in her face, then leading her away to her fate.

The only problem was that she hadn't done it. Or had she?

She couldn't seem to remember. No matter how hard she tried, the last few minutes remained shrouded in an unholy fog, black and menacing. Violet shivered as doubt trickled down her spine, branching out to twist her stomach into knots.

She scoured the ceiling, the walls, the floor, but there was no way in – and no way out. Towering shelves crowded her on all sides, their books the only witness to the crime.

No one could save her.

Heavy footsteps thudded against wood floors, ticking down the time until the end. Violet sank to her knees amidst the growing pool of blood. She bowed her head, like a convict at the guillotine waiting for the blade.

The Guards didn't bother knocking. Instead, they crashed against the door, splintering the wood. It gave way with a resounding crack, revealing Violet stooped beside the senator's body and drenched in his blood.

Chapter 1

Three Days Earlier

Violet tucked herself into the delicate curves of shadow at the edge of the stage. Beneath the curtains, a sliver of light dipped and danced, beckoning like a lover in the night. A hum suffused the scene, spiking each breath with the sweetness of anticipation. It was almost time.

The purr of voices, the heady longing, and the intoxicating gusts of alcohol-tinged air made the world melt away, dripping into a hazy dream. Up here, there was no past, no future, only the here and now, brilliantly alive and agonizingly fleeting. For a time, you could forget your worries, your burdens, yourself.

Except Violet didn't need help forgetting. She'd already lost a lifetime.

The darkness clawed at her memory like it always did, her old friend and stalwart companion. It held her tight, its emptiness coating her completely. Reflexively, she prodded at its edges, searching for a hint of memory, but it resisted her efforts, giving her nothing but echoes of a former life.

The sound of footsteps pulled Violet from her thoughts. She collected herself, stowing her emotions behind a cool façade and the barest hint of a smile.

Sable drew up behind her, placing a hand on the small of her back in an intimate gesture. The warmth of it seeped through the thin fabric of her silky green dress, sending a shiver across her skin.

Bending his head to her ear, he whispered, "Burn bright, my little star," before gliding through the curtains and onto the stage.

The buzz of conversation eased as a spotlight shimmered to life, illuminating Sable in all his glory.

"Ladies and gentlemen," he began, his voice sultry and low. "Welcome to the Alcor Club, home to the best drinks and *live* entertainment in the galaxy."

The crowd chuckled hungrily, eager for the show. The Alcor Club was, indeed, rare – one of the only venues on the Echelon that still employed flesh and blood performers rather than flawless holographic beauties. Most clubs didn't bother. Tech was cheap, they reasoned, and it didn't talk back when you asked it to bend the rules of morality.

For some, though, *real* music would always win – even with its flaws. Which is why the Alcor Club remained such a draw, filling to capacity almost every evening.

"Tonight's entertainment is truly something special. If you haven't yet had the pleasure of hearing her sing, you are in for a treat. Please join me in welcoming our very own vixen, Violet, to the stage."

A chorus of applause, hoots, and whistles rose as the

room sank back into darkness. When the spotlight flickered to life again, it found Violet stationed in the center of the stage, her hands resting lightly on an old-fashioned microphone stand.

She began with a ballad, mournful and gray. The music flowed through her like oxygen, the notes as natural as breathing. With a simple melody to guide her, she wove a story of love, of desire, of despair. The audience stood transfixed, their eyes glazed with the sheen of memory, the lust of fantasy, the thirst of envy.

Violet moved her hips in time with the music, and the crowd swayed in tandem, hypnotized by the sight. Some wanted to be her, others to hold her, yet more to own her. But up on stage, she was untouchable, an idea more than a person, a dream made real for an evening.

It was intoxicating. As one song bled into another, Violet could feel the crowd shift. Their dazes turned to dancing, their desire to delight, and the room transformed into a realm of blissful chaos.

For song after song, Violet held them in thrall, guiding their emotions and directing their thoughts. Power flowed through her as she fed on their attention, devouring their devotion. By the end of her set, a euphoria had settled over her, flooding her system with the most wonderful high.

She glided offstage to passionate applause and drunken calls for more. It was better to leave them wanting than full, to keep them coming back for one more bite. Night after night.

Violet's cravings leaned in a different direction, though. She needed a drink.

Changing out of her slinky ensemble, she made her way to the bar, quickly catching sight of Sable's familiar form. He was slinging drinks alongside several server droids, chatting – and flirting – as he worked. A swarm of thirsty patrons clustered around him, ogling his muscled arms and the line of inky designs that disappeared beneath his fitted shirt.

Violet had never asked about them, but she'd noticed prison markings among the dark patterns, indicating at least one tour in the Grove. She wondered what he'd done to deserve such a sentence – and what it had done to him in return.

Sable turned his gaze on her, and her thoughts vanished, replaced by a sudden warmth. He finished shaking some concoction, then sauntered over, giving Violet his full attention. The heat in it crept up her neck and threatened to spill out in a blush across her cheeks, but she held it at bay.

"You were great up there, V," he said, using the nickname she reserved for friends – and lovers. Although, for the time being, Sable remained firmly in the first category. Not that he hadn't tried to change her mind.

"I know," V replied, cocking her head in a smug display. "Although I could bring in even more business if you gave me more shifts."

Sable shook his head slowly, not breaking eye contact. "You know you're not the only act on my roster, V. I have to give everyone their time in the spotlight. Besides, you don't want to serve your best wine every day. People would get spoiled."

Violet didn't respond. While it was a flattering sentiment, she didn't appreciate being compared to wine – no matter how fine.

As she debated how to turn the conversation in her favor, a reedy figure took a seat beside her, his proximity demanding her attention. She turned ever so slightly toward him, taking in his graying hair, his red-rimmed eyes, his swaying form.

V sighed, all too familiar with what came next. Sable busied himself making drinks, still managing to keep a protective eye on her. It was sweet, but V could handle this on her own.

"You're wonderful," the man said, steadying himself against the bar. "That voice, that hair, those legs."

He ran a finger down the side of her thigh, and indignation rose bright and scorching in her chest. She tamped it down, adopting a mask of composure.

"How about I buy you a drink, beautiful?" he slurred, moving his hand up to rest on her waist. "Or we could get out of here. Go somewhere a bit more…interesting. I know where we can find an anti-grav chamber if you're up for some fun."

V swallowed her first response, which included several violent expletives. Ignoring all her instincts, she leaned in closer, drawing her lips to his ear.

Dropping her voice, she whispered, "I would rather throw myself out of the airlock and suffocate than spend one more minute with you. Now, kindly remove your hand from my waist before I decide to remove it for you." She squeezed his wrist to emphasize the words, feeling bones shift beneath her fingers.

The man's eyes went wide and he scrambled off his chair, scurrying away like the rodent he was. V turned back to the

7

bar to find Sable watching her with interest.

"You could have at least let him buy you a drink before kicking him to the curb," he said, amused.

"Oh, he's buying me a drink, alright," V said, tossing several units onto the bar. "Get me a freeze," she demanded. "Or two."

"V…" Sable said, drawing out the letter in warning. "You've got to stop doing that. The Guards don't take kindly to theft, and the Grove is no place for someone like you."

Sable's comment bounced off V's skin, barely leaving a scratch. She'd been stealing for as long as she could remember. Although, to be fair, her memory only went back a year or so. But in that time, she'd honed her skills to near perfection, teaching her fingers to slide gracefully into pockets and purses. Now she could steal almost anything – given it was small and concealed in an easy-to-reach place on someone's person.

"Start paying me more and I'll stop," V teased. "Cross my heart." When Sable didn't respond, she repeated, "Freeze. Now."

Sable sighed and shifted away, pouring two shots of an ice blue liquid. He slid one across the bar to her, saving the other for himself. They shared a look, then downed the drinks in one gulp, wincing as the liquor shocked their systems.

A familiar frosty feeling awoke in V's gut before branching out, shooting icicles up her chest and into her arms. Prickles danced across her skin as it finally reached her brain, freezing her synapses and bringing the world to a halt. Time slowed for a few glorious moments before snapping back into place.

A buzz lingered in her system, tingling in her veins. Gradually opening her eyes, she glanced up at Sable, tracing the smudged outlines of his torso up to his face. He was beautiful – and he knew it. His black hair fell in waves to rest lightly on his shoulders, and his perfectly manicured stubble accentuated his strong jaw.

Sable's slate gray eyes stared back with a mixture of hunger and amusement, a question clearly written on his face. V shook her head with the barest hint of movement. Sable just shrugged, his shaggy eyebrows lifting as he smirked. By now, he was used to her rejection.

Suddenly, an alarm sounded, deep and resonant. The note endured for several seconds, until its chorus could be felt in every corner of the room. Then it stopped, cutting to an oppressive silence before the world sprang to life.

V groaned as patrons shuffled around her, downing their drinks and collecting their coats. And, of course, making their final – mostly futile – attempts to lure each other to bed. Sable, on the other hand, turned his attention to the crowd, attempting to speed their egress with a few words of encouragement.

"Curfew is approaching," he said in his booming voice. "Gather your things and go. Any stragglers will be forcibly removed and left to the mercy of the sentries."

Thankfully, the gathered crowd obeyed, filing out steadily onto the street. Violet, too, grabbed her bag and stood, shooting one last look at Sable before joining the queue.

Outside, the weather was balmy – or as balmy as it ever got on the Echelon. The ship's faux sky depicted the dying rays of sunset, with darkness quickly overtaking the light.

It was meant to be summer, although up here, in the midst of space, seasons were relative. Summer, spring, winter, and fall all blended together in a mess of fabricated days and nights, with only mild swings in temperature to distinguish them.

V didn't care much either way. By this point, seasons were mere stories told to frighten children, fraught with foes made of rain and snow, wind and fire, of vile forces that could obliterate homes, destroy continents, and ruin planets. Generations had passed since anyone had felt the bite of frost or walked in a cool summer rain. Yet for some reason they couldn't abandon the pretense.

Despite the relative heat, Violet drew up her hood and stuffed her hands into her pockets. On either side of the street, shops were shooing away patrons, lowering their iron gates, and powering down their brilliantly colored signs. In a matter of minutes, the world turned from luminous to gray, losing its neon glow and receding slowly into shadow.

Drawing up to the sole checkpoint along her route, V held out her left arm to the scanner, exposing the black tattoo that marred the milky skin of her wrist. The simple symbol served as her identification and her permit to pass. It was also the only thing she knew about herself – the only link to her name, her provenance, and her past.

The system processed her scan in an instant, cataloging her entrance before allowing her through. V moved on, pulling her sleeve back down to cover her wrist. Around her, countless others did the same, timing their movements one after another like a wordless, choreographed dance.

V arrived home mere minutes before the alarm sounded

again, signaling the start of curfew. She shuffled inside, letting the door slide shut behind her as she began her trek up four flights of stairs.

Home was a generous term for the building in which she lived. Without memory or family – or money – she hadn't exactly had the best pick of properties. From the outside, it was neat and pristine, like most of the Echelon. But inside was a different story.

Holes dotted the ceiling, walls, and floors, providing convenient passageways for rodents and their winged friends. Plaster littered the floorboards like some avant-garde creation, and each step shook more free, adding depth to the decrepit masterpiece.

The door to her apartment creaked as she opened it, announcing her presence. She didn't try to dampen the sound, praying it would give her roommate enough of a warning to hide anything he didn't want seen – or anyone. Yet for once, Mouse seemed to be away, allowing her the rarity of solitude and free reign of their glorious abode.

In reality, the space was just one large room, with a minuscule bathroom tucked off to one side. Several moldering cabinets had been salvaged from the dump to form their kitchen, offset by a dented aluminum countertop and three stools with varying degrees of stability.

Farther back, a sagging yellow couch lay opposite a yawning window. Like always, V found herself drawn to the opening, to the darkening city, to the bleak and desolate lanes.

Buildings stretched for miles, like a forest of glass and steel. Their lights had stopped blinking, their screens had died, and their holographic signs had vanished from the sky, leaving the ship shrouded in gray.

V savored the stillness, letting the calm wash over her in waves. She breathed deeply, the sharp tinge of rust and the earthy scent of mold tickling her senses. The familiar sounds of footsteps, music, and murmured voices flowed through the thin walls to create a soundtrack of life, a background din that centered V in the here and now.

Yet she could never hide for long. The past's gnarled fingers closed around her shoulder, forcing her to turn, to look, to stare into the darkness in search of light. The last year stood bright and sharp within her mind, but beyond that lay a world of shadows, of smudges begging for shape and figures pleading for faces.

V strained to grasp the edges of memory, but her fingers found only ghosts. Tendrils of her life hung around her like smoke, hauntingly intangible, and the harder she tried to remember, the faster they slipped away.

V dragged herself out, rubbing her face as if it could rub away the hunger. She had spent months combing the ship for a hint of her life, her family, herself, and it had nearly consumed her. She couldn't go down that path again.

Stalking over to the wall, she tapped lightly on the screen bordering the window, and the scene changed from a dismal cityscape to a tranquil blue sea, lit by the light of a plump white moon. Stars glittered above the water, their reflection tossed about by the gentle waves. The rhythmic sounds of the surf and the quiet call of gulls flooded the apartment, transforming it into its own small island, with V as its only inhabitant.

With her demons suitably sedated, V made her way to the side of the room, tapping a small white button on the wall. A panel broke free, sliding neatly into the floor at her feet and revealing a cozy sleeping compartment. She turned the button and pressed again, this time freeing a drawer from its plastered prison.

V donned her pajamas and slid into bed, shivering at its cool embrace. She drew up her rough blankets, inhaling the scent of soap and home, before commanding the compartment to close. It did as it was told, slowly cutting off the light and submerging her in shadows.

Chapter 2

Violet woke with a scream. A cold sweat had broken out on the back of her neck, and its beads trickled down her body, carrying remnants of unease.

She struggled to untangle herself from the blankets, which had wound around her legs like shackles. Her breathing was ragged and her heart stuttered, beating out the aftershocks of terror.

She was safe. It wasn't real. It was never real.

V released the wall holding her hostage and spilled out into the apartment, freeing herself from her tomb and its monsters. The space beyond was dim, but the light from the faux moon illuminated its corners and edges, holding true darkness at bay.

She had known the nightmares would come. They always did. No matter where she was, they found her, sinking into her subconscious and drowning her in twisted dreams. Except they didn't feel like dreams. They felt alive, crawling with sights and sounds so tangible that they tore at the fabric of reality.

Sometimes there were monsters, rotting creatures with too long limbs and tongues designed to kill. Sometimes there were people, beautiful beyond belief but dripping with blood until it flowed in rivers around her. Sometimes there were children, with eyes stained black and mouths agape, straining with withered arms to grab her.

But tonight there had been no monsters, no children, only her – paralyzed and numb, unable to move or speak as faceless figures sliced her skin and stole her blood. She had struggled to wrench herself from their grasp, to scream, to run, but they'd held her down, laughing at her panic.

Eventually, she'd broken loose, running, tripping, then falling into a pitch-black pit. The drop had lasted forever, one moment stretched so tight that it vibrated in V's bones. Then she'd landed, crashing into obscurity, which had closed in on her from all sides. The walls, the ceiling, and the floors had been coated in a buzzing blackness that seeped into her veins like tar, binding her to that living prison.

V shook her head, trying to clear the images from her mind. Unsurprisingly, it didn't help. She needed something stronger. She needed to run.

Grabbing her clothes, she turned, only then spotting the figures in Mouse's bed. In the dim light, she could only discern the outlines of bodies, but she counted three, criss-crossed and intertwined, with limbs overflowing from the den.

V just shook her head at that, as well. He was tempting fate by returning after curfew, but that was his business, and

V knew he could take care of himself.

She changed quickly, then slipped into the night, pulling a dark hood over her short blond bob. She scanned the area cautiously, searching for sentries, before stepping out onto the street. With a deep breath, she leapt into a run.

The tightness in her chest loosened as she devoured the ground beneath her feet. Each step drove her dreams further from her thoughts, casting them out into the night, and the melody of her heartbeat sang through her body, calming her mind.

She had discovered early on that she could, in fact, outrun her demons. Figuring out how to evade the sentries had taken longer. The small, floating spheres patrolled the city at night, prowling the ship for errant citizens. But their patterns were predictable – and their cameras imperfect – and V had long since learned how to plan around them.

Now the only thing left to worry about was her thoughts. The pounding of her steps, the beating of her heart, and the soft whoosh of her breath always seemed to pull her back to the beginning.

One Year Earlier

Violet woke up on the street, the hard pavement biting into her back. The few pedestrians that sauntered by noticed but didn't speak, their frowns and sneers berating her with silent judgment.

She struggled to sit, every cell and particle protesting

the move. She felt broken and bruised, like every bone in her body had cracked and every muscle had torn, yet her skin showed no signs of injury.

The questions settled over her like a fine layer of grime, coating her in confusion. Where was she? How had she gotten here? And how was she supposed to get home?

Home. The concept felt fuzzy in her mind, its edges dancing just beyond her reach. She dug through her thoughts, combing the grains of sand for a hint, but the deeper she looked the emptier she grew.

She had no home, no family, no name. She was no one.

She turned, hunting for her face in the glass of a nearby shop window. Someone gazed back, wild and scared, but it wasn't her. It was a stranger, a girl drawn with pale colors and straight lines.

She brought her fingers to her narrow lips, across the bridge of her button nose, over two dark brows set atop green eyes, and down the length of tangled hair, which draped across her shoulders in a curtain of gold. And she stared as the creature composed of light and glass did the same.

Yet she felt nothing. She was a stranger in her own skin, and it fit oddly across her soul, pulling and pinching at her psyche.

She began to walk, to skirt past people and carts and motorbikes. This was familiar. This was the Echelon.

She knew this city, this ship. She couldn't place herself within it, but she could trace its outlines in her mind, following its history back through the centuries to a ruined Earth. It was a colony, one of a handful forced to take to the stars in search of a home. They had spread out across the galaxies to live amidst the dust, to roam unbidden through the endless expanse of stars.

All this she knew. Yet her own name was a mystery.

She fell into a faceless tide, letting it pull her this way and that as she dredged the depths of her mind, combing it for clues. But there were none to be had. Whoever had done this to her had been thorough, merciless, unyielding. They had left nothing behind to cling to, nothing to give her hope.

Then she saw it – the checkpoint. She glanced at her wrist, finding the familiar tattoo etched upon her arm. Breaking from the pack, she made a beeline for the border, her long legs making quick work of the journey. In no time, she stood before the silver scanner, proffering her arm like an offering to this inanimate yet omniscient god.

It accepted her gift graciously, devouring the mark and its data. Within an instant, it responded with an offering of its own.

Violet Innova. Age 24. Parents unknown. Residence unknown. Status: Nonthreatening.

She couldn't help but stare at the name. Violet. Just like the face, it didn't seem to fit, and it kept sliding off each time she tried to adhere it.

A shove from behind broke her from her reveries, and she lurched forward, barely managing to stay on her feet. She glanced back to find her name gone, erased from the screen and replaced by another. She had an overwhelming urge to see it again, to prove to herself that she was real, but she knew it would do no good.

The woman she'd been was gone.

V let the stars guide her back to herself. At night, when the artificial sky dimmed above the main deck, you could finally see the universe beyond. It was muted, dulled by the shield erected to protect them, but it was there – and it was astounding.

A million stars danced across the heavens, glittering with all the splendor of sapphires. Blues and blacks and purples and greens embraced in luscious swirls, making love amidst the dust and dark matter. The planets in their path seemed to bask in the revelry, adding fire and ice to the watercolor scene.

V let the world drop away until she was one with the stars, until she floated amidst the rocks and rubble in tranquil orbit. The Eridian Galaxy welcomed her like it always did, with a show of radiance, quiet strength, and endless beauty.

The Echelon had been drifting through this galaxy for longer than anyone could remember, on a bleak course to nowhere. There was, after all, nowhere to go. The road was littered with the lifeless husks of planets, where glass rained and acid flowed and lava climbed in soaring towers, ready to scorch and consume.

So this was it – their home, their existence, their future. Forever adrift on an infinite sea.

V's attention was caught by the tell-tale whirring of a sentry, and she leapt into action, moving before her mind could process the sound. Her steps were barely audible as she hurdled gates and vaulted over low walls, putting space between her and the hovering patrols. Although they didn't shoot to kill, their censure was far from harmless. Their gaze brought scrutiny and attention – and pointed questions to which she didn't have the answers.

The night air was clean and dry, and it surged through her lungs as she ran, bequeathing strength and speed and spurring her on. A smile played at the corners of her lips, and her blood coursed in the rapid cadence of escape. She was boundless, a river rushing through a manmade jungle. She was free.

Gradually, she pulled away from her pursuer, hearing its hum fade into the last legs of night. Dawn was imminent now, although the sky still bore the bruises of darkness, lingering lazily on the cusp of day. V slowed, relishing the final moments of beauty before the sun awoke and drenched their world in simulated light.

She arrived home just as the first rays began to shine. She silently ducked inside her building, taking refuge in its dark embrace. Her wearied legs ached as she climbed, and she panted her exhaustion into the stale, recirculated air. Easing into her unit, she collapsed onto a stool and dropped her head to the table, relishing the chill against her fevered cheek.

"Have a nice run?" a small voice asked from across the counter.

V didn't stir. Instead, she kept her head down, releasing an exaggerated sigh.

"It was invigorating, as always," she purred back. "You should try it sometime. Really gets the heart rate going. Especially when you throw a few sentries into the mix."

Even with her head down, V could feel Mouse grimace.

"Thanks, but you can keep your nightly excursions. I've got other ways to get my blood pumping."

V couldn't help but snort. "Yeah. I've noticed," she said, finally raising her gaze. "Who are your friends?" She inclined her head toward the bed, where the figures lay curled together in sleep. "I haven't seen those two around before."

Mouse smiled coyly, shrugging his shoulders. Yet his brown eyes gleamed bright and mischievous, telling a different tale entirely.

"A couple new friends, back from a tour in the Grove," he replied. "They were in need of some innocent fun, and I couldn't help but oblige."

"How benevolent of you," V said dryly. "Although I don't think anything you do could be described as *innocent*."

"How dare you!" he cried in mock offense. "I am a perfect gentleman." He placed his hand on his heart in a fluid gesture. "If you don't believe me, ask them yourself. I'm sure they'd love to fill you in on the details."

"Trust me," V said, shaking her head, "I've heard enough already. These walls aren't as thick as you think. When you even bother to close them, that is."

"Don't put on that scandalized act with me," Mouse shot back, pulling his tattered orange robe farther up on his shoulders. "We both know you're no saint."

"If I were, I wouldn't be able to afford the rent," V said, digging a handful of units from her pocket and sliding them across the counter. "I do what I have to."

Mouse looked at the units disdainfully before carefully slipping them into his pocket. "You know that's not what I meant," he said breezily as he began to move about the kitchen, preparing breakfast for the gathered throng.

As he perused the barren cabinets in search of nutrition packets, V considered him. He was shorter than she was, made up of lean muscle stretched across a thin frame. His long nose and prominent ears evoked the air of an affable rodent – no doubt the source of his sobriquet. Per usual, most of his curly brown hair was hidden beneath a colorful cap, which was pulled low over his forehead yet left his bushy eyebrows free.

Currently, his only garments included the robe and a pair of flowing brown pants, leaving large swaths of smooth skin exposed – a fact with which he was exceedingly comfortable. In fact, Mouse gave off the air of someone who would be comfortable anywhere, from the starched and staid halls of the Senate to the bustling underground markets that sold everything from cats to corpses. (So long as it was illegal, it was fair game.)

V still didn't know how much of that was an act. Despite their months together – despite the fact that he had saved her from the streets and given her a home, no questions asked – she still hadn't been able to break through the walls that surrounded his past.

V knew it had involved a stint in the Grove. The marks on his arm told that plainly. There were other marks too, buried beneath the surface, remnants of a life flecked with pain. Yet of those she caught only glimpses, like a comet streaking through the sky, a momentary scrap of fire and heat hurled across the tundra.

Mostly, though, Mouse was just Mouse, effervescent and full of life, eager to share his opinion – and his bed.

Thankfully, though, he'd never taken that sort of interest in her.

Mouse freed a few packets from the back of a cupboard and began emptying them into glasses, curling his lip as the dust plumed in acrid clouds that lingered in the air.

He took her mounting silence as reticence and continued, "Come on, V. You have to stop living in the past – or lack thereof," he said, waving away her amnesia as if it were a mere annoyance and not a central tenet of her existence. "Embrace the present. Embrace your dark side. And by all that is holy, embrace that god damn bartender!"

V bristled. "Sable is nothing but trouble, and I already have enough of that in my life."

"Oh, come off it," Mouse exhaled, rolling his eyes. "Sable is no more dangerous than I am. Or you, for that matter. He's just a man – a very attractive man – who wants to show you a good time. Besides," he said, his eyebrows creeping up in amusement, "sometimes *trouble* can make for the best kind of fun."

V let loose a noise from the back of her throat, which sounded exceedingly like a growl. Mouse threw his hands up in surrender.

"Fine," he exclaimed. "Live your own life. Keep your scowl and your armor. But someday, something's gonna come along that knocks you out of that safe little cage. And, darling, I can't wait to watch."

He spun on his heel to face the sink, topping the glasses with water before giving them a furious stir. With a flourish, he slid a glass across the table to V, which came to rest safely in her palm. A satisfied smirk played on his lips as he scooped up the remaining three and made a beeline for his bed.

V stewed, staring into the chunky green liquid. Annoyance bubbled up, thick and tart, while an itchy irritation spread like a rash across her skin.

Sometimes, Mouse felt like a friend: caring, considerate, and honest to a fault. Yet he could also be an outright pain in the ass. Selfish, self-righteous, self-obsessed. She didn't need his advice – or his condescension. She could handle her own affairs…or lack thereof.

V grabbed the glass and downed its contents, cringing as the liquid connected with her taste buds, conferring the essence of chalk and minerals and underripe greens. She chewed on the chunks, struggling not to gag as they broke into sand-like grains. The whole experience was over in less than a minute, but the pungent, slightly sweet tang of it lingered on her tongue, taunting her with its presence.

Food packets, commonly known as "dust," were a staple of their diet, a quick, cheap way to acquire all the nutrients your body needed without the hassle of preparation – or any real enjoyment. The crystallized food came in a variety of colors and *flavors*, evoking hints of vegetables and fruits and things that may have once been meat. They curbed your hunger yet left you wanting, always aching for more.

V filled her glass with water and drank deeply, trying to rid her mouth of the taste.

You could buy *real* food, of course – bread and cheese and meat and produce. Items without the unsettling texture of curdled sludge. But those things cost units V didn't have. They were a rarity on a ship that could barely sustain its citizens, let alone herds of cattle. They were a dream, and V couldn't waste her time with wanting.

A giggle from behind her made her groan. It sounded as if Mouse wasn't through with his playmates – and they weren't through with him. Averting her eyes, V hopped off her chair and walked briskly to the bathroom, turning on the taps to drown out the noises.

V luxuriated in a short yet gloriously warm shower, rinsing away the tension that coiled in knots along her shoulders. She scrubbed at her body and her short blond mane, inhaling the sharp, clean scent of the soap as she worked. By the time her allocated water reserve ran dry and the stream trickled to a stop, she felt refreshed and renewed, ready to take on the day.

She dressed in a hurry, all too aware of the uncomfortable sounds emanating from somewhere beyond the wall. V fell out of the bathroom, stumbling to catch herself as she ran. By the time she reached the door, her heart was beating in frantic bursts and her breath was catching in her chest. Her fingers closed around the handle with joyous relief, and she dove into the hall, slamming the door shut behind her.

Chapter 3

V rapped her knuckles against the door and waited, her heart rate slackening until its rhythm bordered on normal. There was nothing quite like the threat of someone else's sexual encounter to get you going in the morning. V almost didn't need coffee – or what passed for it in these parts.

Before she could wander off in search of caffeine, though, she had one stop to make. She heard shuffling and rustling – and crashing – from beyond the door before a frazzled woman unchained the lock and poked her head through. Her frizzy red hair stuck up in every direction, and her face was dotted with swaths of a sticky yellow paste. When she caught sight of V, however, she broke into a beaming grin.

"V! Thank the stars!" Riyah exclaimed, opening the door wider and beckoning her in.

V ducked inside, stopping to give her friend a quick hug before assessing the situation. After a short deliberation, she landed on one word: chaos.

Dishes cluttered the countertops and a rainbow of colored powders decorated the cabinets, while blankets and wooden toys carpeted the floor. Clothes dangled off the sagging couch, the battered chairs, even the flickering lights, which cast uncertain rays across the room.

And, of course, there was the swirling cyclone of energy that buzzed around the space, twirling and dancing and heading straight for V. It crashed into her leg at full speed, latching on and squeezing. V let loose a burst of laughter before bending down to pry the boy from her leg and lift him up.

"Aunt Vibet! Aunt Vibet!" he cried, bouncing merrily in her arms – while adorably failing to pronounce her name.

"It's nice to see you too, Leo," she giggled. "You've certainly been busy this morning." She gestured to the mess in the kitchen. "What game have you been playing today?"

"I a monster. Rarrr!" he declared, curling his hands like claws. "Down, down!" he commanded, and V did as she was told, setting the boy down and watching as he bounced away, sporting a lopsided smile.

"It's been like this for hours," Riyah sighed, exhaustion coloring her words. "I barely got an hour's sleep. And now I can't even convince him to sit down and eat."

"I'll trade you," V replied in jest. "I take Leo, you take Mouse and his exotic band of *friends*. Although I have to warn you – you won't get any more sleep up there."

Riyah chuckled. "I'll take it! Anything to get a break from the madness!"

V knew that her friend was joking, yet the purple circles beneath her eyes and the wan tint to her skin showed a palpable fatigue, like some invisible force was slowly sapping her strength. Her cheeks, once rosy, had slowly caved inward, leaving two severe cheekbones to dominate her face. Yet the gentleness in her eyes remained, softening the harshness of her exhaustion.

"Where's Asher?" V asked, feeling his absence in the room. "I can't remember the last time I've seen him."

Something in Riyah deflated, and she collapsed onto a stool, her baggy clothes pooling around her padded frame. She rested her head in her open palm, releasing a sigh that vibrated in V's bones.

"Working," Riyah said, conveying paragraphs with a single word. "He hasn't been home in days. I know we need the money, but..." she trailed off, shaking her head.

"But you also need him here," V finished, knowing all too well the toll it took to be alone.

Asher was employed by the Echelon to repair and restore the tunnels that snaked beneath the ship's main deck. It was grueling work, with long hours and low wages that barely kept them afloat.

There were worse jobs – on the assembly lines or in the dust factories. Or even the off-worlders, those tasked with leaving the ship in search of coveted resources and fuel. Those whose lives were never guaranteed for another day. Yet not having Asher there to share the load was its own kind of torture.

Riyah smiled sadly, something powerful shining behind her eyes. The look pulled at something deep within V, but she ignored it, turning to levity to lighten the mood.

"Well, I might not be Asher, but I'm here for you – and

I'm much more attractive, if I do say so myself. And taller, which is always helpful."

Riyah snorted in amusement. "Well, you're certainly taller."

"How dare you!" V cried in mock outrage. "I'm ten times the man Asher will ever be."

"You're delusional – that's what you are," Riyah shot back. "Did you just stop by to torment me, or were you actually planning on being helpful?"

"You insult me and now you want my help?" V asked. "I have half a mind to walk out of here and never come back."

"Oh, come off it," Riyah parried. "You only had half a mind to start with. If it split any further, I don't think you'd remember your own name."

"Touché," V said, impressed. "Ten points to Riyah."

"Why thank you," she replied, bowing her head in gratitude. "Now, are you really here to help? Because I desperately need some things from the market, and taking this terror outside is utterly impossible," she murmured, pointing toward Leo.

In their brief absence, the boy had captured a pillow and freed its stuffing, which littered the floor like mounds of fluffy snow. He cackled as he rummaged inside for more padding to play with.

"Fine," V said, rolling her eyes. "Write me a list and I'll see what I can do. No promises, though."

Riyah began scribbling frantically on a loose scrap of paper, her tight writing cramped even further by the tight margins. By the time she'd finished, the scrap was drenched in ink, with mere hints of white peeking through.

V took the proffered list and whistled. "That's quite the inventory. Who knew kids were so needy? No wonder the Policies only let us have one."

V chuckled as she ran her eyes over the list. It took a moment for Riyah to join in, and when she did the sound was hollow and forced. V felt a pang of shame for making light of their financial strain, and she sobered.

"Don't worry," she assured Riyah. "I'll take care of it."

"You'd better," Riyah warned. "Or else I'll have to sic Leo on you – and I'm pretty sure he's feral."

V glanced at the toddler, who now had cotton sticking out from between his lips in little white wisps, like he was foaming at the mouth.

"Then I should get to work. No time to waste!" V declared.

She waved to Leo, who shouted an almost incoherent, "Bye, bye Vibet!" through his fluff-filled mouth. Bidding adieu to her friend, she exited the apartment and tramped down the last few flights of stairs to the street.

She merged with the masses flowing to and fro, letting the current pull her along. The crush of bodies was constant, closing in on her from all sides and squeezing until no space remained between them. V smiled.

As her eyes danced across the crowd, pinpointing marks and purses and pockets, her fingers danced accordingly, playing mischief like a chord. There was nothing like a spot of petty larceny to start the morning off right.

Half an hour later, her pockets weighed down with units and her slender wrist sporting a slick silver watch, V approached the Market Sector. Its edges abutted the Business

District on one side and the social sectors on the other, with residential units sprawling out in the distance. They each shared space toward the center of the ship, spiraling out in a concentrated collage of buildings and streets. Yet the market was their hub, the beating heart of this blind metal beast.

Even before she entered, the tumult struck her like a wall, with sights and sounds and smells all vying for her attention. Neon lights flickered from every shop window, while billboards and holograms spoke, selling all manner of lies. Brightly colored motorbikes whizzed through the throngs, hovering just above the ground. And overhead, the high-speed trains barreled through their tunnels, whistling as they wove through the city.

It was pandemonium, a world painted with fluorescent strokes and garish greed, with poverty and luxury and speed.

Buildings protruded from the ground in jagged bursts, some pristine and clean, others a jumble of mismatched stories. Elevators of glass soared and dropped in a daring ballet, held aloft by the faintest of cables. Balconies and platforms and curly steel stairs hugged the buildings like ivy, growing hungrily up their sides.

And the people. Everywhere V looked, there were people. They clung to their shops, their goods, each other. They bought and sold and traded their services for money. They pulsed around her in sticky clumps, their hands and eyes hunting ravenously for something else to own.

V had learned early on, though, that in the Market Sector, it was best to keep your hands to yourself. Even now, the sentries buzzed above her, scouring the scene. Their tireless eyes poked and prodded, saddling her with the leaden weight of inspection.

Yet it wasn't the sentries that gave V pause – it was the people. The Iridium Guards hidden in plain sight, dressed in plain clothes, feigning plain lives. V could feel their gazes like an itch creeping up her spine, yet she could never spot them. Once or twice she was sure she'd found one – looking too hard, concentrating too closely – but they'd disappear in an instant, fading into the background without a trace.

V kept her hands in her pockets and her head down, shuffling along, just one more face in a sea of many. Invisible. Forgettable.

For the first few months, she'd let herself be seen. She'd kept her head high, her hair uncovered. She'd yearned to stand out. She'd screamed a silent scream, praying that some-one would hear it and recognize the sound, that someone would finally claim her.

They hadn't. The only eyes she'd caught had been sinis-ter, the looks leering, the hands coarse and greedy. The sen-tries and their Guards cared little for her virtue – and even less if it was violated.

Now V clung to the crowds, covering herself with their safety. She was unknown, anonymous. She was safe.

Well, safe from her fellow shoppers at least. The sales-people were a different matter.

"Miss! Do you know what your lover gets up to when you're not around? Because with the Nanogem Ultra, you'll be able to see everything," one man crooned from a shop beside her. "It's utterly undetectable. I guarantee it. Only 30 units for *ultra* peace of mind."

The man held up a finger in her direction, and the screen

behind him lit up with her face, plastering her angry eyes on the wall for all to see. V flashed her teeth in warning, and he hastily pointed the camera at another unsuspecting target, freeing her from its spell.

A few feet down the road, a smattering of scantily clad men and women idled before a shop, tempting passersby to step into the darkness. The barest flicker of their flawless skin gave them away. Holograms. V barreled through, enjoying the bursts of light as the figures erupted into shards of code before coalescing once more.

V ignored the retinal implants, the personal droids, the contraptions that could tuck and trim and tease. The only things that pulled at her, drawing her to a stop, were the bikes. Not the ones that whirred around her, but the ones waiting behind shop windows, virgin and new.

Looking at their sleek silver curves, their slashes of cerulean, their elegant fins, V could almost feel the rush. The grips were cool beneath her fingers, the machine purring against her legs, her body bent forward across its hull. Her hair whipped behind her as she split the air in two, parting it like a river.

Tearing herself away from the display, V pushed on, working her way toward the affordable end of the sector. Technology and toys gradually gave way to food stalls and apparel, then secondhand tech, then powder pushers.

V paused, shelling out hard-earned – and hard-stolen – units in exchange for the processed dust masquerading as food. Orange ones, red ones, purple ones that made her mouth feel like it had grown hair and taste like she had gnawed on an old log. Blue ones that were at least tolerable

– for an hour or so, until your body remembered that it wasn't quite food, and the blue dust gave way to blue debris.

The children had it better. At least they got tickets for fruit and bread, for milk and rice and the occasional taste of meat. Yet those tickets didn't last long, not in a world consumed by scarcity and need.

Riyah's tickets had gone the way of most, sold to the highest bidder to fund the luxuries of subsistence. Medicine for an earache. Clothing for a growth spurt. A bottle. A toy. A cradle.

V dug into her pocket, drawing out the dwindling units to pay for a stack of protein sticks and some vitamin-enhanced paste. She cringed as she counted out the last of Riyah's coins, adding a few of her own to make up the difference. It wasn't much, but it was all she could give.

Riyah had been her first real friend – apart from Mouse, who regularly wavered between friend, acquaintance, and mortal enemy. But with Riyah, it had been different, immediate. A collision in the hallway, a laughing baby, a timid smile.

V hadn't known she'd needed someone until Riyah. She hadn't known she'd been lonely until she wasn't. It was a curious thing, unexplainable and obscure but powerful enough to move mountains. It was more than friendship. It was family – and V would do everything she could to protect it.

Chapter 4

The Alcor Club was howling by the time V stepped inside, giving herself over to its familiar embrace. The deep beats clung to her, pounding through her body as she surveyed her kingdom.

The room was crowded with bodies – packed onto the dance floor, packed into booths, packed against each other for solace. Their heartbeats joined with the music, melding until they all breathed and beat as one.

V pushed inside, immersing herself in the gentle chaos. The dance floor pulsed with heat and sweat, and she skirted its edges, admiring the throng and its synchronized rhythm. Above them, the lights danced as holographic shapes twisted and broke in a mesmerizing ballet.

The noise faded to a mellow hum as she entered the dressing room, exchanging her street clothes for a midnight blue jumpsuit that clung to her curves. She freed her hair from its prison, then applied a liberal stroke of red across her lips and dots of shimmering gold across her cheeks.

By the time the last deep notes called out across the crowd, V had transformed herself, slipping from the comfort of her skin into something slippery and bold, a creature made of steel and starlight. She took to the stage amidst cheers and shouts. The room was thick with restless fervor, with bodies poised on the edge and longing to fall.

This time, she didn't bother with ballads. These people didn't want her soulful melodies. They wanted noise loud enough to drown out their thoughts, to fill the ringing silence in their lives, to beat back the hunger and the thirst. For the moment, she was their cure, and she poured herself out for their pleasure.

It was equal parts electrifying and exhausting. As one song flowed into the next, she could feel the energy pulled from her veins, dissipating under the bright lights and constant stares. The melodies bled her dry, and the crowd fed like animals on her blood, demanding more.

The final chords of the final song brought sweet relief, and a contented, satisfied sigh resonated from the gathered throng. V floated offstage to a chorus of applause before the deep beats once again stole their attention. She shuffled through the swarm, fending off hands and eyes and advances as she strained to extricate herself from the crowd.

V collapsed onto a stool at the bar, utterly unable to speak or think or move. Her head fell onto her arms as her bones melted into jelly, rendering her limp. Not even the sticky counter or Sable's amused laughter could compel her to budge.

A shot of freeze appeared before her and she drank,

barely tilting her head to consume the cold liquor. It chilled her heated skin and numbed her mind, casting her further adrift.

She didn't notice the man beside her until he spoke, his resonant voice biting through the haze.

"I quite enjoyed your performance," he said, the words clear and crisp, unadulterated by drink or drugs. "May I buy you another round?"

V didn't look up. Instead, she sighed, tracing the familiar patterns etched on her mind in search of a suitable response. Or, rather, a suitable rejection.

"No offense, but I'm really not interested. I sell songs not sex. If you're looking for company, you're not going to find it here."

Sable cleared his throat, and V looked up through groggy eyes to find him staring at her in disbelief, his mouth agape. With a sinking feeling in her chest, V turned toward the speaker and froze.

Seated beside her, in the pristine gray of governmental garb, was a senator. And not just any senator, but one of the Echelon's most respected officials, Senator Apollo Quinn.

Violet was royally screwed.

Her brain stuttered, bringing up every piece of intel in hopes that it would help her. She flashed through images and facts, through colors and scraps. It was a whirlwind, but through it she managed to scrape together fragments that formed a hazy picture.

The Senate was their governing body, their semblance of democracy. They fed the poor, clothed the needy, kept the Echelon aloft. They made the *hard decisions*, the ones whose consequences kept people in their place. And, most importantly, they enforced the Policies, the rulebook of directives meant to safeguard the peace and ensure their continued survival.

Its senators were elected to life terms – if "elected" was even the appropriate word. More accurately, they were chosen from a pool of the privileged, from the sons and daughters of the elite, whose parents had trained them from an early age to rule. They were educated in history, diction, and commerce, and schooled in charm and deception.

Still, decency managed to claw its way in, to break through the cesspit surrounding the Senate and plant itself in their midst. Of the 30 members who made up its ranks, a handful were atypical, a departure from the norm, each eccentric in their own way. In the case of Apollo Quinn, it was that he had come to politics late in life, adopting the role after decades buried in the biological sciences.

Years of genomes and chromosomes and biomes had brought serenity to his character and a calm stability that made him popular among the populace – if not always the Senate at large. He'd been known to court controversy with his votes and err on the side of the people rather than the powerful.

He'd been dubbed the Mad Scientist Senator by some of his less reputable colleagues in a blatant attempt to discredit him, but the name had done nothing more than amuse him. In fact, he did his best to embrace the moniker, supposedly spending hours entrenched in all manner of experiments deep within his penthouse lair.

Unfortunately, none of this gave V the slightest hint as

to how she could dig herself out of the black hole she'd created. She still couldn't fathom why he was here, in a low-rent club where none of his colleagues would be caught dead. Trying to untangle the possibilities only made her head throb. So, instead, she turned to humility to save her. And copious amounts of groveling.

"I'm sorry, sir," she said, bowing her head – and changing her tone. Her words dripped with sugar so sweet that she could almost taste the rot. "I mistook you for someone else. Please accept my deepest apologies for the vulgarity."

The sentiments felt foreign on her tongue, and she fought to keep her face blank as she raised it once more. She feared that she'd find outrage or anger painted on his features, but instead she found something else entirely. Curiosity.

He scanned her face as if searching for something. In a heartbeat, though, his eyebrows sank in a subtle sadness as his curiosity mellowed into courtesy.

"Don't worry, my dear," he said, his resonant baritone biting through the noise. "I've heard far worse in my time. Believe me: You couldn't shock me if you tried. And many *have* tried."

A polite laugh rumbled from V's throat as she struggled to unwind the tightness in her chest. Apollo paused, as if expecting a response, but V's mind was a cavern of crickets. She willed herself to look away, to keep her cool, but his ice blue eyes held her in thrall, freezing her in place.

Deep wrinkles framed his eyes, betraying his age, and a messy coif of long white hair framed the sharp lines of his face. He had an energy about him, a vigor that betrayed his keen intelligence, but it battled with a weariness that seemed to seep from his bones.

He drew a breath, preparing himself, before diving back in. "You really were astonishing. I had no idea...someone could sing like that," he said clumsily. "The hologirls seem, well, hollow compared to you."

V found the sentiment charming – but also incredibly uncomfortable. She began to shift her attention to Sable, but the senator cleared his throat, dragging her back.

"I have a proposition for you," he declared.

V stiffened at the word, suddenly suspicious. She had given the man the benefit of the doubt based on his kindly reputation, but even the kind ones had their kinks.

"I'm having a party, and it would be the greatest honor to have you perform. To sing," he clarified, sensing V's reluctance. "I'll make it worth your time. How does 300 units sound?"

V's mind went momentarily blank at the mention of money. That sum was almost ten times what she made on the best of nights at the Alcor. She salivated at the thought of everything those units could buy. Real food, new clothes, perhaps a morsel of insight into her past.

The offer was alluring, to be sure, yet there was more than money to consider. Socializing with senators brought scrutiny and questions. She would be thrust into the limelight and stripped of her safeguards. She would be illuminated, with every word and deed laid bare for their leaders to see. One wrong move, one toe out of line, and she'd be thrown into the Grove for impertinence without even so much as a trial.

Sable looked on as she thought, disbelief dancing on

his features. He would take the risk in an instant, she knew, throwing safety to the wind for coin. V envied that brazen recklessness, that utter conviction. She didn't know why, but something held her back, like a warning call rattling deep within her bones, signaling danger.

As the seconds stretched on, Apollo sighed. "The party is in two days," he informed her. "Take tonight to think on it and scry me tomorrow with your answer. I'll be waiting."

He turned to go, but V stopped him with a sudden, "Wait!" He turned, clearly hoping for a decision, only to hear her explain, "I don't own a scryglass."

Apollo stared at her in astonishment, as if she'd just declared that she had two heads.

"I'll have one sent to you," he said as he recovered. "Consider it bonus." He nodded once before blending back into the crowd.

V sat there, stunned into silence, replaying the encounter on a loop. Behind the bar, Sable poured another shot of freeze, sliding it across the counter. She drank without thinking, letting the liquid burn a frozen path through her chest and clear the unease from her mind.

"You're going to do it," Sable said with certainty. "I don't know why you're fighting it."

V bristled, agitated that he thought he knew her better than she knew herself.

"What? You think I can be bought that easily? Just a scryglass and handful of units and I'm yours?"

Sable looked amused at her attempts to upbraid him. "No," he stated almost smugly. "But you could never turn down an offer of adventure."

"I'm just saying," Mouse said, shaking his head, "these people can't be trusted. They're not like us."

Mouse sat opposite Riyah and V at their kitchen counter, sipping from his bottle of beer. The drinks were a treat, pilfered from the Alcor, and V reveled in the pleasure of the liquid gold. She should have felt bad for stealing from Sable, but his cocky attitude and arrogant smile had grated on her nerves, requiring retribution. Besides, he could afford the loss, and right now, V needed the drinks more than he did.

That's why she'd convened this consortium. They were her sounding board, and they weighed her options alongside her, gently easing the load.

"Us?" V inquired, trying to follow Mouse's train of thought – and resolutely failing.

"Ussss," Mouse said slower, gesturing to the trio. "Let me put it this way. There are two types of people: those who make the Policies and those who break them. One guess as to which category we fall into."

Riyah choked on a sip of her drink, coughing loudly to dislodge the liquid from her throat.

"Speak for yourself," she said when she could breathe. "Some of us actually want to play by the rules."

Mouse continued, patently ignoring her. "We're natural enemies. No good can come from fraternizing with them. Take my advice: Steer clear of the senators."

V turned to Riyah, expecting a rebuttal. The woman was quieter than usual, and she sat fiddling with the label of her beer, lost in her own little world.

Riyah's feelings on Mouse were complicated, to put it mildly, vacillating hourly between amusement and exhaustion. V had learned to expect tension, eye rolls, the occasional passive jab. Silence, however, was not her typical retort.

"Riyah?" V nudged. "What's going on in there? You seem to be thinking some deep thoughts."

Riyah came to, snapping out of her daze with a jolt. She tried to smile, shaking off V's concern, but the expression didn't quite reach her eyes.

"The senators are powerful," she said, avoiding V's gaze. "They don't just deal in units. They trade in favors. Performing for them could put you in their good graces, and you never know when that could come in handy." There was something intense in the way she said it, as if she knew something V didn't.

"Just playing devil's advocate," Riyah added in a last-ditch attempt to cushion her words.

"Oh trust me, honey," Mouse bit back. "Those devils don't need your advocacy. They've got this world wrapped around their grubby fingers. They can have anything they want."

"Then why me?" V asked suddenly. When Mouse and Riyah only stared, she continued, "If Apollo could have any singer on the Echelon, why would he travel all the way to the Alcor Club for me?"

"Because you're incredibly talented," Riyah said in breezy flattery. "I bet someone raved about you, and he came to see for himself. And once he'd heard you sing, he couldn't help but want you."

Mouse snorted, and V felt like doing the same. She was

good, yes, but Riyah's view of her was a bit of a stretch.

True to form, Mouse offered a different theory, one with less wholesome intentions.

"It's not about singing. The man just plain wants you. It's as simple as that. He wants you under his roof, at his mercy, and, ultimately, in his bed."

Riyah paled at the thought. "You're disgusting," she spat with more than her typical vigor.

V couldn't help but agree. "That can't be right. Apollo was the perfect gentleman. He did nothing – said nothing – to imply that he wants me for anything other than my voice. Plus, he's old enough to be my grandfather."

"And for all *you* know, he could be," Mouse teased, laughing at his own attempt at humor.

"You're such a child," Riyah retorted, glancing toward the couch where her own child was out cold. Something bleak flitted across her eyes, filling her expression with grief. A knot of unease tied itself around V's heart and squeezed.

"Hey, are you OK?" she asked, reaching out to cover Riyah's hand with her own. It was cold.

Riyah took a breath, then another, clearly contemplating her next words. When she looked up, the sorrow was gone, replaced by a firm resolve.

"Take the job," she commanded. "For me."

V's brows knitted as her friend held her gaze, making a silent confession. Only, V couldn't figure out what it was.

Then the puzzle clicked into place, each piece interlocking to form a terrible picture. Her stomach sank as Riyah's words bounced around her brain, imbued with fresh meaning and fresh malice.

"You never know when that could come in handy." But Riyah did know. She needed that favor, needed to be in those unholy good graces. She needed a fucking miracle.

"I'm pregnant," she whispered, jaw tensed, head held defiantly high, and her hand gripping V's like her life depended on it. Because in a way it did.

Chapter 5

The Policies were nothing new. They'd been conceived upon the Echelon in its early days, before the Milky Way had faded to a dream in the distance.

The Policies were their laws, the rules designed to enforce order within the endless cosmic chaos. They set up the Senate, outlined its power, put people in their place. They controlled resources, businesses, and citizens.

The first Policies were steeped in morality, outlawing murder, robbery, rape. The building blocks followed, spelling out the currency, the taxes, the sentries. Yet those were merely background noise for the Policies that came after.

As they drew further from the people they had once been and the planet they had once inhabited, their laws, too, grew further from what they'd known. Trade and travel between Earth's various vessels were abolished, with disease and contagion charged as the culprits. Without the clear necessity of contact, communications dropped until the Echelon was alone, its own island surrounded by a lonesome sea of stars.

Then their resources dwindled, leaving bellies empty, throats dry, homes dark. They'd grown too big for their boat and too hungry for its rations.

People died in droves, dropping dead in the streets from starvation. Crime grew as the desperate rummaged for fodder to feed their aching guts. Retribution rained down in the streets as those with broken hearts sought to break other's necks.

This hadn't been the plan, of course. The plan was to spread out, to settle down on habitable worlds, to live. Yet the universe, it seemed, didn't want its planets ruined by their disease. The worlds they'd found had been desolate, barren, and unforgiving. They were made of fire and ice, and they fought back against the humans with twisters of rock, avalanches of lava, and seas of blistering acid. The alien worlds fended off their invasion, casting the Echelon to the stars for an infinite voyage.

Aboard the ship, life descended into squalor as starvation set in, consuming sanity and reason. Rolling blackouts cast their world into shadow, and the darkness bred monsters that fed on the light.

To the Senate's credit, they'd tried to help. Their scientists had formulated the powders that passed as food to stretch their dwindling supplies. They'd limited buying and selling and cracked down on the black-market vendors that dealt in faux foods. They'd even expanded agriculture, stealing convicts from their cells to work as laborers on the land.

That was the beginning of the Grove. To many, it seemed superior to rotting away in crowded compartments tucked beneath the surface of the ship. Felons could feel the dirt between their toes, the fake sun shining on their faces. The reality, however, was far more insidious than simple farming.

Prisoners weren't just workers; they were slaves, dispersed across the land under constant watch without rest or shade or water. Their sentences were measured not in years but in yields, with each plant holding the promise of freedom.

Hatred bred violence, with crops at the core, and each inmate guarded their treasure. The frail were left floundering while the hearty thrived, reaping bushels from borrowed labor.

Unfortunately, even these measures weren't enough to save the souls aboard the Echelon. Children were dying in their beds, in the streets, in the arms of those that loved them, and population control became paramount.

The One-Child Policy was instituted and strictly enforced, with neighbors paid to turn on neighbors and friends fined for their silence. Exceptions could be made, of course – for a price. Yet for the others, those not born to privilege and fortune, the consequences were severe.

Pregnant women were seized in raucous scenes staged to make a point. First children wailed as they watched their mothers dragged through the streets. Spouses begged and tried to barter while the faceless Anomaly Detection Force ignored them. It was neither kind nor pretty nor humane, but it was effective.

The women would return in time, with no child – and no memory of what had transpired.

Yet even this couldn't save them. Death still stalked the Echelon, leaving bodies in its wake. The husks, emaciated and gaunt, were carted through the streets like a symbol of the Senate's failure.

They told the people to wait, to have faith. So the populace placed their fate in the hands of gods with two faces, with no other choice but to comply. Yet somehow, as years turned to decades, the death rate dropped and life prevailed upon the Echelon.

The sound of children's wails withered as their numbers fell, leaving playgrounds vacant and classrooms hollow. Giggles ceased alongside growling bellies and innocence died beside disease. They'd traded their futures for their present, and it was palpable.

Yet beneath the surface, something sinister was at play, with no Policy behind it. No one spoke of it in the light, but it was still blinding. Others began to disappear, as well, lost to the ether of the Echelon. The elderly, the poor, the infirm. Those with too many tours of the Grove and those lost within the confines of their own minds.

It was a quiet thing, patently covert, and no one ever dared to tell the tale. Yet it purred a whispered warning through the wind: When you cease to be useful, you might simply cease to be.

V had never seen it, but she'd heard the stories. She knew that if Mouse hadn't found her, hadn't saved her from the streets, she might have joined the ranks of the missing, falling into that nameless void.

Now, however, she wasn't the one at risk. Riyah's fate hung in the balance, teetering on the brink. She would likely live, but she would never be the same. They would rip her from her family, her purpose, and steal her light. They would take away her choice, her power, as if it had always been theirs to wield.

Asher and Leo would feel the pain acutely, left alone to traverse their fractured worlds. Asher no doubt knew the part he'd have to play. But Leo? Could he even understand the gravity, or would he cry for her every day, waiting stubbornly at the door? Would he refuse to eat, sleep, dress until Riyah returned? And when she did, would he notice the sadness in her smile, the permanent grief that made a home in her eyes?

It broke V's heart to even think of it. That someone could control Riyah and her body like a game piece on a board was unfathomable, and the anger of it wound around her ribs like a snake, constricting her lungs until she could barely breathe. Without a family of her own, this little company of outcasts was the closest V had to a tribe. And after this, they would never be the same.

V knew what she had to do. She'd known it from the moment Riyah had asked. She had to accept Apollo's offer. She had to curry favor with the elite. She had to plead Riyah's case and pray to the stars that someone would listen. And if they didn't, V had to do everything in her power to make them sit up and take notice.

A knock on the door woke V from her fitful sleep. She sat up slowly, clinging to the wisps of her nightmare. She could still feel the fingers on her skin, the blood on her hands, the monster at her back.

The knocking came again, measured and even. V shook herself, trying to dislodge the dread that had nested in her chest. She glanced around, realizing she was alone, before padding to the door and peering out. Through the small hole, she could just make out a man, dressed boldly in a suit of deep maroon, his face schooled into a blank expression. He held two packages, both wrapped tightly in gleaming silver, and V's curiosity soared.

She opened the door slowly, and the man remained firmly where he was, the bones in his body fused into place like a statue on her doorstep. A minuscule sweep of his eyes and a flicker of his brow were the only movements that marked him as animate. V glanced down, conscious of her meager garments and sleep-rumpled state – but not concerned in the slightest.

She mirrored his posture, upright and immobile, waiting for him to speak. After an extended moment, he obliged.

"Ms. Innova?" he asked, the question bordering on a statement.

"Yes," she replied, her statement bordering on a query.

Their monosyllabic meeting halted abruptly as he brought his wrist up to her face. V remained still as dots of light erupted from his scryglass, scanning her features. A beep of acceptance rang out, confirming her identity, and the man lowered his arm.

"These are for you," he said, holding out the packages with a curt bow. "Courtesy of Senator Quinn."

Violet reached out, gingerly taking the boxes. On top was a small cube, delicate and light. The promised scryglass, she presumed. Beneath it was another parcel, long and flat and infinitely intriguing.

The instant the packages were safely in V's possession, the man clasped his hands behind his back. With a nod, he turned on his heel and marched toward the stairs.

Frowning at the strange interaction, V stepped back, letting the door swing shut between them. Gently, she set the packages down on the counter, considering them briefly before attacking them with gusto. She could never resist a gift, no matter how many strings were attached.

Tearing through the glossy wrappings of the smaller box, she opened it to reveal a sleek silver scryglass nestled in a cushion of black. It was delicate and thin – and obviously expensive. A childlike glee leapt to the surface as she secured it around her wrist.

Its paper-flat screen was clear except for a faint prismatic sheen, which captured the light and turned her wrist to rainbows. The silver band fit snugly, and she could barely feel it on her arm, its weight a feather's kiss upon her skin.

V was impressed. It was beautiful, state-of-the-art, a wonderful inducement. She only briefly considered how much she could get for it before turning to the second parcel.

Her fingers slid over the slick silver paper before tearing it aside. She cast off the lid with excitement and considered her prize. Scooping up the matte black fabric, she held it aloft before her. It was a dress.

The garment was somehow both angular and sleek, and the strange fabric was cool to the touch. Its high collar dropped into a plunging neck, and gauzy sleeves floated gently above the shoulders. It cinched tightly at the waist before trickling down in flowing waves to touch the floor. Wide slits along the legs sheared its elegance to ribbons, lending a sinister bite to its deep black bark.

Apollo was presumptuous, to be sure, but she had to admit that the man had taste. The dress was stunning, like a dark shard cut from an inky abyss, and V couldn't wait to wear it.

A tiny card floated from its folds to land lightly on the scuffed wooden floor. V bent to retrieve it, cautiously unfolding the delicate paper to reveal a single line of tight black script.

"A little gift to entice you to say yes. I'll be waiting. – AQ"

A shiver trickled down V's spine, warning her of some unseen danger. Yet she'd made up her mind. Riyah needed her, and V needed to do this for her friend.

She was about to ring Apollo when she remembered her attire. Although she felt no shame in her appearance, she thought it best to save the show for his party. Within a minute, she'd fastened her hair tightly behind her head and donned a slightly more modest ensemble.

"Put me through to Apollo Quinn," she demanded of the scryglass before she could lose her nerve.

"Right away, ma'am," a feminine voice chirped from her wrist as the scryglass began hunting for its target.

It didn't take long. Within a handful of heartbeats, minuscule beams of light erupted from her wrist, coalescing into a head and shoulders.

Apollo wore his gray senatorial robes and a smirk. He knew her answer, and V had a feeling he'd never doubted it.

"Violet," he said, his booming voice echoing from her wrist with harsh clarity. "It's a pleasure to hear from you. I hope my gifts were to your liking."

He spoke formally, the stiff words mirroring the stiff set of his shoulders. V couldn't read him, and it grated on her. She wanted some reassurance, some guarantee, but only darkness stared back. Taking a deep breath, she jumped off the cliff.

"I've made my decision," she said, forgoing pleasantries and ignoring his blatant request for gratitude. "I'll do it. For 400 units."

That got a reaction. Apollo's eyebrows momentarily disappeared beneath his mop of white hair before dropping to rest above his piercing blue eyes.

"350," he shot back, a light hint of amusement creeping into his voice.

"400," V stated, unwilling to back down. This was not a negotiation, and she didn't intend to waver. Yes, she needed his favor, but first she needed to show strength. By stating her price, she was setting the boundaries – and seeing if he would play.

A beat passed as they stared each other down, each weighing the other's sincerity. Apollo was the first to blink.

"400 units it is. Then we have a deal. Take the train to the Senatorial Sector tomorrow evening. I'll send you the coordinates and procure you a temporary pass." He paused, carefully considering his next statement.

"This event is more important than you know. Tread lightly, Ms. Innova, or this evening could spell disaster for us both."

Chapter 6

Violet tried to knock a hundred times, and a hundred times she failed. Standing before Riyah's door dressed all in black, she felt like a demon of death, an omen of dark days to come.

She wanted to hug her friend, to promise that things would be alright, but she couldn't. Not yet. Those words held a hollow ring, and Riyah could easily slip into their void. V needed to put action behind her words, to do instead of say, to make plans instead of promises.

So she spun, turning her back to the apartment and marching upstairs. As soon as the door shut behind her, she let her head fall against its surface with a troubled sigh.

"You might want to try a smile," came a voice from across the room.

V opened her eyes wearily to see Mouse tucked into the couch, his arms and legs folded as he considered her.

"Did you just tell me to smile?" V asked, irritated at the thought.

"Oh, it's not for me, darling. It's for your adoring audience. If I'm not mistaken, they're paying you to be charming. The least you can do is give them a smile."

V barred her teeth in response. Mouse had made his disapproval perfectly clear. To say he didn't understand her decision was an understatement. Even in the face of Riyah's revelation, he'd maintained his stance, calling all senators scum and dubbing their hired help insane.

His anger made no sense. Then again, his moods rarely did. Still, V hadn't expected this resentment, this bile. This felt like something different, but she didn't have the time or energy to examine it. So she took his comments in stride, letting them bounce off her matte black armor – and firing back at every opportunity.

"Keep your venom, Mouse. Bitterness doesn't become you."

"I'm not bitter," Mouse said with a mirthless laugh. "In fact, I'm the only one seeing sense here. Trust me – this will all end in tears."

V ignored Mouse and his melodramatic prediction. Pulling her hair tight against the nape of her neck, she twisted it around her finger before securing it with a tie.

Out of nowhere, a trilling voice piped up, causing V to freeze.

"Your train will leave in 15 minutes from platform 152. Don't be late," her scryglass commanded, equal parts motherly and annoying.

V gathered herself, checking her face in the mirror before turning it on Mouse.

"I know you don't approve, but it doesn't matter. I'm

going. And I *will* find a way to get us through this."

"You're fooling yourself." This time, Mouse's words weren't spiteful but sad. "Riyah is already doomed. And if you go, you'll be sentencing yourself to the same fate."

V shook her head and turned to go but stopped in her tracks at two whispered words.

"Good luck."

She didn't look back.

V rarely took the sky train. It jostled her nerves, going that fast that high, with the city whizzing past in a blur beneath her. It made her vision spin and her stomach lurch. Yet Apollo's orders had specifically commanded her on board. So she kept her eyes trained on the horizon, not daring to look down.

Her carriage was almost empty, its glories reserved for the Senate, their guests, and the hired help. But since the affluent apparently had their own means of transport, the car carried only three – V and two servants, one man and one woman. They were waitstaff, if V had to guess, just two more people selling themselves to survive. They sat shoulder to shoulder across from her, unspeaking yet oddly tense.

The man was startling, all sharp edges and smooth copper skin, with deep brown hair that curled in wild locks around his face. The woman was striking, too, but in a way V couldn't quite place. Her broad shoulders and toned arms strained beneath a crisp white shirt, betraying her strength. Her hair was buzzed at the sides, with the rest of her mane swept back into a coal-black braid that fell past her shoulders. V's eyes darted from her angular features to her gloved hands to her hard, dark eyes, searching for the source of the strangeness, but she couldn't put her finger on it.

The woman glanced up, meeting her gaze, and V swiftly looked away, suddenly self-conscious. She tried to refocus on their destination, which loomed large in the distance, but one eye remained on the couple.

A few minutes later, however, all thoughts of strangers were driven from her mind as the Senatorial Sector rose within view. At their speed, the details were blurred into mere ghosts of shapes, but the silver towers, connected by impossible glass walkways, glittered in the light of the simulated sun. They rose, tall and proud, like sharp metal shards jutting from the depths of the ship, a living, breathing forest of modern man.

In another minute, the train began to slow, eliciting a sickening jolt from V's stomach. The moment their car came to a stop, the strangers jumped up in unison and bolted for the doors. Their movements were hurried but precise, and the pair was out of sight before V could even process her surroundings.

Waves lapped at her stomach, ebbing and flowing, and she tried to calm them with a breath. With a conviction she didn't quite feel, she straightened her shoulders and strode off the train. The doors closed behind her with a whoosh, as if sealing her into a tomb.

The platform was nearly empty, with no sign of the couple she'd just seen. Yet sprawling windows surrounded her, looking out at the city below.

They were higher than most of the buildings, save for a towering few, which stretched brazenly toward the faux sky with silver fingers. The rest looked small in comparison, mere men among monsters, but V knew better. Inside, they were likely the height of luxury, the palaces where senators played while the rest of them starved.

Tonight, though, V would be playing alongside them. Bracing herself, she spun and glided toward the exit, with the ribbons of her dress caressing her legs in quiet whispers.

Two Guards were stationed at the doors, and they stared straight at her, wordless and intense. As she approached, they stood at attention, the right one holding out a scanner in silent invitation. She proffered her wrist in response with choreographed grace.

"Welcome, Ms. Innova," the Guard boomed, his deep voice echoing through the vacant chamber. "Senator Quinn is delighted to have you join him for this evening's festivities. Please follow the directions on your scryglass and enjoy your stay."

V didn't know if it was her or her nerves or his apathetic tone, but his words rang with warning, like a bell tolling in her mind. *Get out. Get out. Get out.*

She ignored it, pressing on past the men and into the elevator beyond. Her scryglass beeped out instructions, leading her down, then up a walkway, then across a sprawling building before positioning her in front of an elevator once more. This time, the ride was longer, and she spiraled toward the sky in a cloud of tension.

Soon enough, the journey ended, and the lift deposited her into a luxurious lobby. Its walls were dressed in a plush purple velvet, save for the space taken up by the door, which was inlaid with a gleaming golden pattern. V steeled herself and rang the bell, its tinny song sinking into the folds of fabric.

The door opened to reveal a man, his dapper blue suit and slicked back white hair encompassing her vision. He wore a smile, genial and sincere, and it sparkled in his eyes as he greeted her.

"Welcome, Violet," Apollo said, extending a hand. "I am so pleased that you accepted my offer. With you here, this is bound to be an unforgettable evening."

"Thank you," V replied, releasing his softly wrinkled hand. "It's a pleasure to be here." The butterflies in her stomach beat their wings at her half-truth, but she stubbornly ignored them.

"Now, most of my guests have yet to arrive," the man continued. "I've asked you here early to allow you ample time to get situated. Feel free to acquaint yourself with the stage and setup. If anything is lacking, my staff will be more than happy to help."

So far, this gig certainly had a leg up on the Alcor. Maybe her concerns about this evening would come to nothing. Maybe she'd prove Mouse wrong – and his words of warning would finally stop repeating in her mind.

"Please help yourself to any food or drinks, and don't be afraid to mingle. You are, after all, my guest. However, I do ask that you reserve me a moment of your time. I have a certain *private* matter to discuss with you."

Well, that sounded ominous, V thought. Her brain tripped over pleasantries as she attempted to order her thoughts into a question.

"May I ask what it is you would like to discuss?" she inquired, the formal words sounding stiff as they stumbled off her tongue.

Something bordering on sadness crept into his eyes as he considered her question, but it was gone again in an instant.

"Oh, we'll have plenty of time to talk about that later. For now, just enjoy yourself – and this wonderful party. If you'll excuse me, I have a few last-minute details to attend to. A host's duties are never done!"

He turned on his heel with alacrity and bounded away. V stood there for a moment, processing his words – along with his strange demeanor.

There was something off about him this evening, something unbalanced, like an energy that crackled in a minor key. Maybe it was nerves, a natural reaction to the pressures of such a party. Or maybe she was projecting, placing her own concerns on him. Still, she couldn't shake the feeling that something more was at play.

V chided herself for giving in to her doubts and made her way forward. She stood on a balcony that ringed the room, a sort of viewing gallery overlooking the action. Placing herself along the balustrade, V gazed out across the space, sizing up the scene.

Workers flitted below, hurrying to complete their final tasks before the elite descended en masse. It was a gentle sort of commotion, a ballet of rippling linens, tinkling glasses, and near collisions. Yet the action was muted and the chatter hushed, like the room was saving up its echoes.

The lights suddenly dipped, and V held tight to the

railing as the room descended from reality into a delirious dream. Orbs she hadn't noticed floated before her, casting a fuzzy glow on the scene. Under the mellow pressure of their light, everything transformed, morphing from mundane to magical in the blink of an eye.

Chapter 7

The railing turned to fireflies beneath her fingers, melting from wood to pure radiance as she watched. The walls around her dissolved in a brilliant cascade, replaced by a forest of trees. She could see their knotted bark, hear the wind rustle through their leaves, smell their bright green life.

V knew it was a trick, a mirage, but she didn't care. It was breathtaking.

A soft breeze tickled her neck, making stray hairs dance across her face. The air was sweet and soft with just a hint of moisture, like the jungle after an evening rain. Or so she imagined. Even her own dress came to life, with minuscule glittering particles capturing the light and casting it back in rainbows.

A hint of movement at the edge of her vision made her start. Twirling, she spied a band of small animals parading from the halls to place themselves atop the banister, like living scenery in this picturesque play. Yet their gestures gave them away. Everything was too precise, too measured. They were machines dressed in the lie of life, mere robots reminding them of what they'd lost.

A hare brushed against V's ankle and a finch fluttered past her ear. Down below, larger animals positioned themselves on their marks, like actors taking the stage, waiting for their audience. A fox, a deer, a docile wolf, a silent black panther.

Most of these creatures had perished along with their planet, just more victims of men's insatiable greed. Now their memories were bought and sold as holo pets, mere status symbols for the rich. Other creatures had been saved from the ruins of their world only to live in stasis beneath the surface of the ship. Yet more lived only to die, their mere existence a sacrifice.

These were different. They were mechanical in nature, programmed to be lithe and almost alive. V could tell they were gems plucked from Apollo's mind, a bittersweet result of his research and resources. They were small bits of him scattered across the room, waiting to dazzle and delight.

Unconsciously, V gravitated toward the stairs, propelled by curiosity. The ground beneath her feet rippled as grass grew where boards had been and brilliant flowers bloomed alongside dirt paths.

She descended the stairs, which now resembled earthen steps carved into a hill, and emerged in the heart of the forest. Here, the song of the trees beat like a drum, thrumming through her veins. Crickets chirped, wind whistled, and animals called out through time in a heartbreaking melody.

Above her, the ceiling had turned to stars and the orbs

became its moons, and together they rained down a story that V ached to believe. It was a tale of lost things found again, of fractured worlds made whole.

It was wondrous and terrible, and for the moment it was all hers.

Soon enough, though, others began to join her amongst the trees, spoiling this paradise with their presence. The animals around them didn't startle or flee, and their fearlessness betrayed the forgery. Drinks began to flow, and food appeared on trays carried by dapper staff, waking V from the fantasy.

The crowd was quiet as she checked the stage, testing its equipment and boundaries. With each minute, though, the noise swelled, building on itself until it drowned out the dream. The animals remained calm, unbothered by the intruders, unnaturally still. Meanwhile, the brazen guests goggled and groped, recording the scene with their scryglasses to reenact at their leisure.

V tuned them out as she withdrew into the wings, clinging to the notes that coursed through her veins. The melody was her life raft, and it ebbed and flowed across the banks of her mind, lending clarity and calm to her uneasy soul.

"It's almost time," said Apollo, suddenly beside her. "Take a deep breath. My guests won't bite. They have manners enough for that, at least." He winked, his eyes sparkling with a mirth reserved only for her.

V turned to the gathered throng, assessing them. Their numbers now soared into the hundreds, with people packed on both levels, all clamoring for attention.

"You've certainly assembled quite the crowd," V

responded, nodding at the mob. "All friends of yours?"

Apollo snorted in an utterly ungentlemanly manner. "People like me don't have the luxury of friendship. I have admirers, allies, and enemies, each parading as one another. Honestly, it's exhausting."

V raised a quizzical eyebrow. "You call this exhausting?" she asked, amused. She let her eyes find the food, the fauna, the finery before locking back on him.

Apollo flashed an odd expression, but it disappeared in a sliver of a second, replaced by a sudden calm.

"Don't judge me too harshly," he responded, a hint of ice cooling his tone. "There's more to this story than you know."

V was about to ask, but she didn't get the chance. Apollo took that opportunity to leap onto the stage, his movements oddly graceful. Despite the chaos, his guests clocked his presence almost instantly, and an anxious hush descended. The creatures of the forest stilled as anticipation took root and blossomed into eager restlessness.

Apollo didn't leave them waiting for long.

"Friends, welcome," he boomed, adopting the façade of a showman, cheerful and gregarious. "It is my deepest honor to have you here. I know these last few months have been challenging, but I hope that – at least for tonight – we can relax and enjoy each other's company."

To V, the words felt hollow, like a politician's promise, although their content sparked her interest. What did he mean by *challenging*? To her knowledge, the Senate had been calm, conducting business as usual, but he made it sound as though something sinister was at play.

"To start this evening off right, I've prepared a special

treat," Apollo continued, rubbing his hands together. "I've invited a remarkable guest all the way from the Alcor Club. Please join me in welcoming the one and only Violet Innova."

A deafening roar burst from the crowd as V ascended to the stage. The lights dipped, giving way to a spotlight that caressed her edges. The room turned to stars in her vision and its people faded into one amorphous form.

A familiar thrill twisted around her heart, making it flutter. As the din diminished, she traced the shape of the crowd, sketching its blurred outlines as it swayed. She let the tension build until it wavered on the brink of unbearable, and then she leapt.

Her voice was steady and strong as she wove her spell. The magic settled softly at first, like an early morning dew, before seeping into their souls and spurring them to movement.

V kept the pace light and fluid, carefully avoiding the songs that called for change, the ones that would rain reality down on this dream. Instead, she embraced the safety of the familiar, belting the ballads they clung to and the anthems they adored.

Time began to lose its grasp, blurring in and out of focus. V yearned to prolong the moment, the adoration, yet she knew her time was finite. So she savored the feeling while she could, knowing as soon as she stepped offstage, it would begin to slip away.

All too soon, she found herself facing the final song. By then, the crowd was well past captivated, drunk on spirits and high on the melody. V knew she needed to close with a bang, to leave them dazed and delirious and demanding more. If she hoped to gain their help in saving Riyah, she needed to pry them open and brand herself on their memories. She needed to be unforgettable.

The words came without conscious thought, ingrained as they were on her mind. It was *her* song – the first song she'd written, the one that had won her the job at the Alcor. It flowed from her veins like blood, thick and metallic, coating everyone around her.

> *Twist me up and tear me down*
> *Words falling like forgotten sounds*
> *Fate sets me up, then knocks me 'round*
> *Come sail away with me*
> *Sail away with me, my love, come sail away with me*
> *Sail away, sail away, for tonight I will be free*
>
> *I've lived a thousand times to die*
> *In each you've surfaced by my side*
> *Now it's time to close my eyes*
> *Come sail away with me*
> *Sail away with me, my love, come sail away with me*
> *Sail away, sail away, for tonight we'll both be free*
>
> *When this world passes soundlessly*
> *Without a thought of destiny*
> *A shadow on a waveless sea*
> *You'll sail away with me*
> *Sail away with me, my love, come sail away with me*
> *Sail away, sail away, for tonight we'll all be free*

The last few words lingered, suspended in midair as the music died. Anxious to never outstay her welcome, V dashed offstage, disappearing beneath the thrall of awe that held the crowd in a trance. It hovered for one more heartbeat before bursting in a raucous chorus of applause.

Then, as if by magic, the spell that held them stationary broke, and movement, conversation, and laughter enveloped the scene. The sea parted as friends, allies, and lovers gravitated into each other's orbits, forming disparate pods throughout the cavernous space. Waitstaff danced between them with laden trays, fueling the party toward its boisterous end.

A silver tray skirted the edges of her vision, and she followed its gleam, her stomach growling. Beside her, a waiter carried bite-size morsels, and she unabashedly grabbed two, marveling at the snow-white puree surrounded by pastry and topped with minuscule black eggs. She ate the first in one bite, but took the time to savor the other, letting the salt bite her tongue and the cream caress her lips as she chewed.

As soon as she'd swallowed, she wanted more, so she went in search of servers to quell her rising hunger and quench her aching thirst. Within no time, she'd accumulated a small feast, squirreling away crumbs in the pockets of her dress to present to Riyah when she returned. Smoky meat wrapped tightly in sweet leaves, luscious pillows of pastry cocooning a spicy center, sweet dark treats that coated her tongue with pleasure. She washed it all down with a fizzy green spirit that was so far from freeze they couldn't possibly be classified as the same thing.

Another tray swept past, laden with golden spheres,

and she leapt without thinking. When her eyes finally lifted from the food, she froze, lips parted and hand outstretched, staring at the server. It was the man from the train, the one whose copper skin and curls had captured her attention.

V murmured a quiet thank you before shoveling the bite-sized ball into her mouth. She crunched her way through the crispy coating to find a gooey center, stifling a moan as a wave of pure bliss traveled across her tongue. The man's eyes met hers, flickering for an instant before dancing away to inspect the crowd. He seemed to be searching for someone, raking the room with the intensity of a scout. Then, with a nod, he was gone.

V swallowed, shaking herself from her stupor and reminding herself of her mission.

She didn't meld with the crowd. Instead, she clung to the gaps like an old friend, watching from the safety of their arms. She was an explorer, an adventurer charting a new world with its unfamiliar faces and curious customs. She cataloged everything – those who talked, those who listened, and those who watched it all unfold from on high.

V spotted the woman from the train making the rounds with a tray of silver drinks, which shimmered beneath the light of the floating moons. In the darkness, her skin looked ashen, almost gray. She seemed out of place, distracted, just like her companion, but V didn't have the capacity to care. She was on a hunt of her own, and her eyes were trained on a larger target.

As if privy to her thoughts, Apollo appeared behind her, placing a palm gently on her shoulder. When she turned, she found his kind eyes considering her, a silent question in his gaze.

"A wonderful performance," he said, his deep voice cutting an easy path through the din. "You had the audience absolutely transfixed."

V smiled, flattered at the sentiment.

"If you're not busy," he continued, "I would like to have that word now."

"Actually," V countered, an idea blossoming in her mind, "would you mind introducing me to some of your guests? I'd appreciate the opportunity to...become better acquainted with your circle." The formal words sounded unnatural, like a language she didn't quite speak, but she managed to get her meaning across.

Apollo looked pained at the request, but it quickly passed, replaced by a calm resignation.

"Of course," he replied gallantly. "Your wish is my command."

For the next quarter of an hour, he obliged, presenting her with the Echelon's elite. She met senators and their partners, a treasurer, a housing minister, and several leaders of the Iridium Guard. V paid attention to everyone, to their names and faces, to their interest in her – and the likelihood of using that to her advantage.

V was awash in plans and schemes, in praise and invitations and the prospect of favors. With these people in her palm, she could leech off their power, slowly siphoning it to Riyah. She could save her friend with songs and smiles. She could be the hero.

She was so intoxicated with her own ingenuity that she barely registered as Apollo led her to the outskirts of the room. V looked up to find a door, solid and real amidst the forest of dreams, and turned a curious eye on her companion.

"Now that I've done you a favor, it's time to return the courtesy," he explained. "I think you'll find this immensely intriguing – and particularly advantageous for us both."

There was a light in his eyes and a key in his hand. Sneaking a surreptitious look around, he fit the key into the lock, directing her inside before securing the door behind them. V's stomach flipped and her palms began to sweat as she took stock of her new surroundings.

Shelves crowded them on all sides, with stacks of books straining to touch the ceiling. Hints of vanilla and earth wafted around her, the scent of pages pulled from the past. V yearned to feel the spines beneath her fingers and explore their depths. Yet she kept her hands clasped, her body angled toward his, her shoulders set.

"I am so sorry it has taken me this long," he began, running a hand through his hair in a fit of emotion. His posture had changed and bent, and his voice had softened into something resembling sincerity. Only, V had no idea what he was saying, so she stayed where she was, silent and still.

"I didn't think it would be so complicated," he continued, finally looking up. "I didn't intend to leave you out there, confused and alone. But I have it now – and we can finally begin."

V's uncertainty deepened into utter bewilderment, and a note of warning rang in her mind. She took a step back, covertly scanning for a weapon but finding only tomes.

Meanwhile, the man shuffled to a shelf in the corner and pushed its books aside. Behind them, a scanner sprang to life, mapping Apollo's face. It barely took a heartbeat to process his features before emitting an approving chirp.

Things were getting stranger by the second.

When Apollo turned around, the cubbyhole was closed and obscured, and the man held a matte black object. It was rectangular and thin, and he cradled it with such care that V wondered if it was a weapon.

He approached her cautiously, and she backed up farther, until the hard wood of the shelves bit into her shoulders. V sized the man up, calculating his age and ingenuity and trying to decide if she could take him.

"Now," he began again, looking toward her, "I know you have questions, and I promise you'll get your answers. But first, there's one thing I must do."

V froze at his words, eyes trained on the gadget. At the push of a button, two prongs shot from its tip, crackling with a menacing energy.

V flailed gracelessly as Apollo approached. She wasn't sure if she was trying to attack him or distract him or disarm him, but she managed none of those things. He evaded her thrashing limbs with surprising ease, drawing up to her side and placing the device against her neck.

"I'm sorry," Apollo whispered sadly. "This is going to hurt."

And he was right. As the device whined to life, a thousand daggers pierced her flesh and traveled up to her brain, coating her vision in black.

Chapter 8

V was on the ground, her head pounding. It felt like her brain had been shredded, then reassembled in the wrong order. Everything was fuzzy and distant, and her memories hurt to recall.

Yet she was alive.

She reached up and rubbed her hammering head, her closed eyes, her dry lips. Her hand came away slick with something that felt like blood, but she couldn't find the source. Nothing appeared to be broken or bleeding. She quickly assessed her body for other signs of damage but found none, only a lingering ache that beat through her temples and traveled in bursts beneath her skin.

V groggily opened her eyes, blinking at the muted light. The world spun for a moment, lurching side to side as if trying to find its bearings, before regaining its balance. Sitting up slowly, V scanned the scene, hunting for clues to explain her prone state. She didn't have to search for long.

A high-pitched whine suffused her senses as she spotted Apollo, his body lying lifeless beside her. All thoughts and words escaped her as raw emotion surged, sending her crawling across the floor. She was at his side in an instant, her shaking hands searching for signs of life. Yet she wasn't destined to find any. The dagger plunged to the hilt into his heart made sure of that.

A silent cry clawed her throat raw at the sight. His icy blue eyes were open, his mouth contorted in a never-ending scream. A cold sweat began to creep down V's back as she knelt there, unable to move from the growing pool of blood.

Who had done this? V jerked her head around, hunting through the shadows, but they were empty. She was alone, drenched in blood and stained with guilt.

Had she done this? She couldn't bring herself to believe it. Yet Apollo had attacked her. He'd come at her with that *thing*. He'd hurt her. Maybe she'd hurt him in return.

V checked his body for clues to dispel her theory, to prove her innocence. There was a cut across his palm, blood under his nails, a tuft of black fabric caught in the band of his scryglass. V glanced over her own apparel, but her garments were intact, adding one more mystery to this puzzling scene.

Panic assaulted her system, sharp and insistent. Movement seemed the only way to tame it, so she leapt to her feet and took a lap around the room, leaving tacky red footprints in her wake. By the time she returned to the scene of the crime, the sirens had started to blare.

Somehow, she wasn't surprised. Her emotions fizzled, the adrenaline cooling to acceptance. Her life was over. The Guards would haul her off, charge her without trial, sentence her to life in the Grove – or make her disappear completely.

And without her help, Riyah was doomed. V would never be able to help her friend. It had all been for nothing.

She sank to her knees beside Apollo as the Guards began to break down the door. The thuds echoed around her, sinking into the spines and pages, yet her mind had gone still. She was aware but distant, conscious but thoroughly detached.

The Iridium Guards burst in and tackled her to the ground, all the while shouting indistinct commands. Before she knew it, her wrists were trapped in thick magnetic bands, then forced behind her back.

Those that had marveled at her performance now marveled at her downfall, parting to gawk and gape as the Guards led her out. Some filmed her on their scryglasses, others stared in horror. Even the waiters from the train peered out from the pack to take in her torment.

Time lost hold of its typical restraint, bolting from one instant to the next. V was dragged into the hall, then across a bridge, then onto a train, all the while straining to keep her wits about her.

The Guards refused to talk. Their steel gray armor and steely gazes told her plainly that they had no mercy for her plight. They weren't there to listen or investigate her claims, so she kept them to herself, even as they begged to break free.

The train slowed, then stopped, then spit them out onto an unfamiliar platform. The Guards pushed and pulled, steering her toward their towering home, its outlines sketched in blue and black against the fading sky.

The Guard House was pure pandemonium, with cadets

and criminals twining in a dance of disarray. There was shouting and crying, ringing and beeping, all berating V's mind, but none of it sank in. None of it seemed real. It felt like a dream, just one more nightmare haunting her life.

Suddenly, she was in a room, thrown into a groaning chair, her shackles bound to the table before her. A door closed and locked, sealing her in, alone. And time passed.

Eventually, her thoughts began to thaw and return to the land of the living. Shock gave way to grief, then sorrow – for herself, for Apollo, for Riyah. Gradually, though, something sharper snaked its way across her chest, squeezing her heart. Anger.

This was not her doing. She had not killed Apollo. She was being framed.

The thought acted like an iron rod, driving her spine straight. V finally took in her surroundings, cataloging the wall of two-way mirrors, the industrial table, the empty aluminum chair. The shackles bit into her wrists, and she strained against them, but they stubbornly refused to budge.

Her wrists stung from the effort. Something about the pain focused her mind and calmed her racing thoughts. V composed herself, letting the serenity entomb her. It wasn't a peaceful embrace. It didn't soothe her, but it prepared her for what was to come.

The Guards made her wait, no doubt watching from behind their mirrors to see what she would do. So she did nothing, remaining stationary through sheer force of will.

The curfew alarm blared through the streets, calling all citizens home. It was the only sound that bled into her cell, her only link to the outside world. Soon enough, though, it was gone, replaced by a sober silence.

A minute later, her new world broke open as two soldiers marched in, slamming the door behind them. V looked up, surprised to find Inspectors in place of Iridium Guards, their slick silver suits marking them as superior. They both considered her with quiet disdain, their matching frowns deep and discouraging.

The woman, squat and sturdy, took the seat across from her while her colleague stood, still as a scarecrow. He looked like one, too, with his too-long limbs, wide-open eyes, and scraggly brown hair. He placed his hands on his hips, his frown deepening even further.

It was the woman who spoke first. Folding her hands on the table, she gave V a once-over and sighed, shaking her head.

"Tell us what happened," she commanded, her voice as flat and lifeless as the room. "Don't leave anything out."

The silence that followed was laden with expectation, as heavy eyes considered her from across the table. So V obliged, embarking on her tragic tale.

Although she did, in fact, leave a few details out. Like Riyah and Mouse. Like her true reason for taking this job. She spun a story that shadowed the truth, overlapping at the important points while obscuring others. When she reached the conclusion, she paused, weighing her options – and making her first conscious choice to lie.

The truth would paint her in a hundred shades of guilt, even more than the blood that still speckled her body. If they learned that Apollo had attacked her – or whatever it was he'd done – their minds would fill in the rest, regardless of her word. They would cast her as the damsel striking out in defense, and no claims of innocence would save her.

Although they could just as easily label her story as slander. A senator of such high standing had a character that even the truth couldn't mar. Their ideas of him as a god would trump the accusations of a mortal, and his unimpeachable character might repel even her candid claims.

"He told me he had something to discuss, something advantageous to us both," she relayed, watching as the Inspectors narrowed their eyes in unison. "He took me to the library, shut the door…and that's the last thing I remember. I woke up later with my head pounding, Apollo lying on the ground, and no memory of how it had happened. There must have been someone waiting, poised to attack. Someone who struck me and then him and then fled. Someone dangerous who's still out there, hiding on this ship."

No one spoke, although the woman's eyebrow rose, painting her face with suspicion. The silence stretched, and V's heart thundered in her ears, screaming out her guilt.

"You see, we don't believe you," the female Inspector said, shaking her head. "No one came out of that room. And no one else went in. Besides, the footage from your retinal implant tells a different story."

"What?" The word was out before V could think, confusion controlling her senses.

Retinal implants were for the rich, those who could afford to hack their bodies with the latest biotech. Not for singers performing in lounges and living in one-room shacks. Not for the likes of her. And she told them as much.

"Your lies are getting worse," said the man, finally

deigning to speak. "Why don't you save us all some time and shut up?"

The harsh words stung, shocking V into submission. She didn't understand, couldn't process the development, so she sat there, eyes wide and mouth agape.

"Our techs have been working to gain access to your footage since you entered this room," the man touted. "It wasn't easy. You've clearly put some safeguards in place. Yet with a bit of effort we've managed to retrieve a few…enlightening moments. Shall we take a look?"

The Inspectors seemed to salivate, watching as the wall of mirrors transformed into a bank of screens, transmitting the world as seen through her eyes. She marveled at the clarity, at the déjà vu that seeped into her soul, making her dizzy. They hadn't been lying. She did have a retinal implant recording the world, trapped behind her eyes.

The memory played in perfect detail, down to the same strains of music and the placement of every last guest. V rose out of her body, out of this room, and into that version of herself – so ignorant, so naïve. She followed Apollo blindly, unaware of where it would lead.

V wished she could tell herself to run, to escape, but she was stuck in a loop, forever destined to find death beside her. So she watched mutely, entranced by the memory as it played out on the screen.

Apollo began to speak, and V knew the words before he said them.

"Now that I've done you a favor, it's time to return the courtesy," he said, the words dripping with menace. "I think you'll find this immensely intriguing – and particularly advantageous for us both."

They entered the library, and he locked the door, sealing them into their fates. V could just about smell the books, the beads of sweat trickling down her back, the blood.

"I am so sorry it has taken me this long," Apollo said again, and again she didn't understand him. "I didn't think it would be so complicated," he confessed, looking straight into the camera. "I didn't intend to leave you out there, confused and alone. But I have it now – and we can finally begin."

A burst of static erupted from the screen, wiping it blank. V looked to the Inspectors in confusion, searching for answers, but their expressions held nothing but contempt. The woman sauntered around the table toward V, crossing her arms in a practiced stance.

"Were you having an affair with Senator Quinn?" she asked smugly, as if she already knew the answer.

No, V wanted to scream. A thousand times no. But she merely shook her head, suddenly unable to utter a sound.

Then, without warning, the world went fuzzy, bleeding from concrete shapes into lines of blurry text. V jerked back like she'd been stung, blinking to clear her vision, yet the shapes merely sharpened behind her eyes.

"In two minutes, an alarm will sound," it said. "Be ready."

The lines disappeared, only to be replaced by more. The officers didn't seem to notice, interpreting her odd behavior as yet another sign of guilt.

"When your cuffs unlock, run," the new message read, spurring V's heart into a sprint. "Left, then right, then left again."

For the hundredth time that night, she didn't know

what was happening – yet she found herself hoping for more. When the next words came, a sliver of relief cracked through her confusion.

"If you come across any obstacles, FIGHT LIKE HELL. They will shoot to kill. Good luck."

The words disappeared just as quickly as they'd come, leaving V to wonder if they'd ever truly been there or if she was simply going mad. The latter option seemed more likely by the minute.

"Once again, we don't believe you," the woman was saying, a shark-like smile rising to her lips, as if she'd tasted blood in the water and wanted more. "We think you two were having…relations," she sneered.

"A girl like you and a man like him? It's a tale as old as time. Then what? He didn't give you what you wanted? Not enough units to make him worth your time? Or he wanted more than you were willing to give? Even *someone like you* must have their limits. So you killed him, then you wiped the rest of the footage to prevent us from seeing the full, salacious story."

The insinuation burned a hole through her skin, igniting a fire in her chest. She knew no amount of denial would save her. These people had already written her story, already cast her as the villain, so she kept her mouth shut.

"What? No more excuses?" the man asked in derision. "No more pathetic lies? I'm almost disappointed."

He stalked around the table, towering over her. Then, in one easy movement, he struck her with the back of his hand, sending her head flying. She tasted blood, coppery and warm, and it freed a fresh wave of loathing.

"We asked you a question," he shouted. "SPEAK!"

He reared to strike again, but in that instant an alarm began to sound throughout the station, blaring a call of distress. The lights in the room responded, flashing in time with the sounds.

V's mind inched along, putting the pieces together. It had been two minutes. The alarm was sounding. It was time to go. She didn't know what lay beyond the station, what faceless creature she was fleeing toward, but it had to be better than this.

The Inspectors grumbled their displeasure, clearly annoyed. They glanced at each other, communicating in eyebrows and frowns, before turning toward the door. Without a word, they left her there, securing the cell behind them.

The seconds ticked by, sticky and slow, as V struggled against her bonds, waiting for them to break. When they didn't, the doubt crept in like lava, singeing a path through her mind.

Then V heard the faintest click. Fresh air rushed to cool her burning wrists, and she looked down to find them free.

Nerves licked hungrily at her pounding heart as she rose, almost running to the door. With shaking hands, she tried the handle and – miraculously – it gave. Taking one deep breath, she burst into the hall and made a beeline to the left.

Chaos consumed the station. Guards ran and sentries buzzed as someone shouted orders to the jumbled throng. It was bedlam, plain and simple, and it cloaked V in a mask of obscurity.

Soon enough, the first hallway ended, giving way to another, and V turned right, following the directions in her head. It was working, guiding her through the station and into the safety of the night – but she wasn't safe yet.

"Where do you think you're going?" The woman's cold voice stopped V in her tracks, filling her with icy unease.

The second half of the ghostly instructions beat through her brain on a loop, begging for violence. *Fight like hell. Fight like hell. Fight like hell.*

Spinning around before she could think, V sprinted toward the voice. The world went silent save for the sound of her steps. One, two, three, four. Then she collided with a wall of flesh, knocking them both to the ground.

A weapon dropped and skittered away, but before V could grab it, a punch connected with her jaw, slamming her teeth together. Once again, she tasted blood, but it only spurred her on, fueling her erratic blows. V certainly wasn't a fighter – but for the moment she could fake it.

She was still atop the Guard, straddling the heavy woman like a horse, yet she knew the weight of her body wouldn't hold her down for long. So V curled her fingers and struck, aiming for the gut.

Her punch landed, knocking the wind from her foe. She heard the woman's breath escape in a painful wheeze and moved to strike again, but she didn't get the chance. The Guard grabbed her fist mid-swing and pulled, wrenching V off balance.

V tumbled off her mount, kicking and thrashing as she went. Something connected, and she heard a moan from beside her. Risking a glance, she saw blood rushing from the woman's nose, a feral expression on her ruined face.

V tried to get her feet beneath her, but the Guard wasn't

having it. She sprang from her crouch, claws outstretched, slamming V back to the ground. She felt nails graze her arm and a knee collide with her side, but it barely registered. The pain was drowned out by adrenaline, by anxiety and cruel excitement.

Their grappling grew more savage as the seconds ticked by. V slipped an arm free of the Guard's grasp and sent a chop toward her neck. It collided with her throat, making her choke. V seized her chance and shoved, thrusting the woman away.

In a heartbeat, V was on her feet. She stomped on the woman's ribs, feeling something give. It did the trick, keeping her down long enough for V to locate the weapon and lunge. She felt the cool weight of the energy pistol as it rested in her palm, filling her with power.

"They'll kill you for this," the woman wheezed, trying to stand. "And it won't be quick. They'll make sure you suffer."

The outrage boiled over, with hot, frothy fury sizzling in her veins. V couldn't think or plan; she could only act. With the pistol clutched tightly in her hand, she spun to face her foe.

V saw it in flashes as the lights pulsed, sending them in and out of shadow. The Guard struggling to her feet, her back to the wall. V's arm outstretched. The pistol moving into place.

With a savage cry, V slammed the weapon into the woman's temple. This time, there were no threats or screams as she fell, landing in a heap. She stayed there, unconscious, and a giddy triumph rose in V's chest.

The world began to spin as a loose hysteria bubbled up,

but V tamped it down, willing herself to stay sane. No matter the tumult – no matter what she'd done – she needed to escape. She could worry about the rest later.

V started off down the hall with an off-kilter jog. Her side began to ache, but she didn't have time to inspect the wound. She knew the alarm could end at any moment, leaving her stranded in the station, alone amongst the wolves.

V still cradled the pistol, but it gave her little comfort. She couldn't be sure she'd have the nerve to pull the trigger. Killing was not in her nature. At least she'd never thought it was, but this day was proving her wrong in all sorts of ways.

The path ahead split again, and she veered toward the left, taking the final turn. She couldn't afford doubt, so she traveled on blind faith, working her way down a door-lined hall. Her eyes danced with stars, with each flash briefly illuminating the world then drenching it in black.

It took V one second too long to register the man in the doorway. By the time her eyes traced his outline, he'd already clocked her, his massive form turning fully in her direction. Before he could act, V raised the pistol and aimed it at his chest.

"Don't move," she said, hoping against hope that her voice sounded strong.

His ensuing chuckle shattered that hope into pieces. The smile he wore showcased a mouth full of jagged teeth, and his muscles strained against his shirt as he sauntered toward her, a true predator primed for the kill.

V's hand shook as she gripped the weapon, and he could see it. Despite the dim light, it seemed like he could see every crack in her façade, every chink in her armor. She knew that was absurd, that her raw and splintered spirit couldn't possibly be so clear, yet he kept coming nonetheless, closing the gap between them with measured steps.

V tried to back up but was met by a cool wall. From somewhere deep within her, a soothing calmness surfaced, coating her in conviction. Bracing herself, she closed her eyes and fired.

The kick was gentle. The resounding boom, however, almost shattered her eardrums.

V peeked through one eye, dreading the bloodshed. Luckily, she wasn't destined to find any. Unluckily, the burly man was still bearing down, unconcerned by the generous chunk V had taken out of the wall behind him.

Plaster and brickwork crumbled, littering the hallway and dusting the air with a cloud of particles. Meanwhile, her opponent began to curl his fingers into fists, his smile widening into a wicked sneer.

V moved before he could strike, ducking out of his path and under his arm. He tried to grab her, but his girth slowed his reactions, making his movements leaden.

She danced outside his reach for another heartbeat before he caught up, sinking a sadistic punch into her stomach. Her head went light from lack of oxygen as her body forgot how to breathe. A follow-up strike sent her flying, and she collided with the cracked wall, landing with a thump in the debris.

Yet she still had her gun. This time when she raised it, she didn't close her eyes.

The Guard dropped with a howl as his leg shattered, crumbling beneath his weight. V tried not to look, but she couldn't stop herself from glancing down. The food and drinks she'd devoured at the party threatened to resurface at the sight. But just like the hysteria, she clamped it down, forcing herself to turn.

The pistol dropped from her hands as they shook, and she didn't bother to retrieve it. The thought of using it again, of witnessing more bloodshed in the span of this never-ending day, felt like it might drive her mad. So she picked up her pace and ran.

Her heartbeat mellowed with the familiar rhythm of her feet. She drove herself forward, past windows and doors, driving out her demons as she went. Stale air flowed in and out, powering her lungs and clearing the cobwebs from her mind.

Without warning, the hall opened into a cavernous room. It felt industrial, all beams and chains and cool concrete – and a fleet of motorbikes all lined up in neat little rows.

V itched to climb astride one, to smash the glass garage door and abscond into the night. Except she had no DNA-coded key, no passcode, and no idea how to hotwire a vehicle. Plus, she reasoned, each must be logged within the system, making them easy to track – and easy to recapture.

Instead, she made a beeline for the door, which sat shrouded in shadow at the edge of the room. The handle gave beneath her fingers, and she sent a silent thank-you to the stars. As soon as the cool evening air washed across her face, a new string of text materialized, making her start.

"Head toward the underground markets. No main roads. No straight lines. If you're followed, you're on your own."

V was running before she'd even finished reading. Now this was something she could do.

Freed from the confines of the station, she felt a weight lift from her chest. Her strides were easy and light, taking her through the city like they'd done a hundred times. She drew up a map inside her mind, honed through countless nighttime runs, and followed its outlines toward the edges of the ship.

V zigged and zagged through forgotten lanes, lit dimly by far-away stars. She heard the tell-tale sound of sentries but managed to evade them, ducking out of sight each time they whirred past.

Twice she found her path blocked by a looming dead end, their stones and fences turned sinister in the starlight. So she backtracked, retracing her steps in search of another route through the tangled maze. Each street brought her closer to the underground markets, where sin was on sale and illicit wares suffused the streets. A warning bell sounded in V's mind, but she ignored it, anxious to find refuge regardless of the stakes.

As she drew nearer, another message flashed before her eyes. Startled out of her reveries, V collided with a wall, stopping to regain her breath – and her bearings.

"Almost there," the text said supportively, as if sensing her doubts. "Don't stop. Just keep heading straight."

It was then that V heard the sirens. She wasn't sure if they'd been there all along, muted by her meditation, or if this was their opening call, the initial gambit in their game. Either way, they were clearly on the hunt and she was their target, and soon no street would be safe.

She stumbled forward, her feet forgetting their function, before spilling back into a clumsy run. V told her legs to move, but they were flagging, failing under the weight of her endless ordeals. Her run tapered to a canter, then a trot as the sirens moved closer. They skirted her street, converging just out of sight, yet all she could do was slow.

Out of nowhere, a deep voice materialized from the darkness. "In here," it said, low and demanding.

V didn't think. She just obeyed, following the voice to a door, the door to a hallway, the hallway to a dim shop floor festooned with a mind-boggling assortment of junk. And a woman.

V backed up half a step as she noted the broad shoulders, the black braid, the unusual gray tint to her skin. A cool recognition took hold. It was the woman from the train, the server from the party.

"What the hell is going on?" V began, but the woman held a finger to her lips, forcing V into an unsettling silence.

A second passed, then two, and V's heart continued to hammer, stubbornly refusing to slow.

Then the deep voice came again, startling close. "The coast is clear," it rumbled just over V's shoulder. "It doesn't look like she was followed. We should be safe."

V spun to face the speaker, only half surprised to find the tall, dark-haired man who had captured her attention on the train, then again at the party. He aimed his searing gaze at her, stripping her of her final ounce of composure.

"Now, let's get down to business," he said, his wide brown eyes boring straight into hers. "Who exactly are you? And why is someone trying to frame you for murder?"

Chapter 9

"Who am I?" V repeated, surprise and caution competing for control of her brain. "I think the more pressing question is who are you? And how did you hack into my head?"

The man sighed. The woman cursed. V felt like she was caught in some strange parallel world, in a life that wasn't hers. Nothing that had happened in the past few hours made any kind of sense, and she yearned for some kind of clarity. Instead, confusion coursed around her in thick, incessant waves, lapping at her consciousness.

She let her eyes dance around the room – some kind of repair shop, she gathered – before dipping down to the people before her. They stared back, their gazes catching on every scrape and every speck of blood.

"We're…friends," replied the man, tripping over the word.

The woman let out a derisive sound, something between a snort and a chortle. It sounded ominous.

"Well, we're not your enemies," the man amended. "Not yet at least. But you're going to have to start answering our questions. So I'll ask again. Who are you – and why does someone want us to believe that you killed Senator Quinn?"

"You already know who I am," V sighed, running a hand through her sweat-slicked hair. "You were at the party. You saw me perform. As for who's trying to frame me, your guess is as good as mine. I didn't know a single person there besides Apollo, and our history spans a whole two days."

"You expect us to believe that?" the woman scoffed. "That someone like Apollo Quinn would approach a complete stranger to sing at an event like that? Mere days beforehand? Besides, we saw the footage from your implant – the clip they played at the prison. You two seemed...*close*."

"I didn't even know I had an implant!" V cried, desperate for someone to see the truth in her eyes. "Hell, a year ago I didn't even know my own name. I just turned up on the street like a stray dog – no memories, no possessions. Nothing!" she exclaimed.

Well shit, V thought. She hadn't intended to tell them that part. She let an anxious moment pass as her new captors – or saviors – absorbed the bombshell she'd just dropped.

"Look, I don't know why anyone would want to frame me," she admitted, speaking slowly so they wouldn't miss a thing. "I'm no one. I have no family, no past, and – after today – no future. Maybe they saw me as an easy scapegoat, someone disposable. Someone who wouldn't be missed." It cost her to say those words out loud, and the weight of them nearly crushed her.

The man shifted, his gaze directed downward and his

92

arms folded across his broad chest. This close, V could make out the deep brown of his eyes and the small lines that crinkled around them as he considered her words.

The woman, on the other hand, remained as still as stone. Although she was shorter than V, she was considerably more robust, and the hard muscles of her shoulders remained tensed, as if she was waiting for a fight. A fight she would no doubt win.

V's gaze traveled down her brawny arms to her clenched fists – one a pale white that verged on gray, the same color as her cold face, and the other a patchwork of metallic silver and matte black, with rivets instead of joints and steel in place of skin. The inorganic appendage looked powerful against her sturdy frame, and V hoped she'd never have the chance to see it in action.

V rubbed at her eyes, willing her thoughts to slow from their maelstrom and coalesce into some sort of sense. She teetered on the edge of exhaustion, her body weak, and she yearned for the comfort of her apartment, her bed, her life. It all seemed intangible now, a million miles away. An ache rose in her chest, threatening to choke her. She pushed it down with words, breaking the silence that had fallen.

"How do you know I didn't do it?" she asked, her voice impossibly small. She was grateful, sure, but she couldn't fathom why these strangers believed in her innocence when no one else had. And she had no idea why they would risk their own necks to save hers.

"We didn't know. Not for sure," the man said slowly. "At least, not until now."

"What?!" the woman asked in disbelief. "We don't know

anything, Fynn. We don't know her. We don't know what happened in that room. And we don't know who she's working for!"

V opened her mouth to fight back, but the man – Fynn – beat her to the punch.

"Lyra, her memory has been wiped. She can't remember anything past a year ago, which is exactly when everything escalated. Then Apollo Quinn invites her to the very party at which he's killed? That can't be a coincidence. There's a reason she was dragged into this."

V wasn't following their conversation in the slightest. Her legs wobbled beneath her, threatening to give way, and she sank into a nearby chair, its ratty leather hugging her curves with comforting strength. Meanwhile, the bickering around her intensified.

"Of course there's a reason," Lyra cried. "She's clearly working for someone important, someone with the resources to implant a recording device in her head. Someone wealthy enough to pay her to take the fall."

"Look at her!" Fynn shot back, pointing toward V. "She's not working for anyone. She could barely fight her way out of that station. She isn't a spy – or a killer – but she is important. In fact, she could be the key to all of this."

"Maybe all of that was an act. You ever think of that? Maybe she was waiting for her *benefactor* to spring her when we got in the way."

"Would both of you please *shut up*?" V cried, springing to her feet – and immediately regretting it. The sudden change in position sent her vision spinning, and she flailed wildly, fumbling for something to grab onto. A moment later, something grabbed onto her instead.

As her sights cleared, she saw Fynn standing beside her, his arm wound around her back as he kept her upright. The warmth of him seeped into her chilled skin, making her shiver, and the scent of warm cinnamon and wood shavings enveloped her. She shook herself free of him and sank back into the chair, regaining her bearings.

"I am not working for anyone," she said, enunciating each word. "I'm just a singer, and for all I know that's all I've ever been. I knew I shouldn't have gone to that party, but I was trying to…help a friend," she said, glossing over the details of Riyah's situation. "And while I would do anything to save her, I could never have done something like that."

The image of Apollo covered in blood came back to her, his blank eyes staring unseeing at the world, and she shuddered.

"If you don't believe me, that's fine. I never asked for your help. Just hand me back to the Guards and let them take me to the Grove for what's left of my life. But if you do believe me – even in the slightest – by all that's holy please *stop talking*. It's been a very long day, and I'd really like to lie down."

It was a risky proposition, to be sure. There was no guarantee they'd let her stay. Yet they'd risked a hell of a lot to rescue her, so she had to hope they wouldn't just send her back – not when she might be the *key to all of this*. Whatever *all of this* was.

The questions were piling on top of questions, creating a mountain of unknowns. Yet in this moment, there was only one question that mattered.

"So, can I stay?"

"Of course you're staying," Lyra spat, as if it were obvious. "We didn't go to all the trouble of breaking you out just to let you go. But you're not our *guest*," she said coldly, pulling a set of cuffs from behind her back and starting toward V.

"Lyra!" Fynn admonished, stepping between them. "We don't need to do this. She can help us – but not if we treat her like a criminal." He spoke about V as if she weren't right behind him, sitting an arm's length away.

Lyra hissed her disapproval. "You're too trusting. You know that, right?"

"She's not dangerous," Fynn replied, keeping his cool. "She's just a pawn in something bigger. I can feel it."

"Fine!" Lyra conceded, obviously unhappy. "But if your *pet* gets into trouble, it's your problem. Don't expect me to help." With a huff, she turned on her heel and disappeared into the hall.

Fynn sighed heavily, rubbing his eyes. V yearned for him to turn, to meet her gaze, to explain. Instead, he muttered something about finding blankets and followed in Lyra's wake.

V curled into a ball on the chair, hugging her legs to her chest. A ravenous exhaustion descended, and she yawned, nestling her head on the battered armrest. Behind her closed eyes, bloody images danced in a macabre ballet, straining to keep her awake. Yet even their pull couldn't save her from the darkness of her dreams. Within a minute, she was out, surrendering to sleep and its demons.

96

Violet woke covered in sweat. The scratchy woolen blanket that had appeared on top of her wasn't helping. She quickly kicked it off, relishing the coolness of the room.

Her eyes felt swollen, and she reached up to find her cheeks wet. She wiped away the tears, straining to wipe away the dreams along with them. They had been bloody and brutal, a cruel collage of memories and monsters. And Apollo.

Of course he was there. V had a feeling he would always be there, yet one more ghost fated to haunt her for eternity.

"Remember," he had said, his chest slicked with blood. "I need you to remember."

Then the scene had shifted, transforming into a derelict station. There were no trains, no people, only a wall of black lockers blinking in and out with the lights.

V had moved to open one only to find it crammed with maggots, which flooded out onto her feet. Over and over she tried, searching for something unseen, until she was swimming in a seething sea. Then they were gone, replaced by a woman, then a small girl in military garb, then Apollo.

"Remember!" he'd screamed with his last dying breath.

V felt her own breath catch at the memory. She sat up, trying to inhale, but the air evaded her grasp. Her breaths came short and shallow, and her heart stuttered, attempting to break free of her chest.

She needed to run, to escape, to see the sky, but as she rose she remembered where she was – and what had happened. Her chest constricted until a dizziness took hold, threatening to drag her back into obscurity.

"Breathe," came a deep voice, gentle yet commanding. "You're not alone. Just focus on my voice and breathe."

Fynn. As V's eyes adjusted, his silhouette came into view, stationed on a cot across the room. He sat with his legs slung over the side, his hands gripping the wood along its edges.

"You're safe here," he continued, not moving from his perch. "No one will hurt you. I promise."

With each word, V could feel herself returning, inching back to the land of the living. The anxiety lingered, coursing like an aftershock through her veins, but she could breathe, and she raked in lungfuls of the sweet, cool air.

"Better?" Fynn asked, cocking his head in question. His sleep-mussed hair fell over one eye, and he brushed it back with a touch.

V nodded, not trusting herself to speak.

Her neck throbbed where Apollo had attacked her, and she rubbed at it, feeling two raised bumps at the base of her skull. It still puzzled her – why he'd done it, what he'd hoped to achieve. Why he hadn't killed her when he'd had the chance.

"I think I have something that'll help," Fynn said, finally rising from his cot.

He ducked from the room only to return a moment later, a cloth-wrapped bundle in his hands. He flicked on a weak light and approached V slowly, holding out his offering. She unwrapped it cautiously, still unsettled by this stranger. Until she saw his treasure.

Her stomach growled at the sight of the food. It was glorious.

"Did you steal this from the party?" she asked, oddly impressed.

Fynn shrugged. "They had more than enough. And they

pay us so very little. But don't tell Lyra," he added with a wink. "She wouldn't approve."

V wondered if this was a ploy, a trick to make her trust him – but she didn't really care. Food was food, and in this moment she was ravenous.

Somehow, the delicacies tasted even better cold. She paced herself, trying to make the meager meal last despite the desire to cram everything into her mouth at once. V wished she could contribute her own collection of pilfered treats, but the Guards had emptied her pockets – and seized her scryglass in the process.

"Don't make me eat alone," she said with her mouth full of pastry, gesturing for Fynn to join her.

He conceded, grabbing a piece of meat wrapped in a leaf and popping it into his mouth. He chewed slowly, savoring the taste, and his eyelids closed in pleasure. A deep hum emanated from his lips as he swallowed, and he hastily reached for another.

When they'd finished their feast, they returned to their posts, considering each other from the safety of their bunkers. A slew of electronics and secondhand tech sat between them in various states of disrepair, forming a sort of barrier. They eyed each other cautiously through the debris, neither quite sure what to say.

Exhaustion still ached in V's bones, yet she knew that sleep would be elusive, driven back by the monsters behind her eyes and the morning light on the horizon. Another day would dawn before she knew it, illuminating her disastrous position. So, for the moment, she clung to the night.

"How did you do it?" V asked, breaking the silence.

"Get me out of there, I mean. And how did you access my implant?"

They weren't the most pressing questions, but V had to start somewhere, to shatter the ice before diving into its depths.

Fynn sighed, raking back the curling locks that fell across his face.

"I'm not the technical one," he confessed. "That would be Lyra. But suffice it to say we called in some favors."

V blinked slowly back at Fynn, silently demanding more. She was surprised when he obliged.

"OK, a lot of favors," he amended. "As for your retinal implant, that was a stroke of luck. We tried your scryglass first, but they'd already confiscated it. We thought we were screwed until they switched on the implant. Lyra located the signal and latched on. She knows a thing or two about bio-tech." He glanced down at his arm as if envisioning hers.

A troubling thought nudged V's mind to the next question. "Couldn't the Guards do the same thing to track me down?" Her heartbeat ticked up as she glanced around, half expecting a squadron to break down the door and storm the shop. Except Fynn didn't seem concerned.

"No. You're safe," he replied calmly. "They can't do more than an on-site download of your data. But even if they could, Lyra scrambled the signal so no one can trace you. Trust me, no one knows you're here."

That statement was simultaneously comforting and concerning. On the one hand, no one could find her. On the other, no one could save her. V was in their hands – and at their mercy.

"Why?" she asked, then went on to elaborate. "Why save me? I'm no one. I live in the background, in the space between pages. Why use up your favors on me?"

Fynn shook his head. "Violet," he breathed, his deep voice caressing the letters. "I know you can't see it, but you're part of something bigger. You, Apollo, this murder. It's not happening in isolation. It's all part of a larger plot."

"What is this *big plot*?" V asked, mildly perturbed. "Help me understand. One minute I'm a lounge singer, and the next I'm wanted for murder. A little context would be nice. And maybe some clue as to what I'm supposed to do next."

Instead of an answer, V was rewarded with darkness. The meager light in the room abruptly switched off, leaving V blinking in a curtain of black. She stilled, her irritation crashing against confusion as she hunted for the cause of the disruption.

"It's just another blackout," Fynn rumbled from across the room, still maintaining his distance.

"Another?" V asked in surprise.

"They've been happening more frequently these past few months. Only at night, of course, and not for long. Still, I can't believe you've never noticed."

V shrugged. "We tend to keep the lights off. It's safer for everyone that way."

"We?" Fynn asked, suddenly curious. "You and your partner?"

"Me and my...Mouse," V said, consciously omitting the word *friend*.

"Your mouse?" Fynn asked quizzically. "I didn't realize rodents had any strong feelings about lighting."

V let out a rush of breath that may have been a laugh. "Well, this one is…unique."

"What – he doesn't squeak incessantly? Or scurry in and out of holes? Or constantly get underfoot at the worst possible times?"

This time, V's laugh was definite. "Oh, he does all of that and more. Eats your food, steals your stuff, nibbles on things he definitely shouldn't."

V sobered in an instant. "He told me not to go to the party. It was like he knew something was going to happen, like he could sense it. I should have listened."

"You couldn't have known," Fynn assured her, "and neither could he. What's going on…it's bigger than any of us. You had a part to play, and I'd bet that even if you hadn't gone, you still would have found yourself in the middle of it."

"What do you mean?" V asked, not following his logic. It felt like he was talking in circles, and her brain was dizzy. "What do I have to do with any of this? I've already told you – I'm no one."

"Violet," he growled, the word cutting her to the core. "Don't you understand? The amnesia, the retinal implant, Apollo approaching you out of the blue. None of this is random. It's all connected."

"How?" V cried, still not understanding. "How is any of this linked? It makes no sense!"

"You're important," Fynn said slowly, stressing the words. "You're not the space between pages. You are the story. And I'm guessing your identity is the thread that ties all of this together. Violet, you are the key." As he said it, the bulb blinked back on overhead, drowning the space in light.

Chapter 10

Violet wasn't the key to anything. She couldn't be, right? If she had been, someone would have cared that she'd gone missing. Someone would have looked for her. And that someone would have found her. It wasn't like she'd been hiding.

Instead, she'd moldered away on the sidelines, living on scraps. She'd pieced together a life, a family, when none had appeared. She'd made herself a home.

That was what mattered. Not this mystery. Them. Riyah, Leo, Asher. Even Mouse. They were real – and at this point, Fynn's ideas were mere speculation.

Were her friends waiting up, wondering and worried, stuck in the agony of the unknown? V couldn't shake the image. She yearned to explain, to bear her soul and be believed, to find comfort and support in their company.

Perhaps they could all hole up and hide away, withdrawing to their own little world. Perhaps Mouse and his contacts could conceal them. It wouldn't be the life they'd imagined, reduced to outlaws on the run, but they'd survive. And they'd be together.

Fynn had fallen back asleep just as the first rays of sunlight began to stream through the shuttered shop windows. V had watched as his breathing evened, as his chest rose and fell in a graceful rhythm. When she was certain he was out, she got to work.

Scrounging around the shop, she found a pair of baggy black pants and a hooded gray cloak, along with some rags to wipe away the remaining splatters of blood. Her body ached from her escape and her mad dash to safety, but she pushed the pain away, ignoring its insistence.

In the corner of the room, V spotted a cloudy mirror speckled with age. She positioned herself in front of it and considered the woman staring back from its mottled surface.

With her hair pulled back and the hood draped low over her forehead, she barely resembled the resplendent woman from the night before. Now the makeup was gone, the dress had been shredded, and a stunning purple bruise was blossoming beneath her chin. In the dim light, she looked sallow and weary and small.

Yet there was no time for self-pity. Her window was rapidly closing, and she didn't know when – or if – she'd get another. This was her chance to escape.

V grabbed a few contraptions from amongst the mess of gadgets, pocketing them as she passed Fynn one last time. She hadn't forgotten his kindness – or his secrecy – and she regretted that she'd never have the chance to learn more. More about him and more about what he knew. Yet right now, none of that mattered.

She set her sights on the back door, sidestepping the chains and cables that littered the floor. The door closed behind her with a whoosh and a click, sealing her outside of its safety.

V breathed deeply, embracing the isolation. For the moment, there was no one chasing her, no one studying her, no one demanding answers she didn't have. For the moment, she was free – or at least as free as a wanted fugitive could ever be.

She set off in the direction of her apartment, opting for a circuitous route full of dim passageways and rank tunnels. The few times she was forced into the light, she kept her head down, her footsteps even, her gaze level. She sought out clusters of people and lost herself in the morning rush, hiding in the safety of the crowd.

V's fingers itched to stray across pockets and purses, to search for spare units in the hubbub of the swarm, but she consciously resisted. Mostly. V could never ignore an easy mark.

For the rest of the time, her hands remained firmly in her pockets, clutching the alien tech she'd managed to scavenge. A small metal ball, a bumpy cylinder, a strange mass of metal with a trigger. V had no idea what they did, if they could hurt or kill, if they even worked. Yet their weight was reassuring, a small source of solace in her strange mixed-up world.

The closer she crept to her apartment, the higher her defenses rose. Every sound became a sentry, every person a Guard in disguise. Tension worked its way across her body until every atom was on edge, waiting for the fall.

V ducked into the safety of an alley, its bricks and pipes

and dumpsters as familiar as the back of her own hand. She'd used its cover a hundred times, and she followed the gentle curve to its conclusion, directly opposite her building. From there, it was a straight shot across the street, through the doors, up the stairs.

Except someone was blocking her path. A whole slew of someones, in fact.

The street was packed, lined on both sides with people angled toward the door. Her door. This couldn't be good.

Murmurs danced across the crowd as rumors spread. No one knew why they were there, but they could sense a spectacle, so they gathered like moths to a flame to witness the destruction.

V should have left. She should have turned around and fled. But she couldn't. Theories flew across her mind with terrifying fervor, intent on driving her mad. They pulled at her, and despite the danger she found herself inching closer.

Through a forest of heads and torsos, she caught glimpses of the scene. A fleet of black motorbikes. An ominous mobile prison. Two Guards flanking the door and standing at attention, fingers on triggers.

V's heart plummeted as the cruelest of her theories climbed to the top. Her friends were in danger because of her. They were being questioned, interrogated, threatened. And if they didn't comply, they would be charged as conspirators and thrown into that cell.

A scream rose within her chest, all frustration and rage. Yet it died in her throat as the doors creaked open, revealing a different scene.

A series of Guards spilled onto the street, encircling

their prize. Except these Guards were different. Unlike the ones that had seized V, these were dressed in black instead of silver, with dead eyes and a malicious black heart branded on their helmets. This was the ADF – the Anomaly Detection Force.

The realization came slowly, like V was swimming through sand. The ADF wasn't after her. They couldn't be. She hadn't broken their single precious law, the one that held the Echelon in thrall. V wasn't their target.

The urge to scream resurfaced with terrifying force. Before V knew it, she was pushing through the crowd, shoving her way through the sticky mass until she could see the scene. She immediately wished she hadn't. The whisper of hope she'd been holding onto vanished at the sight of a familiar face and the sound of a heartbreaking cry.

It was Riyah. And they were taking her away.

How could they know? The question rang clear in her thoughts, drowning out the noise. How could they possibly know?

The look on Riyah's face was devastating, pulling V's heartstrings taut. It was despair, anguish, desolation. It was more than V could take.

The look on Asher's face was worse. He followed in the officers' wake, one arm holding up his son and the other stretched toward Riyah in a hopeless plea.

"No! Riyah. Please don't take her. I'll do anything. I'll give you anything. Just please don't take her."

The crowd hung on his words like a drama unfolding for their pleasure. No one moved to help them. No one spoke in their defense. They simply stood there, eyes wide, breathing in sync, and praying they wouldn't be next.

Riyah's tear-soaked response floated through the air to light upon V's ears and shatter her heart.

"Take care of him. Please. I'll be alright. I'll come home. But I need you both to be here when I do."

Leo didn't understand – not yet – but his pudgy hand reached out in search of his mother, mirroring his father's stance. His lip quivered and his eyes went wide as his fingers felt the empty air. Then the cries broke loose, splintering the morning into jagged shards.

V couldn't do it. She couldn't stand by and watch. She had to help.

In that moment, reason fled, leaving only fear and fervor. She would offer herself as a trade. She would fight them. She would do whatever she had to in order to free her friend. V stepped into the street – and into the line of fire.

Except instead of pavement beneath her feet, she found only air. A surprisingly strong hand gripped the back of her coat and reeled her in. V struggled to break free, to make her stand, but the hand only tightened, dragging her back behind the wall of bodies.

Before she could scream, another hand clasped across her mouth, rendering her mute. V struggled to speak, to protest, but her words came out as whimpers in a weak and burbling stream.

"Shut up or I will shoot you myself," came a low-pitched voice. "Running away was idiotic, and running *home* was even worse. What were you thinking? Just keep your mouth shut and come with me, and maybe we'll make it back alive."

Lyra gently removed her hand from V's mouth, moving

the other down to clamp around her arm. V sucked in a breath, then hissed, letting her fury turn her feral. Lyra just laughed, a dry, throaty sound full of arrogant amusement.

"You're pathetic," she whispered. "I'm honestly surprised you've survived this long. Now it's time to go. There's nothing more you can do."

With a sharp tug, Lyra led her through the crowd. The people parted as they passed, then converged on the gaps, quickly filling the cracks.

V's body blazed with indignation, igniting her limbs and demanding action. Leo's cries and Asher's panicked pleas followed her through the throng, tearing her heart in two. Her own safety seemed marginal in the wake of their misfortune, and V would gladly trade it to save them. It wasn't selflessness; it was desperation, pure and simple.

Only, Lyra wouldn't give her that chance. Her grip was firm and her attention focused, and she moved with a certainty of step. Disentangling themselves from the masses, they broke into open air, its cool touch caressing V's heated skin.

They retraced V's steps through the alley, then back across the ship, sticking to its shadows. They didn't run, yet Lyra's agitated pace was definitely above a walk. All the while, V's mind whirled, searching frantically for a way out.

With the arm not currently caught in Lyra's vice of a grip, she reached into her pocket, fingering the gadgets she'd filched. Cool metal met her, reassuring and strong, and she weighed the devices in her palm.

The metal ball fit nicely in the curve of her hand, and her thumb quickly found the trigger. Without a word, she wrenched herself away and flung the ball at Lyra's feet. Crouching behind a stack of crates, she closed her eyes and waited, bracing for the bang. Yet it never came.

Instead of ducking or shrieking or running for cover, Lyra sighed. Striding calmly through the grid of green light that now suffused the alley, she scooped up the ball and switched it off. In another moment, she was at V's side, pulling her up to stare coldly into her eyes.

"Great," Lyra said, her voice as dry as the desert. "You've taken a 3D mapping of the alley. That will definitely come in handy in this elaborate plan to escape."

"You can't force me to help you," V said defiantly, clinging to the emotion like a life raft.

Lyra snorted. "We don't need your help. We need you to shut up and stay out of trouble. Then maybe we'll stand a chance of solving this thing."

"I don't care about solving Apollo's murder – or whatever it is you're investigating," V said. "I care about my friends, and they're in trouble. I need to help them!"

Lyra shook her head, leaning in until they stood nose to nose in the alley.

"You can't help them," she said frankly. "Right now, you can't do anything except make things worse. But you can help yourself – and us. You can suck it up, quit this selfish, center-of-the-world routine, and realize there's more at stake here than one woman's life."

"And how am I supposed to know that?" V asked, more than a little annoyed. "You haven't told me anything about what's happening, about who you are and what you really want. But I'm just supposed to follow you blindly?"

"Yes," Lyra said calmly, as if that was the only logical solution. "What other choice do you have?"

V racked her brain, seeking another course of action, one that wouldn't lead to her imminent death or detention. She came up empty.

"You could be terrorists," V said instead. "Or anarchists. Or…spies. How do I know I can trust you?"

Lyra shrugged. "Call us whatever you want. We're still your best option. And as for trust – well, that's not my problem. It's not as if we trust you. But you may be useful, so we're willing to risk it."

V stared back blankly, unimpressed by Lyra's lackluster pitch.

"Look, our agendas are…parallel," Lyra tried again. "By helping us, you'll inevitably be helping yourself. Everyone wins. Unless you fuck us over, in which case we feed you to the wolves."

V weighed their ambiguous promises against the inevitable danger of consorting with criminals…or whatever they were. For all their faults, they did have resources and connections – and at least the semblance of a plan, which was more than could be said for her.

"Fine," V ground out through gritted teeth. "But you'll have to start telling me the truth. I can't help you if I don't know what's happening."

"We don't *have* to do anything," Lyra laughed. "This conversation is a formality. If you said no, I'd simply knock you out and drag you back, but I wanted to give you the illusion of choice."

Well at least she was being honest, V thought. That was

111

a step in the right direction, however small.

"Lead the way," V sighed, consigning herself to Lyra's charge.

For the first time in their short acquaintance, Lyra did as V directed. She led the way across the city, never daring to let V too far out of her sight lest she break her implicit promise and start to stray.

She needn't have worried. V stuck close, recognizing the relative safety of her presence. Lyra was a force of nature, a whirlwind of metal and might. She wasn't someone to be messed with — at least not if you valued your limbs. The machine or monster that had taken hers must have been a sight to behold. Lyra didn't seem the sort to go down without a fight, and V pitied any person who had faced her.

As they traversed across byways and b-roads, V studied her new companion. Her hair, once again twisted in a braid, swayed with each step, sweeping across the muscles of her back. She walked like she owned the Echelon, all long strides and swagger, and her eyes constantly searched the scene, alert for any threat.

V followed the line of her shoulders down her arms to her balled-up fists, barely catching the tattoo inked on her wrist. The mark, borne by everyone who was Echelon-bred, was faded on her forearm, almost too light to see.

That fact made V stop mid-stride. The ink was designed never to pale or wear, to discolor or disappear. It was forever. V glanced at her own tattoo, tracing the lines that linked her to her name, her age, herself.

Lyra broke her reverie, clapping twice to catch her attention. With a jerk of her head and a look that could kill, she communicated her demands. V raised her hands in surrender and continued on, shelving the detail for later dissection.

The journey back bordered on silent, with only occasional commands to break the calm. "Go left. Left, I said! Watch your step. For all the bloody stars, stop stomping!"

V's relief at spotting the shop was palpable. She dashed inside, sighing as she entered the safe haven. Her heartbeat slowed and the tension within her eased, allowing her to breathe. Until she caught sight of Fynn.

He was seated on his cot, hands tented against his lips, and the look on his face could freeze fire. V instantly put up her guards, sensing the oncoming storm. Silence stretched, sticky and dense, as his eyes connected with hers. Then everything erupted.

"What the hell were you thinking?" Fynn demanded, launching himself off the bed. "You're a wanted criminal. The Guards likely have orders to shoot you on sight. Leaving wasn't just stupid, it was a god damn death wish. You could have been killed."

"Aww, I didn't know you cared," V whispered sarcastically before her brain could catch up.

"I don't," he said a little too quickly. "But your fate is tied to ours. If you go down, everything we've been working for could go down with you."

"Then give me a reason to stay," V insisted, addressing Fynn instead of Lyra – the weak link in this weird little chain. "Tell me what you're working on, or better yet *why*. Otherwise you're just as bad as them. Just another captor and just another prison – and you can't blame me for trying to escape."

"Violet," he growled in the exasperated way V was growing to like, although she'd never admit it to herself. "What we do isn't a game. It's life or death. If we tell you, it'll make you complicit, and your life will never be the same."

V crossed her arms across her chest, defiant. "I'd appreciate your attempts to protect me if my life weren't already ruined," she countered. "Or did you forget in the last five seconds that I'm wanted for the murder of one of the most prominent men on the Echelon? Because that seemed to be a big deal for you before."

Based on the subtle glint in his eyes and the hard set of his jaw, her words were working, worming their way under his skin and taking hold.

"Fine," he grumbled, glancing ever so slightly toward Lyra. "But you'll need to return the favor. Cooperate. Tell us what you know. And for god's sake, stop getting yourself into trouble. There are only so many times we can save your ass." V could have sworn his eyes dipped toward the part in question before hastily flicking back up.

"Deal," V said with certainty, seating herself in the chair and ushering for the pair to follow. "Now spill," she commanded.

Once again, Fynn took up the mantle of narrator as Lyra scowled beside him, silently hating every detail he let slip.

"The first thing you need to know," he began gravely, "is that something is wrong with the Senate."

"Clearly," V snorted, ignoring his solemnity. "Missing people and murder aren't exactly hallmarks of a good government."

"I know you like to listen to yourself talk, *V*, but save

114

your interjections," Lyra growled.

Fynn wisely ignored his partner and continued. "It's more than that, although they may be connected." He took a deep breath, preparing for the reveal.

"Violet, for the past few years, senators have been showing up dead. Apollo wasn't the first, and I doubt he'll be the last. It intensified last year – around the time you appeared without a memory. Someone is preying on our politicians, and we think it's coming from inside their ranks."

"Well, shit," V stated, suitably stunned. "How could we not have heard about this? Wouldn't there be announcements, investigations, elections? That isn't something they could keep quiet, right?"

"You underestimate them," Lyra chided, rolling her eyes. "They can keep anything – and anyone – quiet if they want to. And for the last couple of years, it's been in their best interest to keep their mouths shut."

"Why?" V asked, genuinely puzzled. "What reason could they possibly have for wanting to keep that to themselves?"

Fynn sighed, running a hand through his dark curls. "At this point, it's just conjecture, but if we had to guess, it's precisely because they don't want to hold elections – and they don't want the public to get hold of their plans."

"You've...lost me," V confessed, straining to put the pieces together. Murder, misinformation, malicious plans. It was a lot to process.

"The only way this all makes sense is if someone in the Senate is behind it," Fynn said slowly, spelling it out. "They're systematically eliminating the opposition."

"What opposition?" V asked, no closer to clarity. "We

don't even have political parties. I thought the Senate was supposed to be one cohesive force."

Lyra scoffed. "That's just another lie they tell us to maintain power. They all have their own agendas."

"And someone – or a group of someones – is willing to kill for theirs," Fynn added, closing some gaps in V's mind while opening others.

"So let me get this straight," V said, rubbing her eyes. "A senator – or a clique of senators – is up to something. Not all of their peers agree, so they're killing their rivals. Then they're using some combination of fear, cover-ups, and coercion to keep it quiet?" Fynn and Lyra nodded in unison.

"So why do you two care?" V asked, genuinely curious. "It's not like your lives are on the line. What's in it for you?"

Fynn and Lyra exchanged a loaded look, saying nothing and everything. Their hesitation stretched until it verged on the brink of an awkward silence.

"We represent an interested party," Fynn finally replied, "although the outcome of this stretches far beyond the Senate. Think about the Policies. They were divisive, even among the senators, but no one died for opposing them. So we can only assume that their current plans are a hell of a lot bigger – and that they come with one hell of a cost. As you can imagine, we'd prefer not to see those plans enacted."

"And you think *I'm* the key to this?" V asked, dumbfounded. "I'm no senator. I'm a singer. This is all alien to me."

"I know," Fynn confirmed, "but I still think you're important. I just don't know why. Not yet."

"We need to find out what happened to Apollo," Lyra stated, for once offering a suitable suggestion in place of a

116

rebuttal. "His murder was different. It was loud and messy. It's making waves. If we figure out what happened, who's really behind his death, maybe we'll discover how you fit in – and what we can do to stop this thing."

"You're right," stated Fynn, nodding his approval. "It's time to do some digging."

"At last," V exclaimed, "something we can all agree on. When do we start?"

"We?" Lyra scoffed. "You're a wanted fugitive. Leave this to us. Remember what we said about staying out of trouble?"

"Yeah, that's not gonna happen," V said with a shrug. "If you plan to investigate Apollo's death, then I'm coming with you. You're stuck with me now."

Chapter 11

Violet loved playing dress-up. She loved slipping into a gorgeous gown – and slipping into character. The makeup, the sleek bob, the gazes of a room. It was intoxicating.

But this was just painful.

V stared at herself in the speckled mirror, frowning at her reflection. The woman in its surface frowned back, mousy and homely and altogether forgettable.

This had been the compromise, the cost to join her new comrades on their quest. She had to disappear, they said, to become someone else entirely. Mission accomplished.

V now sported a wig of long, straight hair the color of sewage with an odor to match. With the help of makeup and molded clay, her nose now jutted far beyond her face, its once-gentle curve bumpy and broken. Clothing scavenged from some castoff pile took away her figure, giving her the air of someone down on their luck and possibly deranged.

But the pièce de résistance was not her face or her

clothes or her hair. It was her tattoo.

From all outward appearances, nothing had changed. It remained in place on her left wrist, stark against her pale skin. Yet when Fynn had gently applied another layer, a temporary stain that seamlessly covered the first, he had added something else as well – a new identity and a thin veil of safety.

Hidden within the ink was a stream of false data, with a new name and a new likeness to match this plain persona. It would allow her to pass through checkpoints unseen, like a ghost in this spectral city. Until it faded, she'd be just another face in the faceless crowd, toiling away her life in the shadows.

"How long will it last?" she asked Fynn, who was donning his own disguise in the corner.

"A few weeks at least," he said, coming out from his cover – and revealing his costume.

It was less…intense than hers, with no prosthetics or paint to conceal his beauty. His goal was not to hide, but to disappear, to become normal and unnoticeable in the throng. Yet even shrouded in baggy clothes and hidden behind a pair of horrid glasses, Fynn was not the type of man you missed.

She realized she was staring and promptly looked away, blushing beneath the layers of powder.

"It's impressive," V admitted, focusing on her wrist instead of his face. "The process must have taken a while to perfect," she said, subtly pushing for more.

"The technique has been around for decades," Fynn replied with a shrug. "There's a simple code infused in the ink that can fool the scanners. I'm hardly the only one who knows about it. Hell, the underground markets trade in tattoos like they're candy. Most go to families seeking cover for their second children."

The fading mark on Lyra's arm flashed before her eyes, and a fierce curiosity took hold. Was Lyra a second child, a surrogate sister? She looked nothing like Fynn, so they couldn't be kin, but there was clearly a bond between them.

"How'd you learn it, then?" V asked, prodding deeper. "Did you spend a lot of time in the underground markets as a kid?"

"A bit," he confessed, staring out toward the front of the shop. "It wasn't for me, though. It was for my sister."

"Sister?" V queried, a touch too excited. The morsel was tantalizing, like a string she needed to tug. Fynn seemed hesitant to continue.

"Oh, come on. Who am I going to tell?" V asked, pointing around at the empty room. "It's not as if my social calendar is full these days. Besides," she added on a more serious note, "I have some experience in that department myself." Her thoughts flew to Riyah, and her heart shattered for the millionth time that day.

Fynn's face flashed with understanding, then pity. V hadn't told him the tale, but it seemed that Lyra had saved her the trouble. For once, she was grateful to the woman. V didn't think she could bear to relive the event through retelling.

"I was 5 when Eden was born," Fynn began, sinking into the depths of thought. "It seemed like a miracle that no one turned us in before the birth. My parents were equal parts hope and terror. They knew the danger Eden was in, but they thought *they* could be the exception, the ones to make it work, to keep her hidden."

From the pain in his voice, V could already guess the ending, but it was too late to turn back now.

"We bought her an identity," Fynn went on after a spell. "An ID bracelet with the name of a child who had died, with plans for a tattoo when she came of age. It wasn't cheap. It cost my parents nearly everything they had. But if it kept Eden alive, they would have given anything.

"It worked for a time. Years, in fact. I watched her grow and learn and start to question the world. Sometimes I swear I can still hear her laughing." He chuckled in the sad way of those who have lost something precious.

"I don't know who betrayed us, but the ADF came in the night. My parents tried to fight, to grab Eden and flee, but the Guards were stronger. They ripped her from my mother's grasp and dragged her away. The look in Eden's eyes still haunts me – the confusion, the panic, the pain. She screamed for my parents as they put her in that cell and drove her away."

"What happened to your parents?" V asked, half hating herself for the question.

"They were fined more than they could ever afford and threatened with the Grove if they failed to repay it. But that's not what broke them. They broke the moment Eden went through that door. They've never been the same. They're like ghosts, still alive but not truly living."

He shook his head ruefully. "Maybe it's better for your friend that they've taken her now. Maybe it'll be easier in the end. She'll never be the same, but maybe she'll have the chance to heal, to return to what's left of her family and live."

V didn't think Riyah would agree, but she held the words in, not daring to spoil his story with her pain. She left that honor to Lyra, who came lumbering out of her room with all the gracefulness of a bear, intent on checking their progress.

Lyra wouldn't be joining them in the field. She had to stay back and open the shop, taking in repairs and selling their strange collection of reclaimed gadgets. But she'd be coordinating from afar, using the feed from V's retinal cam to stay plugged into the action.

V had mixed feelings on the idea of someone spying through her eyes. Yet she'd agreed to help them, and they were letting her tag along despite her fugitive status, so she couldn't really complain.

"Take this," Lyra commanded, thrusting what looked like a small calculator into her hands. "And this," she said as she handed over the familiar spherical scanner.

A few other bits and bobs made their way into V's pockets as Lyra bulldozed through the shop like a toddler on the hunt for snacks. By the time she was done, V couldn't remember the purpose of half the items she carried – but Lyra assured her they were all equally important.

"Oh, and don't get caught," she added less-than-tactfully, as if that wasn't obvious. "Breaking into a crime scene won't look good for you, especially when you're the primary suspect. I give you 50/50 odds on getting out of there alive."

"Thanks for the vote of confidence," V grumbled, her nerves fizzling beneath her skin. "It's a pity you're not joining us. Your optimism would do wonders for morale." Her sarcasm stained the words red as she attempted to mask her tension. Lyra glared back, unamused by V's semi-playful teasing.

"It's time to go," Fynn declared, attempting to break the staring match. He put himself between them like an emissary of peace, silently demanding a cease-fire.

V looked away first. Based on the heat blooming on her back, it was clear that Lyra wasn't so easily swayed. Fynn continued on regardless, ignoring his partner's obstinance.

"We should only be gone a few hours," he said, recapping the strategy for Lyra even though she was its primary architect. "If all goes to plan, we'll be in and out without anyone being the wiser. We just need a chance to sweep the scene and look for clues. But if we're caught, you'll need to carry on alone. This time, a rescue is too risky."

Lyra nodded gravely while the tension in V's stomach pulled tighter. She wasn't a spy but a singer, and stage fright was nothing compared to this. She briefly yearned for the simplicity of her former life, before intrigue and murder began to plague every step. She missed her bed, her stage, her uncomplicated days. She missed the people that made her life worthwhile.

Yet V was a big girl with a job to do. The time to sit by and cry had ended. It was time to do this or die trying.

Which was, of course, easier said than done, but the sentiment spurred V forward, and she followed Fynn through the hallway and out the back door.

While their trek demanded stealth, it also demanded speed, with each second on the streets compounding the danger of their discovery. So instead of taking a convoluted course, full of twists and turns, the pair hopped aboard a sky train and rocketed toward their target.

Flying aboard the shuttle with Fynn by her side, V couldn't help but fall back in time. It had only been a day since they'd ridden this way, both bound for the same fate. The intervening hours had turned her world to ash, but they had also sparked a flame of hope.

Fynn thought she was the key, that her story held the answer. He thought she was someone, a riddle to be solved. And he thought *he* could be the one to solve it.

She didn't want to let herself believe that her questions could be answered, that the mystery of her existence could be solved. Yet the promise of a life, a family, a home was too potent to ignore. It was so tempting to fall into that valley of hope and lose herself to the lure of dreams.

To distract herself, she focused on her companion, tracing his sharp edges as they blew past a blurry world. His posture was relaxed, almost calm, but his eyes were alert and wary. They scanned the car with deliberate care, taking in its passengers.

"I am sorry about your friend," he whispered without looking, as if he could sense her stare. "I didn't mean to imply that she has it better than my family. I know it's hell for everyone. But I'm...here if you want to talk."

"Thank you," V whispered in return, studying the set of his jaw. "And I'm sorry about your sister. I can't begin to imagine that loss. Then again, I've lost 24 years of my life, so we each have our burdens to carry."

"I don't know how you did it," Fynn said, finally locking in on her. "The curiosity, the questions. It would have driven me mad."

"Oh, it did," V confessed with a shallow laugh. "The trick is to surround yourself with people who are equally insane so you look sane in comparison."

Fynn snorted, then quickly moved to cover his smile with his hand.

"You're lucky to have them, whoever they are," he said. "And they're lucky to have you. Not everyone on this ship is as fortunate."

V cocked her head in question, sensing something unsaid beneath his words. "What do you mean?" she asked when the gesture alone didn't spur him.

He took a moment to organize his thoughts before he spoke. "The purpose of the Policies was more than population control," he said slowly. "Before, families were big and boisterous. They loved and lived for each other. The Policies severed those ties. Tribes broke down, communities faltered. And without that loyalty, that belonging, we're easy to control – easy to manipulate."

Fynn shrugged lightly, smiling down at her. "You're lucky that despite your past – or lack thereof – you've managed to build your own community. That takes a strong kind of person, if you ask me."

V flushed, suddenly too warm. "What about you?" she countered. "You've got your parents...and Lyra. It may be a small community, but it's yours."

Fynn chuckled at her words. "I didn't so much choose Lyra. She was sort of thrust upon me through a series of unfortunate events."

V was about to ask when a string of text stopped her, flashing before her eyes like a warning.

She flinched. "Our puppet master would prefer it if we stayed on task – and didn't waste time discussing something that is *none of my business*."

She'd honestly forgotten Lyra was there, and her rebuke stung like a slap. The twinkle in Fynn's eyes didn't dissipate, although he wisely shut his mouth, putting an end to their conversation.

V wondered if, when all of this was over, these people would join her tribe, the strange assortment of odds and ends that had somehow become her family. She envisioned Lyra and Mouse swapping tales of illegal tech while Fynn played pirates with Leo. It was bittersweet to imagine, a beautiful dream that couldn't survive the leap to reality. Although sometimes it was just nice to dream.

A few minutes later, the train slowed and stopped, and the pair made their way across the platform and into the city. They'd disembarked early to pass through security on the ground rather than taking their chances in the sky.

Nearing the checkpoint, V's heart began to hammer and her hands began to shake. Fynn glanced down, then in one swift movement captured her hand in his. He held it firmly, and a hint of his certainty seeped into her. It wasn't much, but it was enough to steady her body and steel her mind. Her heart, however, steadfastly continued its sprint, somehow imbued with new fervor.

The Guard in the booth looked bored, his feet propped against the desk and his hands cast lazily behind his head. It was a pose of practiced nonchalance, of purposeful disinterest. It didn't fool V. If the scanners so much as snagged on her ID, he would be there, gun drawn and questions ready, prepared to take her down.

V wondered if he'd seen her picture, if he'd been told to keep watch for the traitor. Was he in there now, checking every scan in search of her face? Would he see through her disguise in an instant?

As they approached, V held out her arm to the scanner, her hand pulsing with tremors of distress. The system paused as every dire outcome cascaded through her thoughts. Then it beeped, tossing those fears to the wind. The Guard didn't even notice as she floated through, her hand once again held in Fynn's.

The remainder of their trek was capped in quiet tension. They passed immaculate streets with immaculate people, who patently ignored the pair. They were invisible, unimportant, unremarkable. They were no one.

They entered Apollo's building without a fuss before finding themselves caught in a maze of luxe corridors, separated by soaring windows and gleaming lifts. Somehow privy to the building's plans, Lyra guided them with retinal commands, quickly steering them to the top. Before V knew it, they were standing before the door, its familiar gold design now crisscrossed with strands of inky black tape.

V froze, berated by memories and assaulted by anxiety. Beyond that door, ghosts lingered but answers beckoned, pushing and pulling with equal force. After a beat, the lure of answers triumphed, and she stepped forward to try the knob. It was locked.

"Use the numeric interface," Lyra typed, barely wasting a moment. When V just stood there, clearly confused, she explained, "It's the number pad in your pocket. Attach it to the door, press the green button, and wait."

V did as she was told, carefully placing the contraption just above the handle before switching it on. Then she stepped back, waiting by Fynn's side as the device did its thing, half expecting it to explode. Instead, it stayed silent, calculating the correct code before releasing the lock with a click.

V didn't bother to hide her awe. "Can I keep this?" she asked in all sincerity, turning it over in her hands. The possibilities blossomed in her mind, revealing all manner of unlawful avenues.

Fynn gave her an odd look that V interpreted as alarm.

"What?" she said with a shrug. "A girl's gotta make a living." With that, she strode across the threshold, leaving Fynn gaping behind her.

The scene on the other side was eerie and wrong. The dream from last night lingered, left to fester in the light. The grass swayed and glitched while the animals crawled and blinked, consuming the last of their power.

In the harsh light of day, the magic vanished, and V could now spot the strings. Everything looked fake and flimsy, a mere façade of truth. Staring at it now, V couldn't believe she'd ever been fooled by the spell.

"It's this way," she said, guiding Fynn to the study. She straightened her back, then opened the door, bracing for the onslaught of memory.

Everything was exactly the same, preserved in a sinister stasis – save for Apollo's body, which was gone. Yet the blood stain remained, dulled to a reddish brown, dyeing the wood with death. The scent of it lingered, metallic and warm, suffusing the air with iron.

Without warning, V was falling back in time, tumbling across minutes and hours. A dizziness took hold as disconnected moments flashed across her eyes like pieces of fragmented time. She landed with a thud, dropping to her knees beside a body that was both alive and dead, there and gone.

Someone spoke, and the voice splintered her senses, dragging her back to herself.

"It's OK, Violet. I'm here. I won't let anything hurt you."

Then he was there, kneeling beside her and pulling her into a hug. He whispered words that never made it past her ears, holding her firmly against him. It felt foreign yet familiar, awkward yet warm, and she leaned into his touch with a demanding sort of greed.

"Just show me what happened," he said after a spell, finally breaking away. "Walk me through the night so I can understand. Maybe we'll find something in your memories."

V didn't want to look, to examine the pain that pulsed in the back of her mind, but Fynn had asked so she complied.

"He said it was a favor," she began, "something I would find…advantageous." She rose slowly, retracing her steps with careful precision.

"He apologized like he knew me, but it made no sense. He spoke like we were in on some secret." V closed her eyes and flashed back to his words, wading through the blur of trauma. "He said he had something, something important, and that it was time for us to begin."

She opened her eyes to find herself back against the shelves, in the same spot where Apollo had struck. Her hand flew to her neck, straining to protect her from the ghost of his weapon. She could feel it now, like prickles in her mind

129

and pinpricks on her skin, coating her in memories of pain.

"That's when he attacked," she confessed, barely above a whisper.

"He attacked you?" Fynn repeated, his voice much too loud in its concern. "What do you mean? Did he hurt you? Did he…do something?" He stood before her, searching, his fingers curling into fists at his side.

"No…yes…I'm fine," she stuttered, flummoxed by his intensity.

The heat of his attention burned, so she turned away, scanning the books for secrets. Her hands grazed along leather spines and delicate pages, centering her in the moment. She breathed, inhaling the scent of aging stories while sorting through her thoughts.

That's when she heard it. The creak of a door bit into her consciousness, splitting her mind in two. Half of her screamed to run, while the rest remained still, rooted in this time and place.

"Someone's coming," she whispered in a rush, spurring Fynn into action.

His eyes joined hers in the hunt for shelter, hurriedly scanning the scene. It was so familiar, this panicked dance, that V nearly laughed at her luck. Two nights and two arrests in the same damned room was almost too much to handle.

Footsteps fell against faux dirt paths, like a drum beat counting down to their discovery. V's heart mingled with the march, falling into sync with their steps. Time sprinted as she stood, staring at the door, suddenly unable to move.

"Over here!" Fynn hissed, low and insistent, pulling her sights toward him.

She found him quickly, crouched into a ball behind a high-backed chair. It took her a second too long to piece it together and understand his command. By the time she moved, the handle was turning, with the door creaking open before them.

With a graceless leap, she threw herself down and tumbled toward her companion. He caught her in one fluid move and clutched her tight – just as the figures entered.

Chapter 12

V closed her eyes and clung to Fynn, praying she hadn't been spotted. A string of heartbeats passed as she waited for the fallout, half certain they had noticed her scramble. Yet as she lay huddled in the shadows, nose to nose with this stranger, no one came to claim her. The figures stayed immobile by the door, lost in their own worlds, pondering some unseen problem.

After an eternity of seconds, one of the intruders spoke, cracking the quiet in two.

"What are you hoping to find?" a woman asked, flat and lifeless…and familiar. V knew that voice, knew its curves and edges, even with their short acquaintance. It was the Inspector from the station, the one who'd pressed her for a guilty plea.

The answering baritone came as no surprise, and V pictured the scarecrow as he spoke.

"Something to help us track down the girl – or at least

explain why she did it."

"You think she's guilty, then? That delicate little singer?" She laughed. "She seems a bit soft for a crime like this, and she definitely lacks the smarts."

V's hackles rose along with her bile, threatening to boil over. She bit her tongue to keep from growling as the insults singed across her skin.

"Eh," the man replied in the verbal equivalent of a shrug. "Does it even matter? The Senate thinks she did it, and we need a win. If it gets us some peace, let's put her away – and take our well-deserved credit."

V felt worse with each word, the injustice stoking the seeds of her anger until she saw red. Fynn tried to calm her with a warning look, but she was past the point of placation.

The male Inspector continued, "Just take another look and see what you can find. Maybe we missed something important."

They set off on opposite paths, combing through every crack. They were meticulous, barely speaking as they hunted, unaware of the proximity of their prey. Yet with each footfall, Fynn and V felt the mounting pressure, knowing it wouldn't be long.

V was desperate, eyes darting around the room for a plan. She could feel Fynn's heart racing at each point their bodies connected, his panic palpable. Then she saw it: Apollo's weapon, the one he'd used to attack her. Its matte black body lay just out of reach, shimmering beyond Fynn's shoulder.

There was no cover to shield her if she stretched, no shelter to hide behind if they fired. No way to get to the object without being seen.

Yet V's fingers tingled, and one word rang out across the silence to stick in her skull. *Remember.* It felt like the remnants of a dream were beckoning her forward, demanding she take what was hers.

As if sensing her budding plan, Lyra chose that moment to butt in.

"Don't do anything stupid," read the text, which flashed before V's eyes. In the surprise, she nearly lost her grip on Fynn and flailed. In the end, it was only his steady hold that saved her.

He held a question in his eyes, grave and insistent. She responded with a glance toward the object. A silent exchange played out in the span of a few seconds, all eyebrows and nostrils, head quirks and nods. It was clear from his frown that Fynn didn't approve, but V didn't need his permission. What she needed was a distraction, something to buy her time to grab the gadget.

V rooted through the contents of her pocket, tracing the outlines of unfamiliar objects. Then, for the second time that day, her fingers found the metal ball and fastened around its smooth surface. This time, however, she actually had a plan. So that was progress.

V flashed the ball at Fynn and made a rolling motion, miming the crux of her strategy. He stayed still, save for a shake of his head, which V wisely ignored.

The Inspectors began to trade their theories, and V used their voices as cover to push the button and bowl the scanner toward them. It rolled quietly across the uneven floors, feigning left then right before coming to rest at the base of a book stack. As soon as it stopped, it sprang to life, spraying the scene with green.

The string of lights started at the ceiling before working its way down, capturing every inch of the space – along with the Inspectors' undivided attention. A second of silence fell, thick and awkward, as their alertness gave way to confusion, which crashed into action. They leapt forward in a tumble of limbs, encircling the sphere with excitement.

V didn't wait to make her move, crawling past Fynn to claim her prize. The distance was longer than she'd expected, and she crossed it in a careful clamber, constantly battling between stealth and speed. Seconds stretched to hours as her shaking hand made contact and her fingers closed around its cool bulk.

Stowing it safely in her pocket, V set off once more to reclaim her place by Fynn's side. Hands stretched out to guide her back, but before they could connect, a shrill "aha!" boomed across the space. V looked up, certain she'd been spotted, only to find the woman clutching Lyra's scanner like some priceless clue.

"Good work, partner," said the man. "Now bag it and tag it and bring it back to the station. Analysis should be able to strip it down to parts and parse it for data."

V could feel Lyra cringe at the words, and a moment later, she voiced her displeasure. "That better have been worth it, V. That scanner was worth a fortune. You owe me some answers."

V didn't care. She knew she'd won the trade-off, although she couldn't articulate why. The strange black box had brought nothing but pain, yet somehow she could sense its importance.

The Inspectors took one more lap, lax in the face of their victory, before calling it a day. Fynn and V let them leave, listening for the door before spilling out onto the floor. They sighed in unison, voicing their relief as they lay sprawled across the scene. V felt giddy, almost ecstatic at her series of close escapes.

Fynn didn't share her feelings. "What the hell was that?" he asked, leveraging himself onto an elbow to stare down at her. "You could have gotten us killed. It's a miracle they fell for that stupid stunt."

"It was worth it. I promise. Because we got this." V brandished the black weapon like some plundered treasure.

In the bright light, without the danger of discovery, it didn't look like much. It was the width of three fingers and shorter than her forearm, with one prong bent at a strange angle. She tentatively touched it, expecting a shock, but the power had drained from its body.

Understandably, Fynn didn't seem impressed, but he swiftly schooled his features. "We better get that back to base," he said flatly. "I'd rather not be here when they return."

"Pfft," V exhaled with a wave. "They're not coming back. Didn't you hear them? They're looking for an easy win. I bet they're already searching for a way to trace that scanner back to me. And when they can't find a connection, they'll just invent one."

She may have been a bit bitter, but they deserved all the bile she could muster. Still, she wasn't about to ignore a good suggestion, so with one last glance around the room, she followed Fynn out of the apartment.

The pair crept carefully back the way they had come, checking around every corner before taking it, but their path remained clear. The Inspectors had vanished, retreating to their lair to find V's guilt in foreign objects. The thought made her want to scream.

Instead, she gave in to the silence that had grown between them, embracing the discomfort. She could tell that Fynn didn't approve of her recklessness or her rash decisions. He saw her as wild and unpredictable, and in a way, she liked it. She would hate to be considered knowable, even by someone like Fynn.

They descended to the street without incident, letting themselves out onto the pavement. The roads were quiet as the afternoon lengthened, with the faux sun still high in the sky. Fynn led the way with impatient steps as V scurried after, perpetually three strides behind.

After slipping through the scanners and out of the sector, they hopped aboard a sky train and blended with its patrons, disappearing into the clusters of citizens. V considered them as they clung to their silence, like separate boulders fighting against the same rushing stream.

No one looked at each other. No one laughed. No one seemed connected, even as they soared above the city, all headed in the same direction.

Maybe Fynn was right, V thought as she watched them. Maybe the Senate *was* trying to isolate them, relegating each citizen to their own small island. After all, people posed less danger alone. Stragglers couldn't disrupt the status quo. Outliers and outsiders could dissent in the dark but would never form an army to oust them.

V looked at Fynn and her sadness doubled, biting into the shell of resentment. He'd had a family, a life. He'd loved and been loved in return. He'd lost more than V could ever know. It was no wonder he was cautious. He couldn't risk losing even more.

Suddenly, V didn't feel so annoyed. She drew closer to Fynn, pulling herself against him to whisper in his ear.

"I'm sorry for…putting you in danger back there," she began, trying to imbue sincerity into inadequate words. "It just felt like something I needed to do. I can't explain it. It was like a lightbulb switched on inside of me. Although, that probably sounds insane."

Fynn didn't disagree. In fact, he didn't say anything. He merely looked down at her, his dark eyes growing darker by the second. They were so close now that their noses nearly touched, and V swore she could feel the spark of static between them.

It was a crap apology and an even crappier excuse. Yet Fynn's lips still quirked into the barest hint of a smile as he held her gaze. Something warm and velvety coated her stomach at the sight, and she answered it with a tentative smirk.

Time slowed for a short eternity as they stood there, neither saying a word. The air escaped from the train, and the people went with it, leaving a vacuum that threatened to consume them. V's eyes flicked to Fynn's lips, measuring the gap that stood between them and the time it would take to cross it.

There were a thousand questions to be answered and a thousand more problems waiting to be solved, but right now none of that mattered. V was drunk on his nearness and his scent and desperate for a taste. And Fynn wasn't looking away.

The train screeched to a halt, tearing V from her reveries. She disconnected from the dream, centering herself painfully in reality. Fynn was not meant for her, nor she for him. They were strangers, cast together by circumstance for the briefest moment until fate had had its fill.

V drew back, letting the warmth cool in her veins until she no longer burned. Her skin still itched and her body buzzed, but she shook it off, refocusing on the rustling crowd. As the doors prepared to open, she let her fingers fall into their familiar patterns, searching for distraction amongst other people's possessions.

By the time they made their way off the platform and into the city below, V was the proud new owner of two wallets and a wristwatch. As Fynn poured his concentration into their route, she combed through her treasures, confiscating the valuables before casually discarding the rest.

Their seamless trek across the ship was interrupted by a pair of Guards, both painfully alert as they patrolled the streets. Fynn and V swerved to avoid their attention, embarking on a wild arc before looping back toward the shop. Finally closing the door behind them was a sweet relief, and V immediately shed her disguise, grateful to be back in her own form – if not her own clothes.

They'd barely been inside a minute before Lyra leapt, invading V's personal space with her hand outstretched.

"Where is it? Show it to me," she demanded without so much as a greeting.

Fynn was unruffled by the brusque welcome, but it took

V a moment to recalibrate and remember what Lyra wanted. Once she did, she fished Apollo's weapon from her pocket, gingerly holding it out for inspection.

The woman grabbed it, yanking it from V's grasp. V made a noise of protest as she instinctively reached to reclaim it, but Lyra was already across the room.

"You're lucky," Lyra said as V righted herself and stopped flailing. "I was able to download the map of Apollo's study before taking that scanner offline. They won't be able to trace it back to you. Or me. Hell, I'd be impressed if they're even able to work out what it is. Inspectors aren't renowned for their intelligence."

"That's…great," V said, not particularly interested. "But what about this device, this weapon? What is it? And why did Apollo attack me with it?"

"I've never seen anything like it," Lyra conceded, turning it over in her hands – before beginning to tear it apart. "It's either the work of a master or a madman, but at the moment I can't say which. Give me some time and I'll find out what it's hiding."

"How long?" V asked impatiently, aching for answers.

Lyra sighed, clearly annoyed. "A few hours, maybe more," she said as she pried the back off and peered inside. "But I'll tell you one thing right off the bat. This is no weapon."

V stared at her in confusion. That didn't make sense. Apollo had used it to hurt her, to bring her to her knees. She could still feel the pain as it radiated through her body, torching every cell.

"What do you mean?" The shrill note in V's voice betrayed her anxiety. "If it's not a weapon, then what is it?"

Lyra smiled as she caressed the contraption, a look of wonder in her eyes.

"It's a thing of beauty," she said in awe. "I don't know what Apollo was up to, but this thing can hold enough data to power the Echelon. And for some reason, he was trying to transmit it all to you."

Chapter 13

Violet's dreams were a mess. Her old nightmares had merged with her waking world to form a shapeless force that stalked her through the night. It hounded her like a shadow, insidious yet out of sight, waiting for its chance to strike.

Once again, the visions returned her to the station which trains had long since abandoned. It should have felt empty, but instead it pulsed with meaning, begging to be explored. V longed to reach out, to fling open the lockers and discover their secrets, yet something stopped her. Fear held her in its grip, warning against the unknown, against the danger of seeking lost things.

Just like before, a figure appeared, silent and still – but this time it wore her face. The phantom reached out a pale hand and touched her cheek, whispering one word on repeat.

"Remember."

V gradually returned to consciousness, unable to shake the word or the feeling of fingers brushing her face. She knew it was a dream, but it felt so real that she could almost convince herself it was a memory, some lost remnant of a past life dredged up to haunt her.

That place felt so familiar, and she traced its outlines in her mind, feeling the lockers against her palms and the cracking floors beneath her feet. It seemed important, but for the life of her she couldn't imagine why.

V blinked at the ceiling, letting her eyes adjust to the low light before pushing herself up. Fynn was still asleep, serene on his cot with his untroubled dreams. She envied that calm, that respite from the storm, and she didn't dare wake him. Dreams were precious, and she couldn't stomach the thought of stealing his. So she padded past him into the far hall, heading toward Lyra's quarters.

A thin band of light seeped from beneath her door, betraying her sleepless status. V leaned her head against the wood and listened as sounds of humming and clacking came from within, confirming her suspicions. She knocked lightly, but Lyra didn't deign to answer, so V let herself inside.

Lyra was lying on her back, her face mere inches from a thin plastene screen. Beneath her, the bed was tidy and clean, its covers unrumpled by sleep. The rest of the room was similarly neat, posing a stark contrast to the loosely controlled chaos of the shop.

V cleared her throat to capture Lyra's attention and steer it in her direction.

"Oh, it's you," the woman muttered with cool indifference. "Is there something I can help you with?" She lowered the screen but made no move to rise, clearly perturbed by V's presence.

V sighed, tired of Lyra's simmering animosity. "Look, I know you don't like me, but can we…"

"I never said I didn't like you," she interjected, finally sitting up. "I don't know you. There's a difference."

"You know more about me than most," V informed her, shrugging as she said it.

"That may be the case," Lyra shot back, ready with a reply, "but it doesn't mean I trust you. And neither does he," she said, jutting her chin in Fynn's general direction. "You may be a pawn, like he says, but I still don't know what side you're playing."

"We have something in common, then," V responded with a smirk. "I don't trust you, either. I mean, you're clearly up to something. Your gadgets, this shop, your fake tattoo. You're playing your own game, and I bet it goes far beyond solving a series of murders." It was an invitation, an opening intended to entice Lyra to play.

"My past and my plans are my own business," Lyra countered, stubbornly declining V's gambit. "I have a mission, and so far you've only been a distraction."

"If I'm such a *distraction*, then why are you spending the night reviewing my retinal footage?" V asked, a hint of triumph trickling into her system. She gestured at the bed, where her visions from the party were playing out in slow motion across the screen.

Lyra tried to retain her composure, but a splinter of frustration fractured her shell. She moved her hand as if to cover up the evidence before realizing it was futile and reluctantly tipping it toward V. It was paused on a picture from V's performance, a view from the stage as she looked out onto a sea of faces.

"I was waiting for my system to finish analyzing Apollo's data drive, and I had some time to kill. So I pulled up the map you managed to take of Apollo's study," she said, navigating to another image on her screen. "At first, it seemed mundane, just another scan of a rich man's room. Then I noticed something."

Lyra handed the device to V, who looked down at the screen, searching for the inconsistency. All she could see was a sketch composed of green lines and numbers set against a backdrop of black. She could faintly make out the outlines of Apollo's study, but nothing jumped out from within it.

"I'm going to need a clue here," V murmured as her eyes lost focus while attempting to trace the lines. "This isn't exactly my area of expertise."

"Clearly," Lyra snorted. Yanking the device back, she zoomed in on a corner of the scene, circling the space with her finger. "Here. There's an anomaly in the architecture of the wall. It's nearly imperceptible, but the blank space beyond it gives it away."

Lyra knew V wouldn't get it. In fact, the woman was reveling in making her feel obtuse.

"Dumb it down for me," V said between gritted teeth. "What is it, exactly, that we're looking at?"

"It's a secret passage," Lyra said slowly, drawing out the words. "It's a back way into the room. It could be how the killer got in and out unseen."

"Aha!" V exclaimed, delighted. A small yet sturdy weight lifted off her shoulders as the final remnants of doubt dissipated. "I didn't do it! You have to admit that's pretty solid evidence that someone else is behind this."

"I'm not ready to rule anything out just yet," Lyra said wryly. "Although this does decrease the chances that you're a cold-blooded killer."

It wasn't much, but V would take the win. They were hard to come by these days.

"What does that have to do with my footage from the party?" she asked, keeping them on track – because when they weren't bickering, they almost felt like allies.

"I can't tell where the tunnel goes or even how it's accessed," Lyra said, fully failing to answer V's question. "From the looks of it, though, it leads up and away from Apollo's place. Which means that if the killer used it, they probably didn't come from the party."

She navigated back to the video shot from behind V's eyes, pressing play.

"I thought I'd take another look at the guests. By comparing attendees against a list of high-profile figures, I can pinpoint any absences – thereby narrowing our list of suspects."

It was smart. V had to admit that this could work, that it might actually get them closer to the killer. Her excitement trilled a quiet melody before silencing at a thought.

"What if they didn't do it themselves?" she asked, hating herself for the question. "Couldn't they have hired a hitman to do their dirty work? Or bought off a member of the Guard? The killer could have been in plain sight the entire time while their money paid for Apollo's murder."

"I considered that," Lyra said, undaunted, "but I don't think it's likely. This was personal. The killer used a knife instead of a blaster, which means they couldn't kill from afar. They had to get close. Plus, he was stabbed through the heart, not the back. Whoever it was, they wanted to watch the life drain from his eyes. They wanted to see him die."

V's mind was working now, piecing the puzzle together. "He had defensive abrasions," she said, thinking aloud. "There was blood under his nails and a gash across his palm. He tried to fight back, but not until it was too late. The killer was already too close to stop. Meaning he knew his attacker."

Lyra nodded, a small smile peeking through her carefully constructed apathy. They were onto something, and both of them knew it. A tiny segment of their hostility thawed as their minds began to work as one. It wasn't friendship – or anything close – but it was a start.

The pair got down to business, carefully combing through the crowd and cataloging the faces. Lyra's software did the bulk of the work, assigning names and designations with the skill of a sleuth, but V also played a part, adding firsthand details to flesh out the scene.

She was amazed at the number of things she'd missed, at the details and dramas she'd neglected to see. She'd been so focused on saving Riyah that the rest had been cast aside and classified as background noise. The truth was, V was only a minor part of this play, a minuscule cog in the larger machine. She was important yet insignificant, notable and negligible, and the labels swirled around her in a whirlpool of unknowns.

Tired of dwelling on her own dilemmas, V turned her attention to Lyra, considering the woman working beside her. In the harsh light of the cheap bulbs, she looked even more foreign than she had at first sight. The tone of her skin toed the line between gray and blue, while her eyes held a darkness that bordered on black.

This close, V could see the ridges of her scalp, the soft skin that gave way to her deep, dark braid. There was no stubble to show that it had been shaved, suggesting a natural occurrence – like her hair merely grew in one solid line straight down her crown. Against her smooth scalp, her ears looked too round, too full, exaggerated into shape by a plethora of piercings.

Lyra caught her staring, and a blue vein bulged in her neck. V flinched but was saved by a sudden darkness as the lights once again fell victim to the whims of the power grid. With Lyra's systems out of action, the women slipped into silence, leaden and full, made worse by their proximity on the bed.

Deprived of her sight, V's other senses kicked in, relaying a picture of her surroundings. Lyra's heavy breathing, the faint scent of flowers and spice, the feel of the firm bedsprings beneath her.

"Where did you learn all this?" she asked abruptly, attempting to ease the sticky discomfort. "The tech," she explained when the silence stretched. "You seem to have a knack for it, but it's not something they teach in most schools. So how'd you stumble across it – this talent of yours?"

V didn't expect much in terms of an answer. Lyra had already confirmed her aversion to sharing. V was simply looking for a way to pass the time until the lights resumed their glow, illuminating a path forward.

"My older brother," Lyra said, surprising them both.

Those three words lingered in the air, unexplained, so V pushed on. "You're a second child?" She tried to hide the interest in her tone, but she doubted it was working.

"Yes," Lyra responded brusquely. "And no." The contradiction hung there for a moment, held aloft by gossamer threads of confusion.

"Did he...die?" V asked slowly, attempting to parse through the haze of uncertainty in search of some kind of meaning.

"No," Lyra said again, debunking V's theory. This time, however, she continued, "We don't talk much anymore. In fact, I haven't seen him for years. But once upon a time, he taught me everything he knew, and I couldn't get enough."

"It sounds like you were close," V ventured, tracing the lines of Lyra's face as her eyes adjusted to the darkness. She might have been imagining it, but it seemed like something akin to sadness was drawing down her features.

"We were," she confirmed, nodding. "I would have done anything for him. Just like you and your friend."

It was a strange sort of invitation, bordering on a command. Her *heartfelt* tale had not been a token but a trade, a not-so-subtle request for reciprocation. She didn't want to build rapport. She didn't want V's pity. She wanted the particulars of V's life, the details that drove her to act. V didn't know why she'd expected anything else.

Hell, she wouldn't be surprised if Lyra's words were a work of fiction, a cunning creation shaped in the moment to advance her own agenda. Although something in them seemed genuine, imbued with a flicker of real emotion.

"Riyah's the only family I have," V stated after careful

consideration. "The idea that someone is hurting her is tearing me apart. And if anyone ever tried to use her against me, I would make sure they regretted it for the rest of their lives."

The silence wasn't heavy now; it was on fire, alight with all the words they hadn't said. It was a standoff, a stone against a stone, steadily grinding each other down. The mood wasn't malicious – not yet – although each held the potential for poison. For now, it was a test, a show of strength aimed at assessing each other's defenses.

All at once, a searing light switched on above them, catapulting them back to reality. As V blinked away the aftershocks, she spotted Fynn in the doorway, his arms crossed as he considered them. She could see the scene through his eyes – two women on a bed staring daggers through the darkness – and the confusion that must come with it.

"How come no one invited me to the party?" he asked, his voice still rough with sleep.

He wore a thin shirt that clung to his solid frame, emphasizing the muscles beneath, and it took a conscious effort for V to look away. Her emotions were swirling, swinging between extremes, and for the moment she didn't trust herself to speak. Luckily, Lyra didn't have that problem.

"We're working," she said, her tone all business. "Pull up a chair and maybe we'll finally get somewhere."

The trio moved into formation and, after a rapid recap, they descended once more into their detective work. Three minds instead of two didn't quite lighten the load, but it did serve to lighten the mood, dispelling the tension of two alphas and replacing it with a tentative calm. By the time the first rays broke through the gloom and made their way to the bedroom, they had almost finished their review of the retinal footage.

Their list had dwindled as they'd steadily checked off names, leaving only a handful of suspects. The esteemed Senator Rigel Griffyn, whose tenure stretched 40 years or more. His colleague Senator Celeste Altair, the latest in her bloodline to preside over the ship. Guard Captain Indus Arctura, who knew the ins and outs of murder from years spent investigating it on the force. The brilliant Sabine Ryker, a fellow scientist and past associate with whom Apollo maintained close ties. And, to round out the list, Corvus Huxley, one of the richest men aboard the Echelon.

They were all significant, influential in their own small ways, key characters whose presence at the party was missed. They would be hard to track down – and even harder to corner – yet it felt like progress, nonetheless. Even lonely names set atop blank paper was better than the cruel unknown.

As if sensing the conclusion of their search, a machine on Lyra's workstation beeped, signaling some kind of completion. Lyra leapt at the sound, bounding to the source as Fynn and V looked on in interest. Her brows furrowed, then deepened further as she deciphered something only she could read.

After a sustained bout of silence, Fynn finally asked, "Lyra? What is it? What did you find?"

Per usual, she didn't jump to inform them of her findings. Instead, she took her time, double-checking her work before dropping onto the chair – and focusing all her attention on V. Her stare was sharp and appraising, stripping V down to parts before building her back up. V felt exposed, raw and unprotected, like Lyra knew something she didn't.

"Apollo's drive was no ordinary device," she started, her words heavy with significance. "It was storage of a sort, a repository for something irreplaceable. Violet, I think this machine held your lost memories."

A torrent of emotions tumbled through her, churning at the thought. Disbelief, then shock, then confusion. Joy, then wonder, then concern. A heavy weight sank through her stomach as the storm converged on a word.

Held. Past tense. As in it no longer stored that data.

But why had it ever? Why had Apollo of all people possessed her memories? What had he done to take them – and why had he decided to give them back?

She wanted to scream, to cry, to curse at the hope that had briefly alighted in her system and the bevy of questions that sprang from its ashes.

Fynn came to her rescue with a question of his own. "Is there anything left? Any memories at all? Anything we can salvage?"

Lyra bit her lip as she dove back into her system, losing herself in the syntax. She surfaced a short time later with a sigh.

"Most of the data was lost when the device was damaged," she said. "Whether it was an accident or a failsafe, I can't tell. Although it does appear that some of the memories made it through, that before Apollo died, he managed to send a short transmission to you."

V let out a harsh, incredulous laugh. Her memories remained the same – blank and desolate, a barren landscape filled with ghosts.

"I don't remember a thing," she stated, leaving no room for doubt.

"That's because he never finished the process," Lyra rushed to explain. "Those memories aren't addressed in your system. They haven't been coded and stored. So they're floating, awaiting activation. They need context and scope before your mind can begin to make sense of them."

"So what do I do?" V asked harshly, still doubtful of Lyra's words.

"You wait," Lyra stated, perturbed by V's tone. "You bide your time until something sparks them. You exercise patience – if that's something you're even capable of."

V's lip curled up at the slight, yet part of her knew Lyra was right. She'd never been one to wait, to let a question linger, to lie back until the answers found her.

"And in the meantime?" V asked, holding onto her temper by a thread. "Do I just stay here, researching the rich and hoping for a clue? Isn't there anything else I can do?"

Lyra faltered for an instant and V seized on it, sensing something more. "What is it?" she demanded. "What else did you find?"

"It might be nothing," Lyra said, hedging her bets, "but it looks like something's buried beneath the code. I could be wrong, but it seems to be a set of coordinates."

It was Fynn's turn to ask. "Why would Apollo hide coordinates in his code? Where do they lead?"

And suddenly, V knew. It had been there for days, lingering just out of reach, waiting for that spark – just like Lyra had said.

"It's an old sky station," V stated, surprising her

companions with her certainty. A vision of it rose in her thoughts as she spoke, pulled from her dreams and solidifying into a memory. "It's been abandoned for years and left to rot. It's the perfect place to hide something."

Fynn cocked his head in question. "How do you know that, V? How could you possibly know that?"

"Because that's exactly what I did. I hid something there, something I knew I would need. And now it's time to get it back."

Chapter 14

"This isn't a good idea," Fynn said for the thousandth time that night. He was pacing and frowning and fighting the urge to barricade the door with his body.

V wasn't deterred. For the first time in a long time, she knew what she needed to do – and she knew she needed to do it alone. Naturally, Fynn disagreed.

"I know what I'm doing," V assured him, placing one hand on his shoulder. The contact seemed to calm him, and he slowed to a stop as she continued. "I planned for this. Somehow, I knew I might find myself here, and I left a trail to follow. We'll stay connected through my cam so you can watch what happens, but I need to do this alone."

"It's not safe out there," Fynn said, as if she needed the reminder. "They're looking for you. At least let me come with you to the station. I'll wait outside while you work. Promise."

"I'm not a damsel in distress," she replied, perturbed at the thought that she needed protecting. "I've had plenty of practice navigating this ship at night. It's practically second nature. You would only slow me down."

Fynn let out a huff as he resumed his efforts to wear a hole in the floorboards. V took that as a reluctant acknowledgment that she was right.

Of course she was right. She'd been formulating her plan all day, sorting out the details and preparing for every eventuality. There had been no more flashes of insight, no clues from her past to guide her. Her memories remained dormant, save for the existence of the station and the certainty that she'd stashed something significant within it.

Lyra had been unhelpful as always, retreating to her room to research suspects rather than lending her talents. For her, the mystery of Apollo's murder took precedence over uncovering V's past, and she made no effort to hide it.

That left Fynn and V alone to toil away the time until curfew, when the city would empty of all but its eagle-eyed spies. A tension hummed beneath the surface as they busied themselves with work, talking but never touching as the minutes ticked by. Eventually, the alarm sounded, calling all citizens home – and beckoning V into the night.

This time, she wore no disguise, no heavy clothes that would limit her movements. From head to toe, she sported sleek black, fitted to her form with precision. Her blond hair was tied back and concealed beneath a cap, conveying the air of a criminal. Now all that was left was to steal into the night, disappearing beneath the cloak of shadow.

A goodbye seemed both too much and barely enough, so V dispensed with the pleasantry entirely, preparing to slip out of the shop without a word. Yet as she perched in the doorway, surveying the barren streets for signs of life, a voice reached out from the darkness to draw her back.

"Wait."

V's brain froze with indecision, whether to wait or flee, but she wavered for a moment too long. In an instant, Lyra was on her, pressing a parcel into her palm.

"Take this," she commanded, flat and forceful. "And try not to die."

There was no sentiment to it, no soft edges, as if the prospect of V's death didn't affect her in the slightest. Yet when V looked down, she saw a different story. Lyra had given her a gun.

"Thanks," V said slowly, her confusion clear, "but I'm not the best with weapons." She flashed back to the Guard House, to the energy pistol, to the mess she'd made of the wall before finally hitting her target.

Lyra laughed. "Then it's a good thing that's not a weapon."

"It's a gun," V stated.

"It's a deterrent," Lyra countered. When V didn't get the clue, she continued, "If you see a sentry, point and shoot. It'll scramble the systems until you're clear. Just don't go giving this one to any Guards. And good luck," she added as an afterthought before stalking back to her room.

V glanced at Fynn, wide eyes meeting wide eyes. Fynn's surprise quickly softened into something else, sending a jolt down V's spine. The force of it drove her toward the door, and this time, no one stopped her as she stepped outside.

Alone at last, V sucked in the cool night air, relishing the relief. The stars sparkled overhead, lighting her way, and she spurred herself into a jog.

The sound of her footsteps on the pavement, her steady breathing, and the soft purr of the Echelon's engines soothed something in her, a tension that had been growing by the hour. She was restless, craving action and answers. And him. For the moment, she let it all go, giving herself over to the night.

She was so lost in her blissful escape that she nearly missed the sentry. V heard its whir a half second before it sailed around the corner. She barely had time to pull Lyra's gun from her waistband before the sentry's beady red eye turned toward her.

V plastered herself against the wall and pulled the trigger, praying she hadn't been seen. For a moment nothing happened. The gun emitted no pulse or sound, merely silence. Then the sentry shuddered, shaking in the sky before swan-diving gracelessly to the ground.

V breathed a sigh of relief as a chain of text appeared across her eyes.

"That was close," Fynn said, stating the obvious. "Keep your guard up and stay alert."

V rolled her eyes and skirted the sentry before taking off again toward the station. The coordinates were ingrained in her mind and imprinted on her psyche. She couldn't tell if she was following the map or a memory, one buried deep and concealed from her conscious mind. Whatever it was, it led her closer and closer to the fringes of the ship, where buildings gave way to the Grove.

Time had taken its toll on these streets. They seemed tired, creaking beneath V's feet as she followed their course.

While a constant wave of repairs kept the Echelon aloft, its flow ebbed to a trickle toward the city's outer edges. This far from the center, money didn't move as fast, and the sectors felt the strain.

There were no checkpoints along the route to slow her passage, yet the sentries more than made up for their absence. V neutralized two more of the mechanical droids, barely slowing as they dropped. In no time, she found herself outside the station, craning her neck to consider it.

Like every sky station, the building was tall, soaring toward the stars and reflecting their light. Yet disuse had given way to disrepair, with little more than steel stilts keeping it upright. The two sides which trains had once passed through now stood open to the sky, with the severed tracks petering into sheer drops. A single set of stairs, encased in broken glass, spiraled up and out of sight, into the belly of the beast.

V had the strangest feeling, an intense sense of déjà vu peppered with sharp certainty. A version of her had been here, standing on this very spot, looking up at this station. V tried to summon her, to manifest that spark, but nothing came. There was only the feeling, the eternal ghost of a girl whom she could never be again.

"Is everything alright?" Fynn typed, concerned by her stasis.

"Yeah," V lied, shaking away the sensation. "I'm just admiring the architecture. Such beauty. Such poise. Such an asset to the landscape." The sarcasm dripped from her words like honey, thick and sticky on her tongue.

"It certainly makes a statement," Fynn countered. "Although I'd say that statement seems more like a cry for help, begging for someone to tear it down. But you're welcome to your own opinion."

V muffled a snort. Fynn was right, of course. They should have dismantled the station years ago and erected homes in its wake, but that would never happen. Like many other priorities, the demolition would be on a to-do list that never got done, mired in the red tape of the rich.

"I'm going in," V stated, forcing her feet to move. "Let's hope it's sturdier than it looks."

With one final scan of her surroundings, V trotted forward and tried the door. Thankfully, it was unlocked, and she slipped inside, immersing herself in the iron-scented air of the stairwell.

Rust decorated the beams like ivy, crawling up the sides and reaching for the ceiling. V stumbled on a sign that had long since lost its battle with gravity. "Danger!" it screamed in loud red letters, followed by a plea for trespassers to leave. V ignored the warning, treading over broken glass on her way to the stairs, which groaned ominously beneath her weight. The sound echoed through the hall like a call to the night, warning of her presence.

V wanted to run, to scale the stories in time with the anxious beats of her heart, but the stairs demanded patience. Time had eaten holes in the treads, consuming their strength, while some steps sat on the verge of collapse. V jumped and hopped in a clumsy dance as she gradually climbed to the top.

By the time the platform rose within view, V's side ached and her breaths came in shallow gasps, leaving her throat raw. She paused on the precipice to catch her breath only to lose it again as soon as she looked up.

Even in the dim light, she knew this space, knew its beams, its tiles, its tracks. She could almost see herself sitting there, legs dangling over the drop, thoughts wild. She could feel its hold on her across the years, tight and demanding in her chest.

"I've been here before," she said, her voice small in the vastness of the space. "I think I came here to escape. I think this was my safe place."

V waited, but Fynn said nothing in response, leaving her alone with a ghost. She ignored the unease that tingled in her veins, forcing herself forward.

Around the corner, set against the same wall as the stairs, was a bank of lockers – the same lockers that V had dreamt about every night since her encounter with Apollo. They were matte black, cold-rolled steel, sinister yet enticing. She couldn't help but reach out, closing her eyes as the cool surface pulled her back in time.

She was pacing, sitting, lying on the floor. She was angry, impatient, in pain. She was crying, screaming, silent. And she was always alone.

The visions stopped as quickly as they'd come, leaving her cold in the mild night. This place had seen her heart break, felt her tears upon its floor, held her up when she felt like falling down. It knew that version of her better than V ever would, carrying her secrets in its shell.

She wished she could pry her memories from its walls, squeeze out the source of her torment and track the cause of her tears. Yet the crumbling fortress stood strong, withholding everything but those secondhand emotions.

Without realizing it, V began to walk along the wall of lockers, her hand trailing in her wake. Her fingers traced familiar lines, charting a course across the surface like it could lead her home. Then suddenly she stopped, held in place by some faceless force that tore her from her trance.

She blinked awake, wide-eyed and alert, searching for the source of the disturbance. What V found was her hand clasped around a lock, her fingers turning white in their fervor. She loosened her grip and looked down, studying the pad in her palm.

"This is it," she said to Fynn across the ether, with certainty ringing through her thoughts. "This is why I'm here."

Once again, though, her words were met with silence. A sneaking feeling told her that something was wrong. Fynn wouldn't ignore her, wouldn't let her flounder alone in a place like this. She might not know him well, but she thought she could say that for certain.

Pushing past the apprehension, V placed her hand on the screen that dominated the lock, hoping to wake it up. Instead, a hot pain shot across her finger. She pulled back sharply, dropping the lock as a tiny bead of her blood sank into its depths.

Two clicks followed in rapid succession as the lock gave way and the locker opened. For a moment, V faltered, fearing the maggots from her dreams, but nothing spilled out. She inched closer, easing the door open and gazing down at her prize.

It was a device, similar to Apollo's yet ever so slightly different. It was larger, clumsier, painted in shades of silver and gray and covered in tiny ridges. Instead of two prongs at the top, there were four, forming a sinister square of points.

V picked it up gently, turning it around in her hands. She was half afraid it would spark and send her body into shock, but it stayed dormant, keeping its secrets hidden. No memories rose to give her context or provide a clue as to its function, yet V's mind jumped to the only natural conclusion.

"I think it's a backup, a copy of my memories," she said, failing to hide her excitement. "It's a second chance."

The ensuing silence confirmed her suspicions. No one was on the other end of her comms. No one could see her. And no one could save her if this all went sideways.

As if on cue, a groan emanated from the stairs, followed by another. V held her breath, standing stock-still in the shadows, praying she had imagined it. Yet it came again, louder and clearer and all too close. There was someone on the stairs.

V closed her eyes, concentrating on the sounds. The cadence was too rapid, too frenzied to belong to just one person. There had to be two or even three of them on the steps, making quick work of the ascent.

She opened her eyes, seeking an escape, but it appeared that she was stranded in this tower. The only entrance or egress was the stairs, and they were currently occupied by an unknown threat. Unless V wanted to hurl herself over the side of the station, she needed a different plan. She needed a weapon.

Except all Lyra had given her was a tool to take down sentries. V didn't know for certain, but she doubted that it would do much good against villains of the human variety. That left her with only her wits, her fists, and her newfound gadget – none of which were intrinsically threatening.

So V did the only thing she could think of. She hid.

With quiet steps, she tucked herself around the side of the lockers, just out of sight of the stairwell. Stowing the device in her pocket, she flattened herself against the steel, holding her breath in hopes that no one would spot her. If they were Guards – as V feared – and their objective was a cursory check or standard surveillance, she might just pass by unnoticed. If they were on a manhunt, however, she was done for.

Within moments, they crested the stairs and emerged on the platform. They were quiet at first, hushed in the way only hunters can manage. Then one of them spoke, breaking the spell with a whisper.

"Are you sure she came in here?" a woman asked in a painfully shrill soprano.

"She's in here, Eris," a man replied, full of confidence and conviction. "The sentry saw her headed this way, and there's nowhere else to hide."

"You better be right, Si," a third voice added far too loudly. "The last two patrols that came back empty-handed got Grove duty for a year. And I'm not going down like that."

"If you don't shut up, Cruz, you're gonna spook her," said Si. "And we need to bring her in alive, not as a mess of bones and blood scraped off the sidewalk."

Eris, Si, and Cruz. Three Guards. Three opponents who knew she was here. Three more than she could feasibly fight off without some sort of miracle.

Hiding wouldn't save her for long. They had her cornered, trapped like an animal, counting down the seconds of her freedom. She could hear them coming, their footsteps echoing in an eerie melody across the empty space. V knew she had to do something.

The moment the first Guard came within view, V made her move, exploding from the shadows with a growl.

Chapter 15

V collided with a solid form, all muscle and sinew and strength. The surprise sent them both sailing, and they landed with a thud on the ground.

V recovered first, glancing down to see a woman beneath her, broad and brawny. Eris, she presumed. The woman was squat but solid – and altogether angry. The lines of her eyebrows fused into one as she glared up at V.

V didn't wait for retaliation. Instead, she leveraged herself up, pinning the woman tightly between her thighs. She had just enough time to deliver two mediocre blows before Eris recovered her composure. When she did, she shook off the strikes like some minor irritation, savagely shoving V aside.

V rolled onto her back, catching glimpses of the two remaining Guards – one dark-haired and sneering, the other stretched and wan. Instead of moving to help, they maintained their places, watching as V gave them a show. Their crooked grins gave off an air of amusement, and V was instantly offended.

Eris shot up with dexterous ease, getting to her feet before V could even get to her knees. She cracked her neck with a terrible snap, then rounded on V, who had only just managed to rise. In the blink of an eye, Eris was on her, stunning her with a punch to the jaw before seizing hold of her shirt.

Lights danced before V's eyes in an erratic pattern as Eris reared to strike again. Her instincts took hold and she thrust her head aside just in time for the blow to glance past her ear. The failure only fueled her foe, who reacted by sinking a knee into the soft flesh of V's stomach. The air escaped her lungs in a painful wheeze, which made her rival smile.

"Give up yet?" she taunted in victorious conceit. "Because I can do this all day. Why not hand yourself over and save us both some time?"

"Go to hell," V muttered, bringing her hands up to Eris' chest and shoving her back with a grunt.

The move severed Eris' grip, and V savored the moment of calm. In a heartbeat, though, the woman was on her again, this time coming at her with a kick. The boot landed squarely on her chest and V flailed, flying through the air with a strange sort of grace before falling back to earth.

She landed on her back, stunned, unable to do anything but stare at the ceiling and struggle for breath. V knew it was futile, that she'd never best one Guard, let alone three. They would subdue her, take her to the station, brand her a killer, then make her disappear. She'd given away her freedom for the chance to remember, and now none of it would matter.

Somehow, that thought made V want to fight, to lash out, to give as good as she got. She certainly couldn't win, but perhaps she could do a little damage. And perhaps that would be enough to soothe her in the darkness.

When Eris came for her again, V was ready. Still plastered on her back, she brought her legs up and kicked with all the force she could muster. Her feet connected with kneecaps, and Eris screeched in pain, tumbling down to join V on the ground.

V didn't waste a second. She used the momentum to spring up to her knees before crawling over to her foe. With a furious lunge, she thrust herself on Eris, driving her hands toward the woman's beefy neck. They closed around muscle and squeezed, with all V's rage funneling out through her fingers.

She sensed Si and Cruz in her periphery, alert but immobile. Unconcerned. They knew Eris was in no serious danger, no struggle she couldn't win. Still, they were prepared to take V down if fortunes somehow turned in her favor.

Of course, that wasn't about to happen. With the strength of a bull, Eris broke V's grasp, nearly crushing her wrists in the process. With V untethered, the woman placed her palms on V's chest and pushed, catapulting her back. She toppled over, landing hard on her side, her right arm trapped beneath her.

A skittering sound broke through the daze of combat, catching Eris' attention. The silver device escaped from V's pocket and slid across the ground, stopping inches from her opponent's feet.

Eris sat up, intrigued, reaching out to claim this new

contraption. Her eyes sparkled as she took in its deadly prongs and fingered the silver trigger, mentally doing the math. V stayed where she was, stuck to the ground as Eris rose, holding out her trophy.

"What do we have here?" she wondered aloud, inordinately pleased. "Some kind of crude attempt at a weapon? It certainly looks like it could do some damage. Shall we give it a try?"

Practically salivating with pleasure, Eris sauntered over to V and bent down. Gripping V's hair for purchase, she placed the device against her neck and pulled the trigger.

The pain was familiar and just as fierce, but V clung to the corners of consciousness, needing to stay awake. The daggers dragged her down, but instead of heading toward her brain, they branched out across her body, imbuing every muscle with agony. V wanted to whimper, to cry, to curse whoever invented this god damn contraption, but she knew it wouldn't help. So she bit her tongue, tasting blood in her mouth as her body exploded.

V struggled to remember, to pull something from the pain that could save her, yet she still couldn't see past the fog. No matter how hard she tried, her memories remained mired in the same darkness that threatened to drown her.

V didn't understand. Why wasn't this working? Why wasn't she whole? The device whined as it labored on its last legs, then finally let loose, with the daggers turning to pinpricks, then tingles beneath her skin. After a moment, its hold on her vanished completely, leaving her panting on the ground.

V felt…different. She couldn't describe it, but something

had shifted beneath her skin. Her memories remained dormant, stubbornly refusing to surface, but a strange sort of force had seized her limbs, and it vibrated through her veins.

Yet it was too late to matter. Whatever change that thing had wrought, it wouldn't do much good with her on the ground, surrounded by Guards who knew they had won.

"Come on, Si," Eris said, sounding smug from her success. "Help me cuff her. We might need to carry this one back to the station." She let out a derisive chuckle as the dark-haired man unsheathed a set of shackles.

Eris leaned down to lift V to her feet, hauling her up with both hands. Then suddenly, something inside V snapped and all hell broke loose.

V couldn't say how it happened. Her hands gained a mind of their own, moving with a stealth she didn't know she possessed. One moment they were hanging uselessly at her sides, and the next they were nimbly sliding a knife between Eris' ribs.

The weapon, freed from the woman's belt with military precision, took its owner by surprise. Eris' hands strayed up to investigate the hilt now jutting from her chest, and her eyes went wide as she found it. Then she crumpled as dark blood began to stain her suit black.

The men behind her stood in shock, processing the abrupt turn of events. V didn't wait for them to regain their composure. With newfound vigor, she pounced, flying across the space with a kick that sent one man careening into the other.

"What the hell?!" Si screamed as the pair untangled their limbs, training their attention on her.

170

V wanted to ask the same thing. What the hell was happening? How had she done that to Eris? And how was she doing this now?

Some sort of switch had flipped beneath her skin, waking her cells from their stupor. Her body seemed to move of its own accord, with little input from her mind. It felt as if her muscles remembered the movements, like a melody she'd once played.

Si and Cruz rapidly regained their bearings, each pulling out a weapon and advancing. They were still so sure, so certain of their success, as if Eris' demise had been a stroke of luck. They didn't understand the danger.

The dark-haired Si pulled out in front, eager to avenge his friend. He held a knife in his left hand and another in his right, maximizing the chances of blood. Behind him, Cruz unsheathed a pistol and trained it on V, ensuring she couldn't escape.

V should have cared. She should have dropped to the ground and surrendered. She should have been shaking in her borrowed boots.

Except she wasn't. A breezy nonchalance had settled across her shoulders, lifting her up. She felt relaxed, energized, even excited. She felt ready to finish this.

Si lunged forward, aiming one knife at her stomach and the other at her heart. V dodged out of the way with dizzying speed, watching as the blur of his body tore past. She whirled around and, with an agile shove, used his momentum against him, sending him flailing to the ground.

Unfortunately, he failed to impale himself on his own weapons. He did, however, lose his grip on one of the blades, which skittered harmlessly into the shadows.

Cruz took that as his sign to fire. V dropped lithely to her belly then rolled onto her back as a blast of energy roared overhead, tickling the hairs on her neck. Si seized on the distraction, launching to his feet to tower over her.

"You've had your fun, bitch," he spat, "and now it's time to pay. We're taking you to the station – alive or dead. It doesn't matter to me in the slightest."

His monologue gave V time to calculate, to play out moves and countermoves in a complex battle plan. It was almost second nature, familiar and easy, and she reveled in the feeling of power. It swept her away, stealing her logic and leaving her hollow, just a creature of hunger and need.

Si moved to stomp on her chest, but V grabbed hold of his leg and twisted, bringing him down beside her. He let loose a whelp of surprise, followed by a groan of pain as he landed. Yet he never let go of his weapon.

He recovered in a flash, bringing the blade up just as V swung herself over. The metal tip bit into the soft skin of her shoulder, slicing a clean cut above her clavicle. The pain took a second to grab hold, but when it did it was fierce and violent, surging through her senses like a flood.

V grunted at the sting but maintained her place atop him, refusing to budge from her bucking mount. As Si struggled beneath her, Cruz amended his plan, abandoning his pistol in favor of a bulbous baton. At the touch of a button, the weapon came to life, glowing with a crackling energy. Cruz closed the distance, gearing up for a swing, while Si aimed his weapon at her heart.

The old V would have panicked. She would have covered

her head and prayed. She would have lost – and likely died in the process. Good thing that girl was gone.

Instead of cowering, the new V captured Si's arm mid-swing and slammed it against the ground, freeing the blade from his grasp. As the black metal club came within view, V rolled aside, barely managing to leave her perch – and grab Si's weapon – in time.

She sprang up a few yards away, getting her feet beneath her as both men struggled to recover. Si spun clumsily to rest on all fours while Cruz regained his balance and refocused on his target.

V watched her actions from outside her body, marveling at her certainty. Without so much as a stutter, she took off at run, knife in hand, barreling toward her foes. With a tiny leap, she left the ground, vaulting onto Si's back. The next moment, she was airborne again, catapulting off toward Cruz.

The knife pierced the side of his neck, slicing muscle and arteries as she dragged it down. It lodged in his collarbone, rending a bloodcurdling scream from Cruz's lips.

V let go as the knife snagged, jarring her arm. She watched with horror as the man tried to free it, losing more and more blood as he struggled against its venom. The sounds coming from his mouth changed from wordless shouts to frantic gasps as he lost his grip on consciousness. Finally, he fell, crumpling into a mess of silver and blood, silent and still against the pavement.

V's newfound knowledge of blows and parries hadn't prepared her for that. The sound of a man dying. The smell of death. It made her hands shake.

Si didn't seem to have the same weakness. He seized on V's hesitation, tackling her from behind and bringing her down. She barely managed to keep from cracking her head on the pavement, getting her arms beneath her just in time to absorb the impact.

Her injured shoulder screamed in pain, pulsing its anger across her chest. V could feel the sticky blood still seeping from the wound, coating her torso in warmth.

Si pinned her down with a knee to the back, pressing her into the tile. He was dense and thick, all muscle and power, and his weight was commanding atop her. V tried to slither out, to free herself, yet her struggles were in vain.

Si's fingers snagged in her hair, viciously squeezing her skull. With a jerk, he pulled her head back before slamming it to the pavement with a crack. Darkness dripped over the edges of her vision, threatening to coat the scene in black. Yet V clung to consciousness, using the pain as her focus.

Si let her head fall to the ground as he turned his attention to her body. One arm held her down while the other struck, stealing the air from her lungs. He pummeled her ribs with skillful precision, releasing a torrent of pain.

The world went quiet save for the sound of his breathing, the crunch of his strikes, her heartbeat in her ears. It would be easy to surrender, to stop struggling, to let him win.

V considered it for an instant, the relief of submission dancing just outside her reach. She considered closing her eyes, relaxing her muscles, releasing her grip. Yet as soon as her lids began to lower, she saw them – Riyah, Leo, Mouse, Fynn. Everyone worth fighting for.

The thought didn't exactly give her strength, but it did

strengthen her resolve. This was not where she died. This was not where it ended. This was only the beginning.

V took a calming breath, waiting for her moment to act. Slowly, she brought one leg up until it rested beside her, freeing her hip from the ground. Si moved to strike again, but V was quicker. Pushing off her bent leg, she rolled to the side, sinking an elbow into his chest. Already unstable with his arm in the air, Si lost his balance and collapsed.

With one last elbow to Si's jaw, V jumped to her feet, sprinting in search of a weapon. Her ribs protested the movement, sending twinges through her back, but she continued the hunt, inching toward the edge of the station.

Outside, the night was cool and calm, and it licked at her blistering skin, catching on the beads of sweat and replacing them with chills. Yet it couldn't quiet her heart, which hammered beneath her broken chest, crying through the darkness to be heard.

Something shimmered at the edge of her vision, and she turned to find a speck of silver peeking from beneath a rail. With the final seconds of her lead, she lowered herself down, dropping to the tracks with a thud. As she bent to reclaim the weapon, she heard Si spring off the platform and land with both feet behind her.

V straightened and spun, dagger in hand, to find her enemy mirroring her movements. Si had unsheathed a dagger from his belt, and he held it aloft in invitation. It glinted in the flickers of light, sending fireflies to dance across the walls in a macabre pantomime of flight.

There were no words now, no threats or calls for vengeance. They were past all that, sunk so deep in the madness that language seemed irrelevant. What mattered now was action, underpinned by skill and strength. This was a game of death, and only one of them would leave unclaimed.

Si advanced, slashing his weapon in wide arcs, driven by wild eyes. His composure had vanished, replaced by a vengeful glee as V began to retreat. Every step took her closer to the edge, to the perilous cliff that waited to pull her down.

She tried to keep her attention trained solely on Si, but the void called out, beckoning for her to look. When she finally did, her stomach leapt into her chest, threatening to choke her. V could barely see the ground, with shadows eclipsed by darkness all the way down.

Si wasn't stopping. He managed to nick her arm, slicing through the fabric of her sleeve to draw blood from a shallow cut, and the tiny triumph emboldened him. He pressed forward, oblivious to the danger, his eyes fixed steadily on her.

V knew that standing there wouldn't save her. All the ducking and dodging was draining her strength, threatening to bleed her dry. So she struck, reaching out through the windmill of Si's blows and responding with her own.

The movement momentarily stunned him. It was enough for V to bypass his guards and sink the blade into his side, cutting through his armor with ease. When she pulled it out, a stream of blood came with it, slicking the silver of his suit.

The pain brought Si back to life. His eyes refocused, clear and sure, and his lips drew back in a snarl. He was done playing, done letting V rule the game. He wanted to end this. He wanted her dead.

A slice across the torso came so close that V's shirt felt the sting, splitting beneath her breasts to reveal her ribs. She struck back with the same precision, tearing through his pants to uncover skin.

Without realizing it, V had given up ground, fleeing precious feet to avoid a blow. Taking one more step, her heel met with open air, nearly pulling her down. She saved herself by seizing hold of the overhanging edge of the platform above, dropping her dagger in the process – and granting Si an opening to strike.

As she regained her balance, her belly pressed along the wall, Si lunged for her, his blade aimed at her neck. V acted without thinking. Some instinct grabbed hold and she pushed herself free, spinning forward.

Si corrected his course, but V ducked below his blow to ram her body into his. His back slammed against the wall, and the force of it freed his blade, which clamored to the tracks at their feet. He moved his hands up to her chest, straining to push her away, but she held tight, the folds of his shirt clenched firmly in her fists.

Si was stronger. He had the muscles and the height and the clear advantage in combat. But V had something he didn't. She didn't know what it was, of course, but it was surging through her veins, moving her muscles to some unheard music.

V's feet slid on the rubble, allowing Si to force her back. She reeled before regaining her balance, but Si was already on her. Within an instant, he had her by the throat, savagely squeezing with both hands. The world grew dim around the edges as V strained for breath, fighting against the arms that held her. Fingernails met flesh as she clawed for purchase, but her efforts were futile. So she stopped struggling.

Bracing her arms on his shoulders and her foot on his shin, she stole his strength, pitching herself in the air before bringing her body back down. One foot met earth while the other met bone, shattering his kneecap with a kick.

Si howled his agony to the night, dropping his hands from her neck as he tilted toward the ground. Except they were once again at the edge, with nowhere to go but down.

Without another sound, Si slipped over the side of the tracks, his body plummeting toward the pavement.

Chapter 16

V knew that she couldn't stick around. Soon enough, the sentries would stumble across the mess she'd made of the Guards and call for reinforcements. Plus, with all the blood she'd lost from her various cuts and gashes, she was feeling… less than stellar. So she made a beeline for the stairs, barely remembering to pocket the silver device on her way out the door.

By the time she reached the bottom, her shoulder was splitting and the world was spinning from the pain. The thought of running back to the shop – or even walking – made her feel sick. She wanted to rest, not run, to sit on the sidewalk and stare at the night as it changed back into day.

There was nowhere to hide, nowhere that provided sufficient cover to guarantee her safety. Every dark corner could be lit by a sentry, with every path and passage as its hunting ground. They wouldn't stop until they found her, and she'd surely be dead by daylight.

There was, however, another option. V's fingers tingled at the sight.

Three motorbikes waited near the base of the station, riderless and inviting. Their sleek black coats reflected the starlight, with the cosmos mirrored in multicolored swirls. V was across the street before she knew what she was doing.

She caressed the handle with the touch of a lover, sweet and soft and wanting. A yearning broke within her, but she pushed it down, knowing there was no way to fulfill it. She had no keys, no ID, no way to make the bikes move.

At least, that's what she thought. Her hands seemed to have a different idea. As she watched, they pushed aside a hidden panel before burying themselves in a mess of wires.

It was the strangest feeling, as if she knew what she was doing yet didn't. As if she'd done this a thousand times before yet couldn't remember a single instance. The movements were ingrained in her muscles, like the methods she'd used to subdue the Guards, and she watched them unfold with awe.

Without knowing how, she bypassed the controls to switch off the bike's tracker before diving into its depths. Reaching the switches that controlled its core, she flipped them swiftly in a synchronized pattern, feeling the rhythm in her soul. After a handful of heartbeats, the motor made a delicious sound, humming happily to life.

V's leaden heart soared as she placed herself atop the bike and felt it purr. For the barest hint of a second, she remembered this feeling, this power. She saw herself astride another bike – her bike – sleek and new and glinting in the sun. She felt the wind in her hair, the freedom in her soul, the ghost of her former self at her back.

The flicker of memory dissipated as she spurred the bike into motion, leaning forward to take command of its reins. She kept its lights low, casting faint shadows across the street as she steered away from the scene.

Before long, the timidness of first touch gave way to exhilaration, and she found herself flying through the streets. It was everything she'd imagined and more. The bike sliced through the air with abandon, consuming corners and devouring city blocks in an instant.

V felt untouchable. She never wanted this feeling to end. She longed to ride until night turned into day and back to night, until the power drained to nothing beneath her feet. She wanted to outrun her foes, her demons, herself. And for a moment, it almost seemed as if she could.

Yet no matter how fast you run, reality will always overtake you.

V suddenly found herself outside Fynn's shop, and the shock of it had her stopping on a dime, nearly tumbling over the handlebars in her haste. She managed to steady herself before bringing the bike around to the back and stowing it in the shadows.

Without the bike to support her, V felt unsteady and unstable, tottering toward the door like she was well past tipsy. The moment her hand hit the handle, it was torn from beneath her, sending her stumbling toward the floor.

Fynn caught her, his strong arms encircling her as she leaned against his chest. Several seconds lapsed as shock mellowed into acute awareness. Both pushed away awkwardly until only Fynn's arm lay between them, connecting their bodies and protecting V from another fall.

"What the hell happened?" he demanded to know, not unkindly but certainly not gentle. "All of a sudden, your feed went black. Not even Lyra could get it back. We had no idea what to do. Then out of nowhere it pops back up, and you're speeding through the city like a maniac. Needless to say, I think we missed a thing or two."

V groaned, the sound half annoyance and half pain. "As much as I'd love to give you a rundown while bleeding out in your hall, perhaps we could do this sitting down? Maybe with a stitcher – or at least a large shot of freeze? Unless you were looking forward to disposing of my dead body. Then, by all means, keep talking."

"Don't be dramatic. You're not dying," Fynn chided her, eliciting an eye roll in reply.

Nevertheless, he guided her into the shop, with one arm wrapped securely around her waist. Leading her to a high chair, he stationed her atop it before vanishing into the hall. V couldn't help but hope that he'd return with a flask of freeze. After the night she'd had, she could really do with a drink.

A minute later, Fynn resurfaced, his arms laden with supplies – yet noticeably devoid of blue liquid. Pulling up a small side table, he deposited his makeshift medical kit before turning to her with a frown. Sizing up her injuries, he dove into the stockpile, emerging with a sinister pair of shears.

Without waiting for her permission, he grabbed hold of the bottom of her shirt and began to cut, slicing decisively through the hem, past the rip beneath her chest and up to the collar. Then he peeled it from her skin, tugging gently at the points where blood had fused it to her body. After a few minutes of focused work, Fynn managed to free it, leaving her in nothing but a thin black bra.

V shivered in the sudden cold. Fynn's warm hands caressed her skin, gently dabbing at the blood that had dried across her chest. When he'd wiped away enough to reveal her injuries, he bit back a swear, fumbling for the stitcher on the table. The long metal rod sprang to life with a sizzle as he brought it toward her shoulder, but he paused before it touched her skin.

"This is going to hurt," he warned, as if she didn't already know. As if pain wasn't coursing through her veins at the thought.

"Then get on with it," she said. So he did.

The tool hissed as it made contact with the wound, and V hissed along with it, reaching out to grasp Fynn's shoulder for support. The feel of fire, glistening and angry, threatened to turn her vision black, but she held on, even as every cell screamed for release.

The scent of burning flesh rose to her nostrils, turning her stomach sour. Her fingers dug furiously into Fynn's skin, but he didn't protest, continuing on steadily like a surgeon. His hands were warm and even as they pressed her flesh together, knitting layers of muscle and skin back into place.

He traced his fingers across her shoulder to check his work, extracting a gasp from V – half pain and half a twisted sort of pleasure. Undeterred, his fingers continued their journey, sweeping down to her stomach to stitch together more tears.

As the pain receded, V became all too aware of Fynn's

183

proximity, the way his hands brushed across her skin, the feel of his breath against her body as he perched between her legs. His dark curls fell across his face, obscuring his expression, but she could feel the intensity in his touch and the concern laced within his tender ministrations.

Finishing the final suture, Fynn studied her body, doing one last scan of her form. V suddenly felt exposed, sitting half naked before a man she hardly knew, allowing him to touch parts of her which few had explored. It was intimate in a way, intensified by her recent escape from death and his clear concern for her safety.

Fynn hummed in approval at his work, and the sound rumbled through V's body, leaving a trail of warmth in its wake. As she tried to quell the feeling, he drew back, leaving just enough space between them for her body to feel his absence.

"You'll be OK," he said, his voice deep and husky in the darkness, like he was trying to convince himself. "You lost a lot of blood but somehow managed to miss your vital organs. You'll heal, but you'll be sore."

V's fingers reflexively crept to her shoulder, feeling the fine line of raised skin, still hot to the touch. The movement stung, and she drew back with a flinch. Fynn didn't miss her pained expression.

"Violet, what happened?" he asked earnestly, finally raising his gaze to hers. "Who did this to you? Why did your feed go dark?"

V tried to put her thoughts in order, to categorize and chronicle the events of the evening, but for some reason they wouldn't fit. Nothing was neat or tidy. Nothing made sense.

Fynn noticed her hesitation and sighed. "Let's start from the beginning," he said slowly. "One thing at a time. What happened when you entered that tower?"

The feeling of déjà vu came rushing back at his question, accosting her with fragments of memory. She closed her eyes, trying to clear her thoughts and parse out the details she knew.

"I'd been to that station before, in another life. But when I tried to tell you...you weren't there. I was alone."

Fynn leaned closer, as if leaning into her story. "We tried everything to get your feed back online. When nothing worked, we thought maybe you'd been knocked unconscious...or worse." He paused, reigning in the emotion that threatened to break free. "But what do you mean you'd been there before? When?"

"I don't know." V shrugged – then instantly regretted it as a stab of pain shot through her shoulder. As she waited for it to clear, an idea blossomed, bolstered by a shred of memory. "I think I knew that something in the station blocked out signals, that no one would be able to see my feed. I think that's why I went there. That's why I chose to hide it there."

"Hide what?" Fynn asked, latching onto the words. "Do you mean the backup? Were you able to find your memories?"

He was curious – too curious – and V instinctively drew back.

"No," she said flatly. "There was no backup. The rest of my memories are gone. What's in here is all I have left," she said, pointing to her head. She studied Fynn as he processed her words, searching for the threads of disappointment but finding none.

"Oh, Violet," he said, reaching out but not allowing himself to touch. "I'm so sorry. I can't imagine what that must mean for you, how you must feel."

V allowed herself to sink back toward him, chiding herself for the suspicion. He didn't care about her memories. He cared about the mystery, about Apollo and the missing senators. And, it seemed, about her.

"I did find…something, though," she admitted, pulling the device from her pocket. With one last look, she handed it over to him, as if offering up a part of herself.

"I don't understand," he said, turning it over. "It looks almost exactly like Apollo's. If your memories aren't inside, then what is?"

"Nothing," V stated bluntly. "Well, not anymore."

Fynn's eyebrow rose in confusion, a question clearly on his mind.

"I had company – of the Guard variety," V explained. "Three, in fact. They thought it was a weapon, and they were eager to try it out on me."

"That's who hurt you? These Guards?" Fynn asked, sounding faintly enraged.

V nodded mutely, shoving down the memories that threatened to surface.

"How the hell did you escape?" Fynn continued, confusion and alarm coloring his words. "Are they coming for you? Should we be worried?"

"No," V assured him, placing her hand on his shoulder. "They won't be coming for anyone ever again. I made sure of that."

Fynn looked baffled, and rightly so. The last time he had

seen V fight, she was flailing away while trying to flee the Guard station, and she'd barely escaped with her life. Now she was telling him that she'd singlehandedly dispatched a trio of Guards? His confusion was clearly warranted.

"A person is made up of more than memories," V tried to explain. Upon seeing Fynn's confusion, she continued, "When that Guard shocked me, she didn't know what she was doing, but she gave me a gift. She gave me back my ability to react, to move, to fight."

V searched for the words that would fit, a way to make sense of what had happened. She reached for the power that now flowed through her system, tracing its outlines in search of a shape. Conjecture and memory aligned in her mind, fusing into utter certainty.

"That device held years of training and muscle memory," V said. "When it discharged, something inside of me changed. My cells reconfigured, my body become whole, and I suddenly remembered that I am a *fucking badass*."

Fynn seemed taken aback – either by her language or her sudden vehemence – but she didn't care. She knew in her bones that she was right, that whoever she'd been before had been trained to hack systems, to drive like the devil, to kill. She didn't know if she'd been a monster or a savior, an angel or a demon, but one thing was certain. V was a force to be reckoned with.

Fynn's face was a puzzle of pieces that didn't seem to fit. He looked perplexed and intrigued and marginally dismayed.

"So you don't remember anything?" he asked, still caught on the wrong thing. "Not a hint of your life before?"

V growled, leaning forward to grab Fynn's face with

187

both hands. "Tonight, I slit a man's throat – and threw another off a train platform. I stabbed a woman through the heart. Hell, I even hijacked a Guard-issued motorbike and sped through this city like I owned it. Forgive me if I'm not thinking about who I was. I'm a little preoccupied with what I might be able to do next."

Fynn let out an almost imperceptible sound of surprise, and V realized just how close she'd drawn to him in her fervor. She abruptly dropped her hands, but for some reason she couldn't drop her gaze. Fynn stared back, his eyes a window to a turbulent storm.

"Violet," he growled, all raw emotion and awe. "Who are you?"

A searing heat bloomed in the pit of V's stomach, sending tendrils of warmth to her cheeks. A drumbeat of desire beat within her chest, demanding action, yet she held back, limiting herself to a look. Her breath turned shallow as she took him in, standing so close yet failing to touch her.

Fynn didn't pull away. In fact, he returned her gaze with an intensity that made her shiver, raking over her chest, her parted lips, her pleading eyes. She no longer felt the pain of her injuries or the shock of how she'd received them. For the moment, Fynn filled every corner of her brain.

The anticipation grew tight and heavy between them until it was almost painful. V yearned to reach out, to pull him against her, but she didn't. She couldn't. She was frozen, held in thrall by the darkness in his eyes and the unspoken command on his lips. *Stay.*

The scent of cinnamon and wood that wafted off his skin was intoxicating, with the power to make V forget her own name. Again. She wanted to close her eyes and drink him in, but she couldn't tear herself away from his gaze.

With the smallest hint of movement, he drew closer, pressing himself between her thighs. Yet even this close, with their noses nearly touching, he didn't kiss her. She could feel his breath mingling with hers, the warmth radiating from his skin, his heart pounding beneath his chest. It was almost too much to bear.

"Violet," he whispered, rough and heady, like a man on the edge of control. "You're astounding." Then he closed the gap, his fingers coming up to twine around her neck and draw her in.

His lips were gentle at first, tentative, as if testing the waters. V leaned in, opening herself up and giving herself over, and in a moment Fynn did the same. His tender touches intensified and his kisses deepened until her body thrummed. It was too much and far from enough, and V needed more.

Her hands wound around his back, pulling him against her. She wanted all of him – to touch, to taste, to feel. To do with as she pleased. She was greed and anarchy and desire, and the feel of him was slowly driving her mad.

Fynn's hands began to roam her body, caressing her neck, her arms, her chest. His touch was gentle yet firm, skirting her injuries while finding the softest parts to stroke. Electricity flowed from his fingers, igniting her cells and sending her closer to the brink.

V's hands reciprocated, finding their way beneath his shirt to touch the smooth lines of his back, the ridges of his ribs, the subtle curve of his hips. She wanted to ravish him, to leave him breathless and begging, to bring him to his knees.

She moved against him, savoring the moan he let loose against her lips. Fynn retaliated with a thrust of his own, freeing a whimper from the back of her throat before kissing it away. Their movements synchronized and harmonized until they rocked together as one, panting their pleasure against each other's cheeks.

There were too many clothes between them, too many layers standing in their way. V wanted them gone, and she made a fumbling effort to undo the clasp of Fynn's pants. He grunted again, impatient and aching for more.

When she finally managed to free it, she hummed, allowing herself a second of satisfaction. Fynn brushed the upraised corners of her lips before diving back in for a deeper kiss. The oxygen seemed to seep from the room, leaving V dizzy and warm, clutching at Fynn for balance.

V yearned to lose herself in his embrace, to forget about the world outside and live in this moment for eternity. To ignore the pull of her past and the mystery of Apollo and surrender herself to her senses. She might have, too – at least for a time – if it hadn't been for Lyra.

Fynn heard her first and pulled away, his hedonistic haze replaced by confusion then alarm as she rounded the corner. By the time she looked up, he'd tucked himself safely behind a table, outside of V's reach.

Lyra took in the scene, her eyes catching on V, panting and flushed, and her head tilted in question.

"What the hell happened to you?" she asked.

Chapter 17

Violet's mind went blank. She'd done such a thorough job of losing herself in the moment that she'd forgotten about the station and the Guards. And the fact that she was half naked and streaked with blood. All she could remember was the heat of Fynn's hands, the feel of his lips, the pressure of him pressed against her.

She blushed at the thought, stuttering a string of nonsense in response to Lyra's question. Understandably unsatisfied, Lyra turned to Fynn for further explanation. Unlike V, his wits were unaffected and his voice was annoyingly even.

"V was attacked at the station. Three Guards intercepted her and tried to take her in, but she managed to fight them off. Unfortunately, though, there was no backup of her memories, so we're no closer to finding Apollo's killer. Although she has learned some new tricks."

The flippant way he said it, along with the way he talked about V like she wasn't even there, sent a stab of anger through her chest, cooling the heat that had flooded her system.

"It's a little more than a trick," V fired back, clenching her teeth to contain the venom. "It's my entire muscle memory, everything I learned about..." But she didn't get the chance to continue, as Lyra cut her off, eager for her own chance to speak.

"It doesn't matter," she said, brushing off V's words like a speck of dirt. "Oh, and you're wrong, by the way," she continued, turning back to Fynn.

"Wrong?" he asked, befuddled. "About what?"

"We are closer to finding Apollo's killer," she said smugly. "Thanks to me."

"What did you do?" Fynn asked, simultaneously intrigued and concerned.

V shared his emotions, although she wasn't about to voice them. Fynn's rapid change in demeanor still had her reeling, so for once she stayed silent.

"I was reviewing some footage and I noticed something."

"Footage from the party?" Fynn asked, doubting the answer even as he asked.

"Not quite," Lyra answered carefully. Fynn and V stared, expectant, and she eventually caved. "I've been looking over footage from the Senatorial Sector, from the cameras placed at the borders."

Fynn looked aghast. "Lyra, accessing those tapes is akin to treason. If we were found with that footage, we'd be shipped to the Grove no questions asked. I mean, how did you even manage to get hold of those recordings?"

Lyra shrugged, downplaying her display of misconduct.

"The Guards use an antiquated code that any monkey could break. Once I found the right frequency, it was child's play. But that's really not what's important here."

For some reason, Fynn seemed stuck on Lyra's scandalous behavior, so V bit the bullet and asked, "What's important, then? What did you find on the footage?"

"It's what I didn't find that matters," said Lyra, rushing to explain. "Sabine Ryker hasn't been spotted since days before the party. It seems our scientist has gone AWOL."

V's brain struggled to piece together the facts, still hampered by a fog of lust and blood loss. She scoured the recesses of her mind for the name and found it lingering with a list of others, all suspects in the senator's death.

Sabine Ryker, a known associate of Apollo Quinn who hadn't appeared at his party. A scientist who could hold a piece of the puzzle that was V's past. If Lyra was right, she'd gone missing, disappearing from the cameras that covered the borders between sectors. It was suspicious, to say the least.

"What does it mean?" V asked, finally conceding. "Is she lying low because she's scared? Or has she gone underground because she's guilty and can't risk being caught?" The mere thought that they were close to clearing V's name sent an eager charge through her veins.

Lyra looked at her with a mix of disappointment and pity, like a promising pupil who had failed at the first test.

"Neither," she stated firmly. "It means that Sabine Ryker is dead, and has been for several days."

V balked – not just at the statement, but at the certainty with which it was said. The hope that had flickered to life was promptly extinguished as the implication took hold.

Sabine wasn't their killer. They were no closer to solving this case. And worse still, there was someone out there hunting anyone who had dared to ally with Apollo.

"I don't understand," V said, praying Lyra was wrong. "Sabine could just as easily be in hiding, afraid that she might be next. Or maybe she's gone full mad scientist and holed up in her rooms conducting some strange experiments."

"Both are possible," Lyra conceded, "but highly unlikely. The timing is too linear to be a coincidence. My bet is that Sabine was the weak link that led to Apollo, with her death a precursor to his. Someone came to her with questions – and coercion – and her answers steered them straight to him."

"That's a plausible theory," Fynn said, shaking his head, "but it's still just a theory. We can't be certain about anything until we have proof."

"I thought you might say that," Lyra said, reaching behind her back. "So I took the liberty of digging a little deeper, and this is what I found." She revealed a screen painted in pixels of black and gray.

V's mind couldn't immediately place the picture, and she struggled to define the shape and give it a name. Then the pieces crashed into place.

It was a body. V's reaction was immediate and visceral, as if her eyes were trying to expel the image. But no amount of bile could rid her of that sight, of the broken bones, the blackened skin, the missing shards of skull.

"What the hell is that?" Fynn demanded, half horror and half revulsion. Unlike V, he couldn't seem to look away.

"It's the remains of an unidentified female who suffered serious traumatic injuries before being burned past recognition. On a hunch, I found my way into the morgue's database and scrolled through the recent deaths. Her body was found shortly after Apollo's, dumped in a drainage tunnel near the outskirts of the sector. From what's left of her, I'd say that this is Sabine Ryker – and this is what happens to Apollo's associates."

This is what could happen to you. The unsaid words hung in the air like a cloud of fog, noxious and haunting. V held her body still, staving off the shiver that threatened to shake her bones.

"You said that we're closer to finding the killer," V whispered, unable to trust her own voice. "Is there something we're not seeing? Some clue hidden in this corpse?"

"Unfortunately, it's not that exciting," Lyra admitted, stowing the screen. Yet the image lingered in V's eyes, branded on her brain. "All it really means is that we've eliminated a suspect, taking us from five to four. Senators Griffyn and Altair, Captain Arctura, and Corvus Huxley. It might not seem like much, but it's progress." She smiled an encouraging smile, but it didn't reach her eyes.

V tried to return it, but the sourness in her stomach sapped her strength. All she could see was the burned body capped with *her* face, lying forgotten in a morgue without a name. She would be killed for a crime she didn't understand, lost before she could find herself. It was a cruel way to go.

Fear made a home inside her heart, burrowing deep as the silence stretched. She wanted to scream, to curse at the stars and demand they listen, to beg for a shred of mercy. And to sleep.

The sudden exhaustion nearly knocked her off her feet,

and she swayed precariously, clutching at the chair beside her for strength. Two hands appeared at her back, holding her up. They were strong yet gentle, familiar yet still foreign, and they guided her to the cot, where they set her softly down.

V wanted to bat them away, to stand on her own two feet, but fatigue held her in its clutches, demanding she close her eyes and deliver herself to dreams. She knew the monsters there were no better than the monsters here, and that death stalked both sides of the line, but she no longer had a choice. With a sigh, she surrendered to the softness of sleep, letting it coat her in its warm embrace.

The last thing she heard was a baritone purr as Fynn whispered, "She's had a long day. Let her sleep. She'll need her rest for what comes next."

With that ill omen, V passed from one world to the next, dragged down into a seething landscape of dreams.

Tonight's terrors were dark and viscous, trapping her in a realm of devils and demons. They danced around her in their finery, dripping with blood and smiling as she struggled to escape. Yet her feet wouldn't move, her hands wouldn't grasp, and her mouth wouldn't open to free her screams.

She was their prisoner, their plaything, their pet. She was their project, and as she watched, her body began to bend and sway to their rhythms, betraying her completely as they laughed. No matter what she did, V couldn't break from their spell, even as she strained with every cell.

Glancing down, she saw her fingers dripping with someone else's blood, her gown stained red from the gore. It made her giddy – the violence, the carnage, the pain. It made her want to dance to the devils' drums and join in their chorus.

She was lost, caught completely in their grasp and drunk on the danger, ensnared in the revelry of lost souls. V was gone, cast into a lightless corner of her mind and replaced by a demon intent on raising hell.

V would have woken up screaming had it not been for the hand across her mouth, holding her down. It was large and firm, smelling of wood and spices, but none of that mattered in her panic. In an instant, she was struggling, her instincts kicking in before her mind could catch up.

V latched onto his forearm with a vice-like grip, ripping his fingers from her face. Once she'd freed her legs from the tangle of blankets, she dealt a blow to her assailant's belly. The figure stumbled back, surprised, and V vaulted off her cot in pursuit, her shoulder aching from the effort.

The man was already off-kilter, primed for the kill. All it took to bring him down was a single sweep of his legs. He fell with the weight of a boulder, eliciting a sonorous thud that shook the floor beneath them. She was astride him before he could protest, pinning his arms with her legs and raising a hand to strike.

"Violet!" a voice exclaimed, stopping her fist mid-flight. "It's me. It's only me."

Fynn's words took a moment to process, slowly seeping through the fog. Gradually, V's eyes lost their glaze and focused, taking in the figure beneath her.

"Fynn?" she asked, certain of his identity but confused by the circumstances. "Why did you attack me?"

"I think you'll find that you were the instigator here, not me," he whispered, ceasing his struggles to stare at her. "Meanwhile, I was trying to warn you."

More details fell into place, forcing her fully into consciousness. Daylight streamed from the windows, suggesting that she'd slept far beyond dawn. Her injuries still throbbed and her muscles ached, meaning the hours of unconsciousness hadn't been enough to heal her. And the man beneath her, submitting to her victory, was the same one who had so recently stroked the curves of her body and sought to claim her as his own.

The memory sent a flush of heat through her cheeks and down her chest, yet she maintained her place astride him. She was acutely aware of how his body felt between her legs, of every place their skin made contact. Yet she was also aware of the way he had distanced himself last night and disparaged her newfound talents. V wasn't about to relinquish the upper hand without procuring some payback.

"Warn me about what?" she asked, less a question than a demand for answers.

"The Guards," Fynn replied with an edge.

A spike of panic lanced her thoughts, and she hurriedly checked the room, as if Guards might be hiding in its corners. Yet the space held no one but them. V breathed a sigh of relief.

The reprieve was short-lived, though, as Fynn went on to clarify, "The Guards are canvassing the street. They're asking about you. V, they'll be here any minute. You have to hide."

V's alarm returned with a vengeance, and she finally loosened her grip, allowing Fynn the space to rise. He sat up but made no move to wriggle free. For a heartbeat, they stared into each other's eyes as their minds whirled. The sound of motorbikes and voices filtered in as their own silence stretched.

"What the hell is happening?" Lyra shrieked, shocking them out of their stupor. "Why is *she* still here? Are you trying to get us all thrown in the Grove?"

Fynn started at her words, casting V off balance and sending her to the floor. She landed harshly on her shoulder, sending pain prickling down her arm and across her chest. She grunted her discomfort as a pair of hands hauled her up from behind, returning her to her feet.

V turned, expecting to find Fynn but discovering Lyra in his stead. The woman kept her hands planted firmly on V's back, steering her sharply toward the side of the room.

"What are you doing?" V asked, affronted. "Get your hands off me!"

"Pipe down and do as I say," Lyra commanded, stopping in front of a chipped blue bureau set against a blank section of wall.

With one hand on V, she groped beneath the cabinet's top, searching for something. A subtle click confirmed she'd found it, and Lyra stepped aside at the sound, taking V with her. An instant later, the bureau swung away from the wall, revealing the smallest hidey-hole V had ever seen. Well, technically the only hidey-hole V had ever seen, but still.

It was barely large enough for a person to scrunch up and squeeze inside – a fact which V learned firsthand as Lyra thrust her toward it. Her body naturally contorted into a ball as she landed on her butt and clutched her knees to her chest.

"Stay here," Lyra ordered, "and don't make a sound." She promptly swung the cabinet shut, sealing V in.

V's heart hammered as her eyes grew accustomed to the

darkness. Pinpricks of light spilled from air holes in the wall, coloring the space one shade paler than pitch black. Still, V could barely make out the outlines of her feet as they strained to keep from tapping out the seconds.

She was cold and thirsty and sore, but she knew that silence would be her savior, so she clung to it. Beyond the wall, Fynn and Lyra moved without speaking, burying themselves in the banal – sweeping, tidying, unshuttering the shop. Minutes passed with nothing but the sounds of movement to mark them.

Suddenly, the bell above the door clanged, splitting the silence in two. V cringed, sensing the Guards like a cold wind as they entered.

"Officers, what can I do for you today?" Lyra asked, seizing the upper hand – and sounding perfectly poised. "Do you need a spare part for your scryglass or perhaps a secondhand holo pet for your collection? We're all booked up on repairs for the day, so if that's what you're after I'm afraid you're out of luck. But I'd be happy to add you to the waitlist if you'd like."

The Iridium Guards ignored her ramblings and got straight to the point.

"We're looking for a fugitive, a murderer," said a deep voice, which resonated through the room, filtering clearly into V's cubby.

Murderer. The word tolled in her mind like a bell, ringing true. She had killed – perhaps not in cold blood, but she had still killed, snuffing out three lives that had once burned bright. There was blood on her hands, a stain on her soul that could never be washed clean.

Yet if she hadn't killed them, they would almost certainly have killed her – or at least led her away to her death – stealing her life without a second thought. There was some solace in that, but it did little to assuage her guilt.

"This woman has been spotted in the area," the man continued, likely pulling up V's picture. "We're asking everyone for their cooperation. We believe she may have allies who are harboring her. She's already killed four innocent people, including three Guards. Bringing her in is our highest priority."

They made her sound like a public menace, like a stain on the fabric of society. They'd branded her a villain and doused her in blame, and they were determined to see her pay.

"Pull up your sleeves," the Guard commanded. "We'll need to scan your tattoos."

A stroke of silence followed as Fynn and Lyra complied, rolling up their cuffs to reveal their IDs – one forged and one real. V waited with bated breath, praying that Lyra's mark was still strong, not faded to the point of suspicion. She heard a beep, followed by a pause as one set of credentials loaded.

"Mr. Fynnrar Eos, age 26, shopkeeper," another Guard reported, reading off his screen.

Fynnrar? V muffled a spurt of laughter at his full name, promising to give him grief for it once this was over. A name like that couldn't pass unmocked, even in such tragic times.

Another beep sounded as Lyra proffered her hand, and this silence stretched longer.

Finally, the Guard reported, "Mrs. Lyra Eos, age 28, repair technician."

V's laughter died in her throat at the words. Mrs. Eos?

As in Fynn's wife? Were Fynn and Lyra married?

It made no sense. She'd never seen them kiss – or even touch. They didn't share a bed or a room. They acted like business partners, united by a common cause not a bond of matrimony.

She didn't believe it – or she didn't want to – yet pieces of the puzzle began to click. The way Fynn had pulled away from her last night. The way he'd pushed her off of him this morning. He was ashamed of her, of what they'd done, and he was trying to distance himself from his deeds.

V felt hot and cold and sick as her body tried to rid itself of the thought. Yet it persisted, pinning itself in place with a nail through V's heart.

Meanwhile, the Guards had begun to scope out the shop, rummaging for clues to reveal V's presence. Her mind flew to the bandages, the blood, the bed. Had they been cleaned up in time or were they sitting in plain sight, like fluorescent lights pointing straight to her?

A pair of boots stopped just outside the bureau, and she pushed herself into its corners, straining to stay silent despite her pounding heart. Without warning, the cabinet doors swung open, and V cringed at the sound, feeling the man's proximity in her bones.

The door to her den was still sealed, yet she closed her eyes and held her breath as the Guard peered inside, searching for secrets. A loud knock sounded against the wall as he rapped his knuckles on the wood, testing the truth of the grain.

V balled her hands into fists as she readied herself to fight, preparing her mind for the pain. Yet after another

202

moment, the man withdrew, closing the cabinet behind him. With wooden steps, he walked away, rejoining his partner by the door.

"Thank you for your assistance, Mr. Eos, Mrs. Eos," the first man stated lifelessly, as if following a script. "If you hear or see anything suspicious, please alert us immediately. We have Guards posted throughout the area to ensure your safety, and they'll be stopping by periodically to check that everything is alright." With that veiled warning lingering in the air, the two men took their leave.

V fumed in the darkness of her snug, waiting restlessly for someone to release her. She wanted to rage, to shout, to ask the questions lighting up her mind. She wanted answers.

As she waited, Fynn and Lyra waited with her, toiling away the time until it was safe for them to move. It felt like an eternity, and V spent it stewing in her anger, allowing it to outshine the feeble rays of heartbreak.

"I think they're gone," Lyra declared, stalking back toward her room. "You can let her out, but you have to know it's not safe for her here. Not anymore. Not if *we* hope to make it through this in one piece."

Her tone made it clear that "we" did not include V. It was them, just as it had always been. Husband and wife. Fynn and Lyra. A two-person team tackling the injustices of their world with no room for a third.

Fynn padded toward the bureau, then released it, springing V from her temporary prison. She tumbled gracelessly to the ground, her legs having long since succumbed to the numbness. They tingled as she tried to rise, yet she batted away Fynn's hand as he attempted to assist her.

Finally, she managed to regain her footing, aided by the very cabinet that had held her captive. V stared at Fynn defiantly, daring him to explain, but no words came. The longer the standoff stretched, the heavier V's question weighed until she was finally forced to speak it.

"So you're married, huh?" she asked, hating how small her voice sounded. "Care to explain?"

"It's complicated," he said gruffly, as if that would satisfy her. Naturally, it didn't.

"Then why not dumb it down for me? I might not be as bright as the great Fynnrar Eos, but I bet I can keep up." The words tasted like acid, and she spat them out with the force of a weapon.

Yet they appeared to fall short, as Fynn kept his mouth shut and his secrets locked away, replacing them with a rigidity V had never expected. He seemed like a different man, a stranger in the shell of a friend, and V winced at the calloused disinterest.

"Is this some sort of game to you?" V asked, throwing her hands up in frustration. "You rescue the damsel in distress, tease her with lingering looks, kiss her like your life depends on it, then toss her to the curb? My life is chaos. I've been searching for something to cling to. And you used my desperation for a bit of fun behind your wife's back?"

"No," Fynn stated coldly. "Lyra's known all along. In fact, it was her idea."

The words didn't register right away. Once they did, she was certain she'd misheard him because no one could be that cruel.

"What do you mean?" V asked, all the warmth stripped

from her words. "What, exactly, was her idea?"

"To seduce you. To make you think that I cared. To gain your trust."

Each word struck V like a savage blow, knocking the wind from her lungs. It had all been fake – every look, every word, every touch. Her body burned with the betrayal, yearning to exact revenge. Her muscles knew what to do, where to strike to inflict maximum damage, yet for some reason she couldn't bring herself to do it.

Fynn continued, providing details that only served to further splinter her heart. "After you ran away on that first day, risking all our lives in the process, we realized that we needed something to keep you here. You needed a reason to stay."

"And that reason was *you*?" V asked incredulously. "You must certainly think highly of yourself."

"It wasn't just me," Fynn responded, his countenance finally cracking into something resembling sincerity. "We told you the truth about the Senate. We needed to know that you would tell us the truth in return. And that you wouldn't expose us if given the chance. You had to establish a bond – if not to the cause, then to someone within it."

V felt like she couldn't breathe, like the room was too small and the air too thin. She wanted to run, to escape, to leave these people and their lies. Instead, she started to pace.

"You devised this plan – together – to trick me into trusting you? You lied to me so I…what? So I wouldn't run? So I'd give you access to my cam? So you could control me?"

Fynn stayed silent at the accusation, his stoic face showing no signs of remorse.

V's mind flashed back to her first night with Fynn, to the words he'd spoken in the darkness. "You're safe here. No one will hurt you. I promise." She'd been a fool to believe him, and she hated herself for her weakness. Still, she hated him more.

"And now what?" she asked, leveling a look at him that could crush stone. "How do you expect me to trust you now?"

"I don't," Fynn stated sadly. "I expect you to leave."

V thought she had hardened herself to his words, but those five cut her like a knife, leaving a trail of pain beneath her ribs.

"Your memories aren't coming back," Fynn said, a nameless emotion deepening his voice. "There's nothing more you can do here. And now, by killing those Guards, you've made yourself a target. You're a liability."

Maybe he expected her to protest. Maybe he wanted her anger. What he got was her silence.

"This goes far beyond me and Lyra," he explained, attempting to justify his actions. "We're part of something bigger, and we can't risk everything just to keep you safe."

Fynn moved closer, instinctively reaching out a hand before closing it around empty air.

"Look, we'll give you supplies, units, tech. We'll help you stay in the shadows."

"Why?" V shot back. "Why do you care?"

"I don't want the Guards to find you," he said earnestly. "You don't deserve to die, not for someone else's crimes. Violet, just because I lied doesn't mean I don't care."

"Save your pity," V bit back. "I don't need it. And I don't need you."

Chapter 18

Even seated atop her bike with the wind whipping around her, Violet couldn't outrun her thoughts. They clung to her like tar, tormenting her with whys and what-ifs.

The simple truth was that she'd been played. Fynn and Lyra had preyed on her need for connection to further their own agenda. They'd manipulated her emotions, mining her for information until the cost of keeping her outweighed her usefulness. If she didn't hate them so much, she might even admire their ingenuity.

V didn't consciously plan her route, instead allowing her emotions to guide her, but she was unsurprised when she came to a stop near the steps of her apartment. She knew it was foolish to hide in the first place the Guards would look, but the comfort of home called to her, and her bruised heart couldn't help but answer.

For some reason, she expected the building to be changed, for the halls and walls to show new cracks and fissures, yet everything remained the same. It was V who had changed.

V stopped outside a unit that wasn't hers, raising a hand to knock, but before she could a set of voices drifted out from between the cracks. They were achingly familiar, tugging at the tears lingering just out of reach. She let herself slide down the door until she landed on the ground, her ear pressed painfully against the wood.

"You have to go to sleep," a tired voice said, deep and unbearably sad. "Please, Leo, just climb into bed and close your eyes. I promise I'll be right here."

"But I want mommy," Leo's little voice replied, wavering on the verge of tears.

"Mommy's not here," Asher answered, as if he'd said it a thousand times, "but she loves you very much, and she will be back. She will make it back." He repeated it like he needed it to be true, like by saying it he could make it happen.

"Where is she?" Leo asked, blind to his father's pain. "Where did mommy go?"

"She had to go away for a while," Asher tried, coating the truth in honey. "The men in black needed her for a very special task. Because your mother is a very special woman. I've known that since the second I met her."

An incoherent murmur escaped Leo's lips, and Asher laughed, a flat chuckle that carried no joy. V's heart ached at the sound, and she longed to break down the door and embrace them both. Yet her presence couldn't solve this. It would only make matters worse, complicating them to the point of chaos. She no longer fit in their world, just like she didn't fit in Fynn's.

"Do you want me to sing you your song?" Asher asked,

already knowing the answer.

"Yes! My song!" Leo shouted, delighted at the prospect. After a moment, Asher began to sing, and the words were so familiar that V whispered them in time, adding a quiet chorus to his solo.

I've lived a thousand times to die
In each you've surfaced by my side
Now it's time to close your eyes
And sail away with me
Sail away with me, my love, come sail away with me
Sail away, sail away, for tonight we'll both be free

It was V's song, the one she'd sung countless times to lull Leo to sleep. It made her feel closer to them, yet somehow so far away. V couldn't stop the tears, and they ran freely down her face, carrying the agony and sorrow that clung to her in a permanent cloud.

She stayed long after Asher's song had ended and Leo had drifted off to sleep. Then she picked herself up, dusted herself off, and began to climb. By the time she appeared on the fifth floor, her face was a mask of indifference, with her tears tucked away and her lips contorted into a fine line.

V opened the door slowly, the telltale creak announcing her presence. The man in the living room turned, and V paused as confusion clouded her senses. This was the right apartment, the right floor, the right building. But that was not the right man. That was not Mouse.

He almost looked like Mouse, except several inches taller – and several decades older. Where Mouse had curly brown hair, this man's was straight and white, darting off in every direction. His face was a canvas of wrinkles capped with thick black glasses that magnified his eyes. But his long nose and large ears were a dead match for Mouse, betraying their familial connection.

"Ora?" he asked, tilting his head as if confused. "Ora, is that you? What were you doing out so late? I told you to be home in time for supper."

V turned around, confirming that there was no one behind her. This man was talking to her, yet she had never heard of an Ora. She inched farther into the room, hands upheld, trying to puzzle out his presence.

"My name is Violet. I'm one of Mouse's friends. I won't hurt you. Can you tell me your name?"

"Ora, what are you saying? I don't understand this game. Your mother and I have been worried sick. We've been looking for you for days."

Violet sighed, scanning the corners for Mouse but finding no one. She was alone with this man, and he seemed to think that she was someone he knew. That she was his daughter. For all she knew, she was – although she highly doubted it.

Sensing he wasn't violent, V bit the bullet and approached, moving slowly so as not to spook him. While she did, she racked her brain, hunting for this man in the fragments she knew of Mouse's past, but she came up empty. Mouse might have been the sort to share his bed, but not his stories, and V had never truly broken through. She studied the man as he studied her, hoping to gain some insight.

"I'm sorry, dad," she said, trying a new tactic. "I didn't

mean to worry you. I was just out looking for Mouse. Have you seen him?"

The man's features fell into a look of confusion as he tried to put a face to the name, but he couldn't quite manage it. The sadness in his eyes was heartbreaking as he shook his head, opening and closing his mouth without a sound. He seemed lost inside his own mind, looking for clues to piece his memories back together.

V knew how that felt. She longed to reach out and hug him, to help him reclaim his life even as she was losing hold of hers. Yet there was nothing she could do.

Abruptly, the door to the apartment shuddered then squeaked, announcing another presence. Without thinking, V placed herself before the man, preparing for battle. Fists raised, feet planted, face blank. She stared down the door, waiting for it to open fully and reveal her opponent.

When it did, a sigh escaped her lips as she recognized the figure. Mouse.

He didn't notice V at first, his hands laden with bits and bobs and an assortment of bags. But the second he did, he stopped short, surprise flickering across his face. Then anger took hold.

"What the hell are you doing here? Do you know how much trouble you've caused? The Guards have been here every day, tearing the place apart in hopes of finding you."

"It's nice to see you too, Mouse," V muttered, shaking her head. "Any chance you'd care to explain your friend?" She motioned to the man, who had lost interest in their conversation and begun investigating the window, clearly mystified. It now depicted a field of vibrant flowers, all flowing gently in the breeze – one of Mouse's favorites.

"He is none of your business," Mouse bit back, depositing his treasures on the counter. "You shouldn't be here."

V cringed at his hostility, sensing no playfulness in his tone.

"Come on, Mouse. I just need a chance to catch my breath, to make my head stop spinning so I can figure out what to do next."

Mouse just shook his head. "I warned you. I told you not to go to that party, but you made your decision. And look where it got you! Three dead Guards. A slain senator. A city-wide manhunt. I'm sorry, V, but I can't harbor a murderer."

The word sliced through V's skin like a scalpel, clean and calculated. "I didn't kill Apollo," she whispered. "I'm not a murderer. Mouse, you know me. I would never do something like that."

Five beats of silence lapsed before Mouse responded, his voice softening ever so slightly. "It doesn't matter. On the Echelon, you are what they say you are. Hell, I'm far from a saint, but these last few years I've kept my hands clean. Or at least clean enough. I can't stain them again by helping you."

The old man chose that moment to insert himself in the conversation, cowering in the corner by the window. "Who are you people? Are you criminals? Are you planning to kill me? Because I'd like to see you try!"

The words broke Mouse from his stasis, and he crossed the apartment in a handful of strides, holding out his hands.

"We're not going to hurt you, grandpa," he whispered in a soothing tone. "You're safe. Just calm down and I'll make you some dinner."

212

The man obeyed, silencing his protests at the promise of food. He clung to Mouse's hand like a child, and Mouse gazed at it sadly before retraining his sights on her.

"V, you can't stay," he said, finally letting the sorrow of the words shade his features. "Your face is plastered on half the screens in the city. To side with you now would be suicide. Just…go to the Alcor. Talk to Sable. He knows people, so maybe he can help."

It was a clear dismissal, a demand for her to leave, and V's heart fractured further, yet she nodded. She could feel her eyes shining as she turned around and walked out of the only home she'd ever known, but she didn't cry – not until the door locked behind her.

This time, her drive across the city was far from freeing. The wind tore at her, reaching out frozen fingers to claw at her clothing and snag on her skin. She strained against its pull, pushing onward even as it tried to hold her back.

A tinge of panic colored her thoughts as she approached the once-familiar checkpoint. The tattoo on her wrist, the one Fynn had falsified, remained in place, but it hardly matched the visage she wore now. This bare-faced, tear-streaked mess, without paint or prosthetics, was a far cry from the woman who would show up on their scanners.

As it happened, though, the Guards had too much faith in their system to care much about a single discrepancy. Curfew was nearing, and the crush of the crowd weighed heavily on both sides. They scarcely spared V a second, accepting her identity as fact rather than an elaborate fiction.

Safe on the other side, V threw herself into the throng as they raced against time, seeking shelter before curfew closed in. V melted into the crowd, allowing the tide to tug her forward. It carried her along at a sprightly pace, branching into tributaries and streams, like veins pumping people through the city.

No one noticed her atop her stolen bike, nameless and faceless beneath her helmet. The darkened screen cast the scene in a thousand shades of gray. It felt fitting somehow, this muted gloom, as people traveled without talking and collided without connecting. Everyone was separate, isolated, even as bodies pressed in from all sides. They were all alone.

By the time V knocked on the door to the club, the lonesomeness had settled over her like a fine coating of dust, making her skin itch and her body beg for contact. On the other side, a rustling erupted, followed by the scrape of a lock sliding open. Sable's face appeared in the crack, and the familiar lines of it almost made V smile.

"We're closed. Go home," he said, his tone stern but not unkind. He moved to close the door, but V stuck her foot in the gap, forcing it open.

Without a word, she flipped up her visor, revealing her face. Sable froze at the sight, his mouth ajar and his generous eyebrows furrowed.

"V, you're here," he said, surprised into stating the obvious. He shook his head, shaking off the shock along with it. "Come inside," he demanded. "It's not safe out there."

V did as she was told, taking off her helmet as the door closed behind her. Inside, the Alcor was silent, but it still held the echo of life. Stale alcohol and sweat suffused the air, and half-empty glasses dotted its sticky tables. V breathed it in, letting the familiar scents carry her back to a simpler time.

"What are you doing here?" Sable asked, arms crossed over his broad chest.

It was the same question Mouse had asked, with the same tone of suspicion, and V immediately turned defensive.

"I'm not a murderer," she declared, jumping three steps ahead to cut him off at the curve. "I didn't kill Apollo."

"Damn it, V," he cursed. "Of course you didn't. I know you. And I know you're not capable of something like that."

V's relief at his words was palpable, and the cord that had wound around her chest slackened. She pushed deeper into the room, claiming a chair at the bar. Instead of taking his usual place across from her, Sable sat beside her, reaching out to capture her hands in his.

"I'm capable of far more than you think," she whispered, staring down at their hands so she wouldn't have to meet his eyes.

They were closer than they'd ever been, their knees knocking and fingers entwined, and the intimacy of it felt foreign. They had always flirted, slowly circling in an endless dance, but they'd never truly touched. Unlike with Fynn, this proximity brought no sparks, no fluttering feeling that rendered her speechless. There was only a gentle warmth, like embers instead of flames, soothing and comfortable.

"The Guards?" Sable guessed, and V nodded, confirming his suspicions. That she might not have murdered, but she'd killed, that her hands were far from clean.

"It was me or them," V explained. "And I didn't want to die." It seemed thin, a see-through excuse for her crimes, but it was all she had.

Sable didn't pull away. Instead, he sighed and shook his head.

"The guilt of it never goes away, even in the Grove," he confessed, shocking V out of her self-pity.

She'd known Sable had gone to the Grove, that the marks on his skin had been earned, but she'd never known the crime. She'd assumed it was backdoor dealings, petty theft, bribery. Some bloodless misconduct for financial gain. Not murder.

"Who was it?" she asked, lightly prodding at the edges of his story. She craved a confidant, someone who understood, someone who saw through her sins to the person struggling beneath.

Sable shrugged. "Some man. Over a woman, of course. He started it – and before I knew it, I'd finished it."

"Was she worth it?" V couldn't keep the question from spilling out, and she regretted it almost instantly.

After an agonizing moment, Sable answered. "I thought so. I would have plucked a star from the sky and handed it to her on a silver platter. By the time I got out of the Grove, though, she was gone, married off to someone else. I guess I'm not the kind of man who's worth waiting for."

It broke V's heart to hear him say that. Sable was a fortress, with a confidence that no one could crack. He was cocky and sure, endlessly optimistic and eternally suave. Nothing could touch him. Or at least that's the man she'd built up in her head.

"But this isn't about me," Sable continued, rousing himself from the memory. "I've served my time. You, on the other hand, are currently the most notorious person on the

Echelon. So why come to me? You in need of a stiff drink or something?" He tried to smile, but a sadness lingered behind it.

"Clearly," V answered, fully serious despite the mischief in her tone.

"Then I better get the lady a drink. Freeze OK?"

V nodded and watched as he skirted the bar to retrieve the bottle and two glasses before reclaiming his seat beside her. With steady hands, he poured them each a dram.

V downed hers in one gulp, closing her eyes as the ice infiltrated her system and a layer of frost crept across her brain. She waited until time snapped back into place before confessing her true motives.

"I need to disappear...and I don't know where to start," she began. "Mouse said you might know people who could help."

Sable let out a choked sound, half laughter and half derision. "Mouse has connections to half the convicts in the city. Why can't he help you hide?"

"He's chosen his side – and it's not mine," V said, listening to the words echo strangely across the empty space.

"That asshole is as selfish as they come," Sable spat, finishing his drink with a flourish.

V couldn't disagree, although her thoughts kept wandering to the old man in their apartment. Mouse had changed in his presence, morphing into someone soft and protective, someone V had never seen. There was clearly something there, a story that wasn't hers to share. So she merely nodded, tight-lipped and tired.

"I have nowhere to go, no one to run to, and barely any

units to my name," V admitted, swallowing her pride and skirting the edges of hysteria. "This is the last place I could think to come. If you can't help me, I'll be back where I started – alone on the streets. And it won't take the Guards long to find me there."

Sable sighed. "I can't let my best employee go down like that. What kind of boss would I be if I left you to the mercy of the streets?"

"I'm your best employee?" V teased, her voice wavering.

"Don't pretend you didn't know," he said, rolling his eyes. "Hell, you're the reason half our customers keep coming back," he laughed. "Listen, I can't promise anything, but I'll ask around. I've earned a few favors over the years, and this seems like the perfect time to cash them in. Maybe we can find some sort of safe house for you until this all blows over."

We. The word radiated warmth, but it carried a bitter aftertaste.

"If they find out you've helped me, they'll throw you back in the Grove. You know that, right?" She had to make sure he understood the stakes of siding with an outlaw like her.

Sable smiled, all teeth and predatory glee. "If they do, at least this time I'll know it was worth it."

V couldn't stop herself. One moment she was seated atop the stool and the next her arms were around him in a tight embrace, her face buried in the inky waves of his hair. He was startled by the sudden contact, but he quickly softened, melting into the hug and surrounding her with warmth. By the time she pulled away, the tightness in her chest had loosened another notch, making it almost possible to breathe.

"Come on," Sable waved, getting up from his seat. "I'll show you where you can sleep."

He led her back beyond the stage, past the dressing room to a narrow hallway that jutted off to one side. At the end, a large door loomed, leading to Sable's office. Beyond it, a small studio waited, neat and tidy with a single bed.

It didn't feel like Sable, not like the Alcor did. It was compact and efficient, with no frills or finery. The colors were muted and gray, simple in a way that Sable definitely wasn't. There were no picture screens of his family, no soft furnishings, no sentimentality. This was basic necessity, a place to lay his head that was separate from a home.

"It's not much, but it's comfortable enough," he explained, guiding her toward the bed. "I'll be right outside in my office. If you need anything, just give me a shout."

He turned to go and was already at the door when V whispered, "Wait." It was small and subtle, but it sailed through the air unhindered, reaching Sable's ears. He paused with his hand on the knob but didn't turn to face her.

"Stay," she said. It wasn't a question or a command, but rather a plain entreaty. V didn't want to be alone.

Sable closed the gap between them in a matter of heartbeats. There was no hesitation in his touch, no uncertainty in his movements. He held her tightly, the way she needed to be held, and kissed her so deeply that she felt it in her bones. She kissed him back, hungry for connection and aching for contact.

The stubble along his jaw scratched against her skin as he lowered her to the bed, burying his face in her neck. She moaned out his name, tangling her hands in his hair to hold him against her.

He smelled like the Alcor, and she inhaled the scent of home as he undid the clasps of her top and slid it over her head. V rapidly remedied the imbalance by relieving him of his shirt, tracing her hands down the hard lines of muscle and ink. The tattooed designs were fluid and free, stretching from his arms down his strong chest.

It didn't feel the same as with Fynn. There was no fire blazing hot beneath the surface, threatening to burn them. Neither was reduced to a creature of need or rendered without reason. This was safe and simple, with no threat of love to shake them. As each envisioned another face behind closed eyes, they let their bodies run wild, exploring, tasting, and touching like it was their last time instead of their first.

Sable teased his fingertips down her side and up her stomach, skirting the scrapes and scratches that marred her skin. His hand landed on the cut that had nearly cleaved her collarbone in two, and his eyebrows furrowed as he studied it.

"Did they do this to you?" he growled, half animal, half man. V nodded, not trusting her voice to stay stable. "Then they deserved everything they got," he stated, so thoroughly certain that it made her shiver.

An instant later, all memories of the mark and how she'd gotten it disappeared as Sable pinned her to the bed, gentle yet firm, and took what he wanted.

Chapter 19

At first, V thought it was another nightmare – the pounding, the footsteps, the shouts. It felt familiar, like an old foe come to torment her in the dark.

The only problem was that most nightmares don't continue when you wake. This one did.

As soon as V realized that the sounds weren't coming from inside her mind, she snapped fully awake, her body tensing where she lay. She tilted her head and saw Sable still sprawled beside her, clinging to unconsciousness, unaware of her panic.

It didn't take them long to find her. She barely had time to rouse Sable and throw on the rest of her clothes before they were knocking down the door and barging through the gap.

There had to be at least 10 Guards, resplendent in silver and armed to the teeth. The procession bottlenecked in the doorway, with five streaming in and the rest blocking the room beyond.

V knew it was futile to fight, that she had no hope against so many men – but that didn't stop her from trying. She was dead either way, so she figured she might as well make her last minutes count.

In the moments before the brawl, when time stretched tight and the seconds spanned hours, she wondered if Sable had tipped them off. They had clearly known where to find her, meaning someone had told them, and she hated to think it was him, but it made sense. His open arms, his bid to keep her there, his promises of help.

Yet as she stood poised to fight, he stood with her, arms raised and ready to follow her to the grave. Or at least to the Grove.

A voice rose out of the ranks to declare the Guards' obligatory message. "Violet Innova, you are under arrest for escaping custody, evading arrest, and for the murders of Senator Apollo Quinn and three Iridium Guards. It is in your best interest to come quietly, without struggle. Be warned, we will use force if necessary."

V was on the move before the man had even finished speaking. Sable took that as his cue and surged forward, fists out and ready to fight. The Guards seemed so shocked by the sudden movement that they didn't flinch for a full five seconds. Then all hell broke loose.

V's vision was flooded by a sea of silver suits, their sheen dulled by the dim lights. In the commotion, it was difficult to discern where one Guard ended and the next began. So V simply picked a spot and struck.

The muscles in her shoulder were sore, yet they still knew

what to do. Rearing back, she delivered a blow to someone's midsection that sent them doubling over. As their head came down, her knee met it in mid-air, thrusting them back with a bellow and a broken nose.

Something orange danced at the edge of her vision, and she ducked an instant before a burly redhead sent a strike flying toward her face. The momentum carried his fist over her crouched form and into another Guard. It collided with his jaw and elicited a sonorous snap. Both men reared back, outraged at the attack yet still crazed by the proximity of their prey.

Beside her, Sable was brawling with the ferocity of five men – and the skill of a drunken teenager. His movements were fierce but jagged, fueled by muscle but untrained in any method of combat. He had somehow sent one opponent to the ground but was quickly being cornered by two others, with three more waiting in the wings.

V returned her attention to her own battle, which was barely better. Fewer Guards gravitated toward her, likely due to her gender, but they would soon realize their mistake. In fact, V would be glad to show them.

The ginger and his unwitting target recovered their bearings and began to bear down on her. Their silent struggle over who would strike first gave her a second to strategize. In a blink, a hundred possibilities passed before her eyes, then settled into the outlines of a plan.

V ducked once more and spun, using her speed to her advantage. The side of her fist met the inside of a kneecap, then the outside of another, striking two birds with one stone. Thrust off-balance, the men teetered like toddlers on unsteady legs, their own assaults forgotten amidst the pain.

V sprang back to an upright position, dealing a round-house kick with precision. It struck the redhead squarely in the side, sending him to the ground, where he landed with a groan.

Meanwhile, the other regained his balance, coming at her with his claws extended. He swiped at the air like a feral creature, completely forgetting his weapons. V, however, was all too aware of the gleaming knives and the gun. It was too small a space to let loose a shot, but the prospect of a blade appealed to her.

As her foe approached from the side, she attacked with an elbow, striking him hard in the sternum. The move served to knock the wind from his lungs, but it didn't derail his advancement. Soon, two large arms snaked around V and squeezed, lifting her feet from the floor.

V's fingers remained free, and their light touch went un-noticed as she stole a knife from its sheath and twisted it to-ward his stomach. As he clutched her tighter, the blade found a home inside his belly, sending a spark of shock through his system. He released her with a shove before pawing at the wound, attempting to stem the surge of blood.

The scent of iron danced in the air as the dagger dripped in her fingers. Rather than waning, the battle strengthened, growing more savage by the second.

Sable was on the ground, bleeding from the nose with one hand lying useless beside him. He was still moving, still straining to fight, but V could tell that he was fading. Soon, his muscles would refuse to respond and the pain would push him to unconsciousness, leaving V alone against this small army of foes.

Something struck her hard in the stomach, and V glanced down to see a freckled fist. She followed the line of it up to a familiar face, with a pair of bright red cheeks, bared teeth, and a bushy orange mane.

The ginger glared down at her with open hostility, clearly unaccustomed to being beaten – especially by the likes of her. V felt a stab of pride at the level of loathing she'd managed to garner, but she knew she couldn't rest on her laurels. Lunging forward, she struck twice in a single stretch.

The heel of her boot slammed down on his foot while the heel of her palm flew toward his nose. She felt the cartilage crack beneath his skin, eliciting a childlike wail. V was about to finish the job, whipping the knife from where she'd stowed it, when a wall of force slammed against her back, shocking her system into silence.

Something inside of her recognized the feeling like a long-lost friend. The stinging force of the gun rendered her fingers numb, and the knife clattered to the floor at her feet. As the world tilted in V's vision, the racket around her ceased, coating the room in a blanket of calm.

V's legs lost their battle with gravity and gave out beneath her, pulling her down to the ground. By the time she landed, the darkness had devoured what was left of her strength, casting her into oblivion.

In the space between dreams, the times that almost passed for consciousness, V figured it out. It had always been there, lurking in her mind like suspicions do, nagging at her thoughts without ever showing itself completely.

It was Mouse. He had turned V in. Just like he'd done to Riyah.

It made an awful sort of sense, although his motives remained a mystery. He was the common denominator, the thread connecting both captures. Within days of him learning Riyah's secret, the ADF had come for her, carting her away like a common criminal. It was a cruel twist of fate that V had branded a coincidence, yet now she saw it for what it was: betrayal.

But that hadn't been the end of it. Like a lamb, V had walked back into his life – and he had led her straight to the slaughter. It was Mouse who had suggested she go to Sable, and she'd willingly complied, strolling naively into his trap.

V wondered how long it had taken him to call the Guards, if he'd hesitated in the slightest or merely hurried to sell her out. The thought made V sick. He wasn't a mouse, but a rat, deceitful and diseased, without a scrap of sincerity.

When full consciousness came, V resisted, keeping her eyes closed and her body still as she puzzled out the purpose of Mouse's deception. Yet she couldn't crack it, couldn't see past the façade into the heart of the beast. She supposed she would have to live with those lingering questions – or take them to her imminent grave.

With a sigh, V finally sat up, allowing her eyes to adjust to the darkness before glancing around. Just as she'd feared, she was in a cell, stashed somewhere deep within the bowels of the ship. From where she sat, she could hear the engines purr and feel them vibrate through her cage. Industrial

226

scents wafted in noxious clouds, smelling of fuel and sulfur and steel.

The stimuli exacerbated the ache that thrummed through V's brain. It felt like her head had been flattened by a sky train – and her body wasn't much better. The energy pistol left its mark in the form of aches and pains, compounded by V's recent injuries. The result was a headache large enough to cripple a city and muscles so tight they nearly hummed.

Even the skin on her wrist throbbed, and she looked down to see a raw red patch surrounding her tattoo. The Guards must have realized her ruse, scrubbing off her false identity in search of the truth. She felt exposed, laid bare before them with nowhere else to hide.

A groan emanated from somewhere on the ground, capturing V's attention. She glanced around to find a crumpled figure curled into a ball in the corner. The moan was deep and pitiable enough to point to a man, and V's heart hammered as she realized who it must be. Sable.

The weakness in her legs wouldn't allow her to stand, so she crawled, clumsily shuffling to peer at the poor creature. She extended a hand, placing it gently on his shoulder, and turned him to face her. The instant she spotted his curly brown hair and oversized ears, however, all thoughts of sympathy vanished.

"You! Fucking! Bastard!" she screamed as she slammed her fists into Mouse. "You did this to me! And to Riyah. You betrayed us – and you deserve to rot in hell."

The fury of her blows faltered as the last of her energy left her, and she sat back on her heels. Staring at the man with revulsion in her eyes, she considered his sad state. He was broken and bruised, with a split lip and a gash just above one eye. It made his young face look old, but it did nothing to soften V's rage.

"Can't you see?" Mouse asked with a humorless laugh. "I'm already in hell."

"This?" V asked, gesturing to the bars. "This is nothing compared to what they're doing to Riyah. Or to what they have in store for me. If you're looking for pity, you're in the wrong damn place."

With a snarl, she shoved Mouse away and retreated to her corner of the cell. She needed space to think, to piece together his presence and make some kind of sense of it.

She was certain that he was the traitor, the one who had turned her in to the Guards. There was no doubt in her mind about that. Yet somehow he'd still found himself trapped in a cell alongside her, destined for a similar fate.

V considered that it might be a trap, a con designed to make her trust him. He could still be a pawn in this game she didn't know how to play. Except the blood and the bruises seemed genuine, and his vanity would never allow him to incur such injuries for someone else's scheme.

"Why are you here?" V finally asked, blunt and unfeeling. "Why would the Guards turn on their *dutiful* informant?" She spat the word like a curse, hoping it would cut – and based on Mouse's reaction it did.

Mouse didn't respond, too wrapped up in his sulking to contribute to the conversation. Yet V was determined to make him talk, so she tried a different tactic.

"Aren't you curious why they caged us up together? Me, a bloodthirsty murderer, and you, the rat who betrayed me?

I mean, it's not like they're short on cells. They could easily have kept us apart. So why throw us in here together, in such close quarters?" V paused for a response that never came before ultimately answering on her own. "It's because they want me to kill you."

Mouse let out an insolent noise, half hiss and half growl. V wasn't deterred.

"I bet they're sick of you," she continued, voicing a theory that solidified as she spoke. "You were a good informant for a while, but now you're more trouble than you're worth. So they chucked you in here with me in hopes that I'll get rid of their *problem*. I am a killer, after all. What qualms would I have about dispatching a former friend?"

"You're wrong," Mouse snarled, his voice huskier than V had ever heard it.

V raised an eyebrow, intrigued. "About what?"

"I'm not the one who's trouble. You are," he shot back. "And you're the reason I'm here."

V felt a sliver of pride at the fact that she'd played a part in Mouse's defeat. It was a small sort of triumph, a morsel of success in this ill-fated match.

"Do tell," V invited, happy to hear more.

"I told them where you were alright, but the Guards thought I'd been holding out on them, that I'd known where you were all along. Some even thought I was in on it from the start, that I'd somehow helped you kill the senator and best their three buddies. After they grabbed you, they came back for me – and for my grandfather."

The resentment in his voice split into sadness at the final four words. V couldn't help but wonder at the mention of the old man.

"You never told me about him," she said, her grip on rage slipping ever so slightly.

"I never told anyone," he countered, sounding infinitely tired. "I was trying to protect him – and I failed."

V wasn't about to forgive Mouse, but she knew that the old man had done nothing to deserve his fate.

"Why was it your job to protect him?" she asked, desperate to know his motives. "What did he need protecting from?"

Mouse sighed painfully slowly, and V was certain he wouldn't respond. Yet a second later, he embarked on his tale.

"He raised me. Grandpa Solamine was basically the only family I ever knew. My mother was…absent. Attracted to the wrong type of men and the wrong type of life. She overdosed on Rapture when I was 10 and left us alone to try to cobble together the pieces of a life."

Something slotted into place in V's mind, and she asked, "Ora?"

Mouse seemed surprised. "How do you know that name?"

"Solamine," she explained. "He was confused. He thought I was your mother."

Mouse nodded, a grim smile spreading across his face. "You do look like her. Especially when I found you in that gutter. At first, I thought I was seeing a ghost."

"That's why you saved me," V realized, "why you picked me up and brought me home. Because I reminded you of her."

Mouse nodded. "Healthy behavior, I know," he said

sarcastically. "You're nothing like her, save for a mild resemblance, but it was enough to remind me of what it was like to have a family."

"I still don't understand," V confessed, steering him back to the point. "Why did your grandfather need protecting? And how did turning on your friends help?" The acidity returned to her voice at the accusation.

"When Ora died, he was already too old to work. No one would give him a job," Mouse replied. "I knew the streets from spending time with my mother, so it was easy to translate those skills into cash. By the time I was a teen, I was buying and selling banned goods with the best of them."

Mouse was cocky even now. V snorted but said nothing, too afraid to break the flow of his story.

"Naturally, I got caught and carted off to the Grove. When I got out, Grandpa Solamine was...different. He'd started to forget things, to wander off, to lose track of reality. I knew it wouldn't be long until they came for him, and I was right."

V could see the scene clearly. Solamine was just one more citizen who had ceased to be of value, who had failed to earn his keep aboard the Echelon. The Guards had come to right the imbalance of resources, intending to snuff out his life to make space for others.

"I begged, I bartered, I sold them secrets in exchange for his safety," Mouse growled, fully immersed in the memory. "And I wasn't sorry. I knew enough about the city and its vagrants to keep the Guards satisfied for years. I kept him alive. Until now. So if you think this isn't hell for me, think again."

Mouse had traded his friends for his family – and

ultimately failed, losing them all. Against her better judgment, she felt sorry for his loss, yet she harbored no sympathy for him. It was Solamine who split her heart, and V yearned to save him despite barely knowing his story.

"None of that justifies what you did," V stated, cold and indifferent. She couldn't forget Riyah's face as they'd dragged her away, and she couldn't forgive Mouse for causing it. "You deserve to rot in here."

"What, you're not going to kill me like you killed those Guards?" Mouse countered, bitter and caustic. "I was looking forward to a fight."

"I'm not a murderer," V said again, singing the same refrain she had last night. "Even if I were, you deserve to live with what you've done, with who you've become."

"Plus," she added, offhand and under her breath, "it wouldn't be a fair fight. Not anymore."

The pair descended into silence, with only the rumble of the ship's engines to give them solace. V felt untethered, cast adrift in time and space with nothing to cling to. Minutes and hours blurred until they lost all meaning, but still no one came. Relief and frustration warred within her as they drew out her torment, making her suffer the agony of anticipation.

Perhaps this was their plan, to let her die in the darkness, waiting for a trial that would never come. Perhaps instead of killing her outright, they had sentenced her to this – a faceless death that bore the shape of hunger and thirst and hope. Perhaps their cruelty ran deeper than she had ever imagined.

Just as V resigned herself to the misery of her final days, the sweet sound of footsteps reached her ears. They were quick, resonating through the tunnel in rapid taps, like someone was running toward them. V sat up, pressing her back against the wall as if that could prepare her for what came next.

A minute later, the shape of a Guard emerged from the fog and made a beeline for their cage. He was out of breath and bumbling, dropping the keys before finally managing to fit them in the lock. As the cell door swung open, he squeezed himself inside – and stared at V.

She'd expected violence, a scuffle, screaming. This was even more unsettling. His gaze was heavy and probing, and he studied her with an intensity that she couldn't quite place. It wasn't sexual or sadistic, merely curious, as if she'd done something to warrant his confusion.

The man came to with a visible shake, snapping himself out of his stupor. His wide eyes mellowed and his posture stiffened as stalked toward V with purpose. Holding out one hand, he waited, clearly hoping to help her up.

"Ms. Innova," he said, lingering on her name a little too long, "I'll need you to come with me. There's someone who is very eager to meet you."

V weighed her options – then realized she had none – so she took his hand and stood. Without so much as a glance toward Mouse, the Guard led her from the cage and locked the door behind them.

Once they were free, the Guard dropped his hand and backed away, as if touching her constituted some sort of crime. V saw the briefest window blink into existence, taunting her with the chance to escape, but she knew she'd never manage it. She was too tired and her legs too heavy to take off down the tunnel. Fleeing would be futile, just another tactic to stall her fate for a few more seconds.

When the Guard motioned for her to follow, she complied, tagging along in his wake. V scanned the scene, half expecting more Guards to fold out from the shadows and flank them, but no one came. They were alone, accompanied only by the sights, sounds, and smells of the inner shell of the Echelon.

Whatever sense of direction V had was lost in the darkness. The tunnels branched and curved in a curious maze, with no street signs or markers to show the way. It was a mirror city, a shadow world that seemed light-years away from the surface.

Normally, V would have yearned to break the silence, demanding to know where and when and how. Yet now, she couldn't bring herself to ask for fear of knowing. Her curiosity curdled into apprehension with each turn they took, and her mind painted pictures of her fears.

By the time they began to climb, V was shaking. She could no longer trust her legs to carry her forward, so she clung to the walls in hopes that they could hold her up. The Guard beside her saw but said nothing, merely slowing his pace to keep time with hers.

His gentleness was disconcerting, although V couldn't complain. It was better than being led through the halls like a criminal on a leash or cursed at by a wall of Guards. Still, the relative silence was strange, and V kept a wary eye out for any trick or trap.

The Guard led her around another bend before stopping abruptly, causing V to crash into his back with a cry of surprise. He reached out to steady her, then swiftly pulled away, still troubled by the thought of contact. His sunken face was blank as he turned away and began studying the empty wall.

V saw a string of buttons appear at his touch, brought to life by some key or code. He typed in a sequence, then waited as an unseen computer considered his request. Soon enough, a whirring noise broke free from the stone, and the blocks began to rumble.

A set of hidden doors opened to reveal an elevator, its interior drenched in white light and gleaming metal. The Guard beckoned for V to follow, and they stood side by side in the tiny space as it began to rise. A few seconds later, it stopped.

On the other side, V expected to find a courtroom or the gallows or the Grove, but she didn't. Instead, the doors dinged open on a strange new scene.

V was led into a lavish home, with a domed ceiling so high that it seemed to touch the sky. The roof was clear, with what felt like a single pane of glass separating them from the cosmos. V longed to reach out and touch it, to stroke the violet veins of stardust and the planet-speckled sky.

The room around her was stunning, although it couldn't contend with the brilliance of the Eridian Galaxy. A plush sofa ran the length of two walls, dressed smartly in a warm beige that counteracted the darkness of space. Subtle halos streamed from sconces in the walls, while the polished white floors reflected them back, coating the room in a gentle glow.

V was so absorbed in the grandeur of her surroundings that she barely noticed the Guard as he crept toward the door. When the ding of the elevator sounded, it broke her concentration, bringing her back down.

"Wait," she exclaimed, holding out a hand to stop him. "Where are you going?"

"This is where I leave you, miss," he responded with a nod, letting the doors close quietly between them.

V was bewildered, alarmed, uneasy. This was so far removed from the scene she'd expected that she couldn't make sense of it. And the surprises weren't over yet.

A woman rounded the corner with a flourish, the gauzy trim of her gown blurring her edges, like she wasn't quite there. Her blond hair was perfectly coiffed and her dress was impeccable, but her soft brow and gently wrinkled eyes were contorted into a look of concern.

The moment she spotted V, though, it was as if the sky had opened up to reveal the heavens. Tears sprang to her eyes as she glided forward, smiling with outstretched arms.

V knew this face. She could trace it to a picture Lyra had shown her. She could even connect it to a name: Celeste Altair. Senator. Suspect in Apollo's murder. And something else that V struggled to put her finger on.

Then the woman spoke, and pieces that had been floating around V's mind assembled themselves into a recognizable pattern.

"It's you. Oh, my stars, it's really you. How I've missed you, my darling girl. My wonderful, beautiful Sky."

V considered the words, the woman, the room. It was all achingly familiar, like a word she could taste on the tip of her tongue but somehow couldn't say. Then in an instant, it came to her, all blinding light and clarity.

"Mom?"

Chapter 20

Violet was in Celeste's arms before she knew what was happening. It felt like a fever dream, real enough to convince her body but not her mind, with the past and present colliding in a raucous din. It was all too much and not enough, and it made her head spin.

The air around her thinned until breathing became a chore and V had to sit, with her mother beside her on the beige couch. The two women stared at each other, groping for words to fit their strange situation yet coming up short.

Celeste's appearance had knocked something loose in V's mind, codifying memories and slotting them into place. V could recall the smallest things – the soft wrinkles around her mother's eyes, her surprising strength, the commanding timbre of her voice. Yet large fragments still floated in space, leaving conspicuous absences in their wake.

She couldn't remember who she'd been or the life she'd lived. And no matter how much she strained, she couldn't recall what had torn her from this place and this person. All V could cling to were bits and pieces of a life and the outlines of a name – her name. Sky.

She expected it to fit like an old sweater, comfortable and familiar, but the edges of it didn't quite match up to the person she'd become. In the absence of this name and this life, V had forged her own way forward, creating something new. Now she was neither Violet nor Sky, but some amalgam of both, with pieces from two puzzles that would never add up to a perfect whole.

The sound of Celeste's voice dragged V back to the present.

"I searched for you," she confessed, smiling sadly. "I never gave up hope that you were out there, that you were still alive. I knew in my bones that someday you would come back to me."

Something about Celeste's statement nagged at V, souring this happy reunion with a tinge of uncertainty.

"I wasn't hiding," V began, dancing around the issue before diving in. "I was out there the whole time, living in plain sight. If you were looking so hard, why couldn't you find me?"

Confusion, then understanding, then sympathy passed over Celeste's face in rapid succession. Instead of answering, however, she turned to her scryglass and pulled up an image before angling it toward V.

All she could do was stare, not comprehending in the slightest. The picture showed a girl, slightly younger than V, with long chestnut hair and pointed features. Her nose was slightly crooked, as if it had been broken, but it did nothing to mar her beauty. V's gaze snagged on the girl's wide green eyes, and she shivered. It was uncanny – and impossible – but V knew those eyes.

"This is you – or was you," Celeste corrected. "This is the Sky I raised, the daughter whose every freckle I knew by heart."

"I don't understand," V admitted, feeling cold and clammy despite the warmth. "How can that possibly be?"

Celeste sighed. "I can only hazard a guess," she said, "but I'd bet that the same person who wiped your memory also altered your appearance. They didn't want you to be recognized – or found. It's likely they got their hands on a mod machine, meant for reconstructive surgeries, and forced you to change."

"But why?" V asked, still utterly adrift. "What did I do to deserve this?"

"Oh, darling!" Celeste exclaimed, reaching out to grasp V's hands. "None of this is your fault. You've done nothing wrong. This was all because of me. Some radical or rebel wanted to send a message, and they used you to do it. You were merely a pawn, and I'm so sorry you got caught up in their game."

The story made sense, yet the pieces refused to fall into place. A rift remained in V's memory, refusing to close, like some crucial part was missing. She groped for it, feeling around in the darkness for the shape of something familiar, but nothing emerged.

"How did you find me?" V tried, hoping for a flicker that would burst into a flame. "If you didn't know what I looked like – or even my name – how did you know I was Sky?"

Celeste smiled and let loose a light laugh, shaking her

head. "Your face may have changed, but you haven't. You are still the same ferocious Sky. My daughter never backs down from a fight, and she is by far the fiercest warrior on the Echelon. That brawl in the bar was pure Sky style."

"You knew it was me because I beat up some Guards?" V asked, still harboring a dash of suspicion.

"I *hoped* it was you," Celeste corrected. "So I had the Guards bring you here. And when I saw you, there was no doubt in my mind."

No wonder that Guard had been so perplexed. He'd been told V was some long-lost daughter, some descendant of a powerful dynasty. And – covered in blood and quickly purpling bruises – she didn't exactly look the part.

"So they just let me go?" V probed, hopeful but disbelieving. "They're not sending me to the Grove?"

Celeste nearly laughed, barely stopping herself in time. "No," she assured V. "No one is coming to take you away. Once I inform the Iridium Guards that it's definitely you, all charges will be dropped. Hell, I wouldn't be surprised if they issued a formal apology for all the trouble they've caused."

The sudden change in her situation made V feel dizzy. A flood of elation rushed through her veins, drowning the dread that had held her captive for days.

"How?" she asked, incredulous. "I'm wanted for murder. That's not something you can sweep under the rug."

"When I told the Guards who you were – or who I believed you to be," Celeste explained, "it put their witch hunt into stark perspective. You had no motive to kill Senator Quinn, and their evidence was circumstantial at best. The unfortunate casualties that occurred along the way were clearly an act of self-defense. They'll be ruled accidental, and your name will be cleared of all charges. You have my word."

The ease with which V found herself a free woman was downright scary. The power her mother wielded seemed infinite, and for the moment it was working in her favor. It didn't erase the guilt of taking three lives, but it did a good deal to diminish the ache. She wanted to crumple then and there, to give into the relief and succumb to her body's calls for sleep, but she had one more question.

"The night Apollo was killed," she said quietly, "you weren't at the party." It wasn't quite a question, but she couldn't bring herself to accuse the woman who had just saved her life.

Celeste seemed taken aback by the statement, but she quickly recovered. "How could I celebrate when you were still missing? I couldn't stand amongst those people and smile when I knew you might be suffering. Although now I wish I had. I wish I'd put on a brave face and stood in that ballroom and watched you perform. I would have known in an instant who you were – and I could have saved you so much pain."

V squeezed her mother's hands and smiled, comforted in knowing she wasn't a killer. Celeste's elimination left three suspects, although V supposed that it was no longer her mystery to solve. With her shiny new pardon, she'd been released from that inky web, with her life no longer tied to its outcome. It was Fynn and Lyra's problem now, leaving V free to find out who she was – or at least who she'd been.

"I can't imagine my little girl singing in a bar for units," Celeste was saying as V tuned back in. "You've always had an amazing voice, of course, but I didn't think you'd be caught dead in a place like that."

V laughed along with her mother, although it felt like a betrayal. The Alcor Club had been good to her, and she'd found something crucial on its stage, a part of herself that was fierce and fearless. Without it, V didn't know where she would be – or what kind of person she would have become.

She tried to tell this to Celeste, but the words wouldn't come. They lodged in her throat, held down by the certainty that Celeste would never understand. The Alcor belonged to a different world, a different life, a different version of her daughter. Yet the memory of her last night within its walls forced V to speak.

"The man I was with when I was captured. Sable," she began. "He was only trying to help me. He doesn't deserve the Grove."

Celeste narrowed her eyes, as if trying to glean the nature of their relationship. An instant later, her face flattened into a placid smile.

"I'll see that he's released," she said with a benevolent nod, as if speaking to a subject. "He must care for you deeply to have put his life on the line for yours," she continued, clearly prodding. "There aren't many like him on the Echelon."

"Ye...yes," V stuttered, slightly thrown by the subject. "He's a very good *friend*."

Discussing her love life with a mother she hadn't seen in a year – and barely remembered – was the epitome of uncomfortable, so V quickly changed the subject.

"Actually, I have another friend you might be able to help," V blurted before she'd even formed a plan.

Her mother pursed her lips, no doubt envisioning another unsuitable suitor.

"Her name's Riyah. Riyah Biela," V rushed to clarify. "She was taken by the ADF."

Understanding found its way onto her mother's face, quickly followed by pity. V didn't care. All she knew was that if her family had power, she was sure as hell going to use it to try to free her friend.

"I know she went against the Policies, but it wasn't on purpose. She is a good woman – a good mother – and a loyal citizen. Is there any chance you could speak up on her behalf, grant her some kind of exception? I would give anything to get her out."

Celeste was already shaking her head, pity still staining her features. "I'm sorry, Sky. Even I can't overturn the punishment for breaking a Policy. Common criminals are one thing, but Anomalies are a different matter entirely."

The fact that her mother had called Sable a common criminal didn't escape V's notice. However, at that moment, disappointment weighed heavier than anything else, crushing her with its force. Celeste seemed to notice, wrapping an arm around her daughter's shoulders and pulling her close.

"Don't worry, my dear. Your friend will be fine. She'll be back to her old life in no time. Trust me. Everything will work out as it should."

The sentiment did nothing to lessen the ache, which ate at her body like hunger, gnawing from the inside. Once again, Celeste didn't understand. V didn't have the words to explain it or the strength to withstand it, so she stood, disentangling herself from this stranger with whom she'd shared a lifetime.

"It's been a long day," she said, rubbing her eyes. "I think I'd like to go to bed."

"Of course," Celeste said, rising to stand beside her. "Do you remember the way? I can show you if you'd like."

"No," V said a little too quickly. "I'm sure I can find it. Goodnight…mom." The word felt foreign on her tongue, and despite the truth of it, it tasted wrong. Instead of examining it, V turned and followed her feet to the end of the hall, then around a bend.

Her room sat at the end of a row of sliding doors. She knew what lay beyond them without looking, her memories unfolding like a map in her mind. Celeste's bedroom, an exquisite bathroom, a study. Then it was her room, her sanctuary amidst the storm. Without turning on a light, she slipped inside, locking the door behind her.

Chapter 21

Violet expected a reprieve from the nightmares. She'd discovered who she was and where she'd come from. Surely that was enough to drive the demons from her dreams.

But no. Instead, they were worse than they'd ever been, haunting her with hellscapes from which she couldn't wake.

In them, a faceless devil danced atop a bottomless grave, calling out her name. V yearned to run, yet her feet wouldn't listen. They carried her closer and closer to the creature, who laughed in a manic craze.

She stopped an arm's length away, unwilling to turn or blink or move lest the monster sense her presence and pounce. Ragged bits of skin hung off its blackened bones, flapping in the wind. The creature looked rotten, like death had laid claim to its body but couldn't seize its soul. The sky overhead churned and spun, mixing black and blue as it growled its displeasure.

V was petrified, a woman made of stone atop a mountain

built of blood. Still, she felt an insatiable need to know who it was that held her in thrall – and what it was they were guarding.

She took a step, then another, peering into the gorge beneath the cracked grave. She could hear screams and cries, and they sang in her veins, calling out for vengeance. Yet she knew she couldn't save them, not without damning herself.

All of a sudden, a set of hands planted themselves on V's back and pushed. She shrieked, arms flailing as she began to fall. Just as she slipped beneath the surface, though, her fingers found purchase on a withered root and grabbed hold. She hung there, suspended above the pit, caught in a trap of her own curiosity as the devil looked down.

It was only then that she saw its smiling face. Recognition turned V's blood cold and encased her chest in ice. Because staring down at her was Celeste.

The smile turned sinister as her mother reached down and pried V's hands from their hold. As the last finger loosened, V screamed, dropping into the depths of the pit.

V came to in a cold sweat, tangled in luxe sheets with pillows strewn around her. She couldn't catch her breath, and her heart beat out a familiar chorus: *Get out. Get out. Get out.*

She sat up, abruptly thrown off balance by the strangeness of the room. Every shadow and corner and fixture was foreign yet familiar, caught in a limbo of mislaid memories. Just like V.

Only the sky, sparkling through the window above her, spoke a language she knew. V had refused to close the curtains when she'd turned out the lights, needing the constancy of the cosmos as they drifted overhead. Now the stars gave her solace and the planets granted peace, slowing her heart-beat to a patter.

V yearned to run, to lose herself in the darkness and the rhythm of her feet. Yet she didn't know what dangers still lurked outside the door. She didn't know if her mother had cleared her name, if word of her pardon had spread. Hell, V didn't even know exactly where she was, although somewhere in the Senatorial Sector seemed likely.

All was quiet in the house, hushed in the way only sleep – and death – can manage. To V's knowledge, she and Celeste were alone, with no hired help or family to clutter up their quarters. V rifled through her scattered memories for visions of a father but was unsurprised to find none. As far as she could tell, it had only ever been them, mother and daughter alone atop the world.

With the prospect of sleep now a distant dream, V hoisted herself off the bed, her muscles stiff and aching. She raised her arms with some effort and stretched, lengthening the cords that connected her joints and allowing them to breathe. When it no longer felt as though her body was bound together with knots and pins, she began a thorough inspection of the room.

The space was neat and tidy, with everything stacked and sorted and stowed out of sight. It was soft in a way that bordered on stark, with white walls fanning out into floating seating and a cantilevered bed. Pinpricks of light emanated from the walls, while strips of icy blue shone from beneath floorboards and furniture, creating a muted sort of glow.

It was elegant and understated, yet utterly impersonal, like any number of influential citizens could have called this home. Nothing screamed Sky or leapt out as obvious sources of joy. It was far more than she'd had, but so much less than who she'd been. She couldn't help but miss her tiny apartment and her cave of a bed – even if they did remind her painfully of someone whom she couldn't stand.

V swept her palm against the wall, freeing a chest of drawers. She opened the wardrobe, the desk, the shoe rack buried beneath the floor, scanning the contents for signs of her existence.

Here, at least, were hints of her, proof that a version of V had once lived within these walls. She could see herself in the colors, the lines of a dress, the heel of a shoe. She could spot the connections between the woman she was and the woman she'd once been.

V fingered the delicate fabrics and inhaled their scent, letting the flashbacks take her to a time when she'd belonged. She saw herself seated in the back of senatorial meetings, training with a team of combatants, studying with tutors of every subject. She flicked through dinners and dances and demonstrations, and a realization dawned.

Celeste had been training her, building Sky up to be a version of herself. Her destiny had been set since the day she was born, almost certainly leading straight to the Senate. She hadn't had a choice, only a path to follow and an outline of a life she would one day lead.

V scanned her fragments of memory for the presence of a friend but found none. There were teachers and trainers and scientists, but no one who could remotely be considered close. She was alone in a sea of blurred faces, surrounded by relative strangers – save for one.

V froze, rewinding her thoughts to the latest flash, to a face that was clearer than most. The memory stuttered and skipped, like a record that was scratched, but the man was always in focus. V saw his lab coat, his long white hair, his gray robes hung up in the corner. She couldn't see what he was doing – or even where – but she knew that face, that energy, that hair.

It was Apollo Quinn.

What was he doing in her memories? Surely they'd crossed paths in their previous lives, thrown into the same circles by circumstance, but this memory showed something else entirely. This was close-quarters contact, one-on-one, an encounter engineered with an aim.

V needed more. Her head ached from the effort, but she forced herself to focus. The scene was encased in shadow, blackened and blurry, but its edges began to give. She pushed and prodded, slowly driving back the darkness to reveal a blinding light.

As she peered through Sky's eyes, she could just make out the lab, stuffed to the brim with beeping machines that spun and whirred. Apollo poked at a set of screens, peering at strings of data that made no sense to her. Yet the numbers and symbols seemed to reassure him, and he made thoughtful noises as he read.

A moment later, he turned, giving Sky his full attention.

"I think we're ready," he told her, his voice muddled by the mistiness of memory. "The projections look promising. It should only take a matter of months. Once I have it, I'll find you and we can get to work."

"Good," V heard herself say with a surety she hadn't

quite felt. "Let's do this."

The memory cut to black without another word, leaving V clawing at the edges. Confused – and desperately trying to remember more – she laid out the facts before her.

Apollo had known Sky. They'd been working together. They'd been on a mission, although toward what end V couldn't tell. Then a year later he'd appeared, with V's memories in-hand and the critical task of returning them.

Apollo had known who V was – who she *really* was – all along. They'd been in this together from the start.

"I am so sorry it has taken me this long," Apollo had said on the fateful night that would prove to be his last. "I didn't intend to leave you out there, confused and alone. But I have it now – and we can finally begin."

The threads of some long-lost story began stitching themselves together, and suddenly it all made sense.

His projections had been wrong. Instead of months, it had taken him a year to build the device that would once more grant her access to her past. So he'd left her there, in the real world, without a link to the life she'd had. But he'd finally figured it out, bringing her back into his orbit so he could return what he'd taken. So they could get to work.

Only nothing had played out the way they'd planned. The data transfer had failed, Apollo had died, and V had taken the fall.

None of this meshed with Celeste's theory that Sky had been stolen to settle some score. Because no one had taken her memories; she'd given them away. It had all been by design, a carefully constructed scheme with only one goal V could see: to escape. But from what?

The answers only led to more questions. Why had Sky needed to surrender her memories? What work were they supposed to begin? What had she been running from – and was it the same thing that had gotten Apollo killed?

V's head hurt from trying to untangle it. The maze was messy and twisted, and it was never meant to be solved alone. Apollo should have been there to make sense of the mystery and take the turns by her side.

A loneliness that looked a good deal like grief washed over her. Apollo's murder had taken away more than the missing link. It had taken her partner, her co-conspirator, her closest thing to a friend. His death was a tragedy on multiple levels, and it sparked something savage within her.

Apollo had been onto something. They both had. Sky hadn't been trying to escape a life she didn't like; she was trying to hide in plain sight while they figured out how to fight. Now, with Apollo gone, it was up to V to continue their efforts alone.

She didn't know what that meant, but she had to start somewhere, so she began to search. She started with her room, combing through the things that made up Sky's life and praying they held a clue. Floorboards and wall panels became casualties as she pried them up to peer beneath, hoping for some hidden gem, some journal or record to lead her like breadcrumbs back to the girl she'd been.

The room, however, had precious few secrets to spare. By the time V had dismantled every fixture and dug through every drawer, she barely had enough to piece together a day, let alone a life. A few appointments saved on a scryglass, a letter from a fleeting lover, a child-sized wrist cuff that she supposed had once belonged to her.

There was nothing that pointed to a sinister plot, no hidden files or coded messages or secret clues. Sky couldn't have planned for a future like this, so she'd left no trail to follow.

V cursed her clouded memory, scraping through the skeletal fragments she'd managed to glean. It felt akin to raking her nails across glass, supplying nothing more than a shrill noise and a piercing headache. She clasped her head in her hands as she knelt on the floor, trying to hold herself together while her world fell apart.

Pieces of who she'd been and who she'd become swirled around without settling, creating a maelstrom in her mind. People from her past mixed with faces from the present, blurring into crowds that shouted wordless commands. V let out a muted cry as the chaos swelled and crested, splitting her head in two.

It took a concerted effort to drag herself out of the storm and center herself in the present. When she did, she found that she was curled into a ball on the hard floor, panting with heavy breaths and clenched fists. Sweat dripped from her forehead and moisture stained her cheeks, but she wiped it away, gradually unfurling until she sat upright.

V wouldn't get anywhere like this. Whatever this was, whatever game she'd been playing, she couldn't do it alone. Sky had known that, and she'd enlisted Apollo's aid. Now it was V's turn to bite the bullet and ask for help.

Except her remaining pool of allies was dreadfully shallow. Mouse was out. Asher wouldn't be of much use. And Sable had already risked too much for her cause. That left only two people.

V let out a sigh that bordered on a snarl. The last place she wanted to go was back to Fynn and Lyra. They had lied and manipulated her and cast her out once her usefulness expired. As allies, the pair was sorely lacking.

Yet, V reminded herself, they also had tech. And skills in the subtle art of spy craft. And ways to get information that she couldn't. V also had a hunch there was something they were hiding, something less altruistic behind their actions. She itched to uncover their secrets and use them like they'd used her, to further her own ends.

Besides, in the day since her departure, the tables had turned. The target was off her back and the balance of power had shifted, leaning considerably in her favor. As a member of the elite, she had resources, connections, and access, plus the power of her mother's name. She was valuable, and Fynn and Lyra couldn't afford to ignore her.

Chapter 22

V was out the door the moment the curfew sirens sounded, not even waiting for the din to die down before she called the elevator and climbed inside. She buzzed with anxious energy, and her body practically vibrated with a blend of determination and dread. She ached for a confrontation, a chance to make a stand, but the pain from her last encounter lingered, warning her of more wounds ahead.

Not wanting Celeste to worry, V left a carefully worded message, to be delivered on her scryglass once she woke. She said she'd gone in search of memories and something to stir them, but she'd be back in time for supper. V knew that leaving so soon could look suspicious, that she'd barely been home a day, but the urgent pounding in her head left little choice.

The Senatorial Sector was stagnant in the simulated dawn. Nothing moved or made a sound, save for the sentries. For once, though, V let herself be seen, choosing to stand tall and shine in the safety of being Sky.

No alarms sounded and no sentries swooped to scan her, so she presumed that her name had been cleared. When she proffered her wrist at the checkpoint, her suspicions were confirmed. Her picture remained the same, but the accompanying data had already been altered.

Sky Altair. Age 25. Daughter of Senator Celeste Altair. Residence: Senatorial Sector. Status: Nonthreatening.

It beeped her through without issue, and she confidently stalked to the other side. Quietly, though, she sighed in relief, releasing the tension that had wrapped around her ribcage.

V continued through the streets, stopping here and there to consider the world, as if seeking signs of her former self. Then, with a dash of stealth and a pinch of good timing, she disappeared, slipping away unseen onto quieter streets.

Picking the Eos' lock took less than a minute – a surprising feat given their fondness for secrecy and high-tech toys. Then she was in, surrounded by the knick-knacks and bric-a-brac that had once made her feel safe. Now all it managed to do was make the world feel like it was closing in, pressing down painfully from all sides.

She arranged herself artfully in a chair, with her long legs perched atop the low counter. Her arms were crossed over her chest and her head rested against the wall in a carefully constructed show of nonchalance. Dressed in a stunning blue ensemble from Sky's closet, with her blonde hair slicked back in the latest style, she was the picture of perfection – if perfection had a penchant for picking locks and waiting silently in the shadows. When the pair finally woke, V would be the first thing they saw.

The idea of them together, sleeping side by side or curled in each other's arms, still sat wrong with her, with a small voice whispering that something was amiss. V chided herself for the thought, blaming it on some lingering hint of envy and casting it aside.

The element of surprise wasn't strictly necessary for her plan, but she liked the idea of having the upper hand. And scaring the shit out of Fynn. So she stilled herself in the silence, holding every muscle taut like a predator anticipating her prey.

She wasn't disappointed.

Fynn rose first, shuffling in with eyes still full of sleep and a mind not fully centered in the waking world. His gaze swept over the scene, and he blinked, taking a second too long to process her presence. When he did, the look on his face was priceless. As was his squeal of surprise.

Lyra plodded in to investigate only to freeze, her shock evident in the stillness of her limbs and the slackness of her features. With her metal arm half raised, she reminded V of a droid that had missed its charging and run out of power mid-task. Yet of the pair, she rallied first, shaking herself from her petrified state to stalk to V's side. Fynn followed, trailing after his wife with his mouth hinged open and his bushy eyebrows slanted in bewilderment.

V spoke first, seizing her chance to control the conversation.

"I would say that it's nice to see you both, but this time I think we should skip the lies."

"Violet," Lyra said by way of a greeting, pushing past the snide comment with nothing more than a mild frown.

"Mrs. Eos," V responded in turn, her tone sticky and sweet. "Mr. Eos," she continued, nodding at Fynn.

Finally finding his voice, Fynn croaked in apparent confusion, "Violet?"

"Yes," V replied gently, as if speaking to a toddler. "We've already covered that bit. Me V, you Fynn, her Lyra. Now that we've cleared that up, perhaps we should get to the point."

"Why are you here, V?" Lyra barked, her tone all business.

"Good," V responded, whipping her legs from the desk to lean forward. "At least one of you knows what questions to ask."

"Save the sarcasm," Lyra cut in. "Just tell us what you want. Your name's been cleared and you've found your family. What the hell do you need from us?"

That caught V off guard. The fact that she'd found Celeste wasn't common knowledge, nor was her new status with the Guards. That could only mean one thing.

"You've been spying on me?" V scoffed, incredulous.

"Of course," Lyra countered calmly, ignoring V's agitation. "We had to keep an eye on you – and boy have you been busy."

V wanted to ask what they'd seen, but from the smirk on Lyra's lips, the answer was clear. They'd used her retinal implant to watch *everything*. Her fight with Mouse. Her capture. The appearance of Celeste. And, evidently, her night with Sable. A blush threatened to break free, but she fought back, refusing to show remorse for any part of the past few days.

V was her own person, unattached and unencumbered, unlike the people before her. She could do what she liked

– and who she liked – and they didn't have the right to say a damn thing.

Glancing toward Fynn, she smiled and held her head high. "Good," she declared. "Then I won't have to fill you in. That should save us all some time."

There was something in Fynn's eyes that almost gave her pause. If she hadn't known better, she would have sworn it was sorrow, but it couldn't be. He had never felt for her the way she had for him. He had never cared. Each lingering look and blistering touch had been a carefully constructed ruse designed to make her fall.

Yet if that was the case, then why did he look so miserable? V didn't have the time or emotional capacity to wade through the complexities of that question, so she stopped asking.

"I'm here to help you," she stated, plastering on a cocky smile.

Lyra scoffed, like V knew she would. "Help us? Those Guards must have knocked you harder than we thought. We don't need your help."

"Oh, really?" V asked, feigning surprise. "So you've gotten to the bottom of Apollo's murder? You've solved the case of the missing senators? And you've finally figured out how everything is connected?"

Lyra chose not to take V's bait. True to form, Fynn wasn't as smart.

"We're no further than we were before," he confessed. "In fact, we've hit a wall."

"Shocking," V spat, her tone bone dry. "I never would have guessed."

"Why would you want to help us?" Fynn asked, ignoring her blatant mockery. "After...everything?" He looked down, seemingly too ashamed to meet her eyes.

"Oh, I haven't forgotten any of that – and I haven't forgiven you, either," V assured them. "But, like you said, what's happening out there is bigger than any of us, and I want to help. So here I am."

Lyra still wasn't convinced. "And what, exactly, are you offering? Fashion tips?" she asked, gesturing toward V's ensemble. "Or perhaps some of your newfound fortune?"

"Not quite," V countered. "I was hoping to share my new findings on why Apollo was killed – and why I got roped into the mess. Although, now that you mention it, more resources certainly couldn't hurt your...operation," she added, tacking on a note of disdain as she glanced at the disarray.

"Wait, you know why Apollo was murdered?" Fynn blurted, clearly curious.

"I definitely know more than you two," V replied, keeping her cards close – and the gaps in her knowledge closer.

"And?" Lyra probed, hoping V would crack.

"And this time, things are going to be different," she informed them. "This time, I'm not settling for half the story. I want answers."

Fynn and Lyra shared a not-so-secret look. They knew what she wanted. The only question was if they were willing to give it.

"What kind of answers?" Lyra asked with a halfhearted show of ignorance.

"Let's see," V said, leveraging herself up and starting to pace. "We could start with who you really are. Then maybe

259

who you're working for. And, to tie it all up, maybe you could tell me the real reason you're so interested in Apollo's death."

She stopped in front of the pair, crossing her arms across her chest and staring in pure defiance. This was the moment of truth. It was the moment they gave in and told her everything or she walked away, forced to go it alone despite the overwhelming odds.

Fynn and Lyra returned to their silent conversation. It didn't take long. After a moment, they disengaged, coming to some sort of conclusion.

"How do we know you're telling the truth?" Lyra asked, coming as close to V as was comfortable – then taking another step.

V smiled, a wicked gleam in her eyes. "You don't. I guess you'll just have to trust me."

V and Lyra stared, waging a battle with their eyes. Neither blinked, and neither backed away. It was Fynn who finally stepped in, clearing his throat as if calling for a truce.

"Fine," Lyra spat, turning her back. "We'll tell you what you want to know. Then you help us finish this. If you double cross us, though, I swear to the stars I'll end you."

V had no doubts that she would. Or at least she'd try. Thankfully, V didn't intend to do anything of the sort. She was about to repeat her list of questions when Lyra jumped in, saving her the trouble.

"You might want to get comfortable," she began. "This story's not a short one."

V settled herself back behind the counter, motioning for her host to continue.

"To answer your first question, I'm Lyra. He's Fynn. We

never lied to you about that. Although I suspect that's not what you wanted to know."

V opened her mouth to reply, but once again someone beat her to it.

"This will go faster if you don't talk," Fynn said sagely. "I've learned that lesson the hard way."

V wondered but didn't ask, heeding his advice.

Lyra ignored them both and continued with a bombshell. "I'm not from the Echelon. I wasn't born here, and I wasn't raised here. In fact, I've only been here for the past two years."

V's mouth hinged open, with her mind momentarily cutting to black. She yearned to ask, but she held her tongue, waiting eagerly for Lyra's explanation.

"My home ship is called the Alasia. We were a sister vessel to the Echelon when the first fleets departed Earth, but time and the cosmos came between us. By the time the Echelon cut off contact, we'd already drifted millions of miles apart."

"Cut off contact?" V blurted, unable to stop herself. "What do you mean? There were outbreaks on the other ships. Trade and travel were outlawed. Communications just dwindled in response." At least that's what she'd always been told.

Fynn sighed as V ignored the one rule she'd been given. Lyra, on the other hand, let out a loud snort.

"You idiots will believe anything your senators say. If you're looking for the real lies, just start with the stories they've sold you."

"If it wasn't disease, then why did they decide to cut

261

ties?" V asked, so curious now that it almost hurt.

Lyra smiled, revealing far too many teeth. "Simple. They were afraid. And fear makes fools of us all."

Fynn could read how hungry V was to know, so he stepped in to explain. "We're not alone out here. There are other species, *alien* species, although I'm told that they don't particularly like that word." He glanced toward Lyra for the barest hint of a second before continuing. "When the first race – the Kura – made contact, everything changed."

"At first, the humans hoped to cohabitate, sharing the Kura's planet and resources," Lyra said, "but it was already overpopulated. They'd been forced into space too, searching for room to spread. Instead, they found us."

An errant thought popped into V's mind, and her brain couldn't stop her from blurting it out. "You're not human!" she stated, pointing at Lyra. The gray pallor to her skin and her strangely dark eyes suddenly made so much sense.

"Bravo," Lyra said slowly, clearly mocking her. "But you're only half right. My mother was Kura, but my father's human. I'm a mongrel of sorts. Not the most popular with either species, but that's rather beside the point."

V's world was tipping, threatening to toss her overboard, but she held on tight, enthralled. The universe was wider and weirder than she'd ever dreamed, and it was magnificent. Still, she didn't understand what all that had to do with the Echelon – and with Apollo.

"Some were curious about this new species. Others saw the benefits of cooperation, like advancements in tech and expanded trade. But your lot got angry. They didn't want these *aliens* ruining their way of life – corrupting their children, spreading their diseases, taking what was theirs. Your senators stressed the importance of separation, and when the other ships disagreed, the Echelon locked its doors, cut off all comms, and fled.

"We thought we'd heard the last of you. Decades went by, then centuries without a word. Then one day, one of your senators sent a message to the Cosmic Conclave, an assembly formed aboard the Alasia. 'The Echelon is creating a weapon,' it read. 'Something capable of killing us all.' It wasn't a threat, like we first assumed, but a warning. And a call for help."

Lyra sighed, rubbing her eyes. "We used the senator's comms link to reply, asking for details. He didn't know much, and we couldn't promise aid without proof, so he vowed to find some. Then everything went silent. No more comms, no more senator. That was the first disappearance."

V was starting to connect the dots, with a hazy picture flickering to life. Yet so many questions remained. This time, however, she kept her mouth shut.

"The Conclave couldn't ignore the threat, but they couldn't exactly invade the Echelon either. So I volunteered to make the voyage. My partner, Nyx, and I would follow the coordinates the senator had given and board the Echelon, tracking down this weapon. Then we'd return with a full report. Only none of it went down the way we planned."

Lyra unconsciously massaged the metal of her arm, as if attempting to soothe some phantom pain. "We used cloaking tech to conceal our approach," she said, jumping ahead. "We thought it would be enough. We were wrong."

Lyra suddenly dropped into silence, her dark eyes going

dim. V didn't understand the change – at least not until Fynn stepped in to explain.

"The Echelon has sophisticated shields. The senator didn't warn them. Lyra and Nyx essentially flew into a kill zone, and only one of them made it out alive."

"Your arm?" V asked Lyra, already knowing the answer.

Lyra waved the appendage in the air, flexing its metallic fingers. "The cost of gaining access to the Echelon. I was the lucky one. There wasn't enough of Nyx left to salvage."

Sensing Lyra's reluctance, Fynn took up the baton, adding another layer to the story.

"She needed help – and an identity, one the Iridium Guards wouldn't question. I was working in the underground markets, securing papers for second children. Lyra stumbled in broken, bleeding, and barely conscious. After some extensive off-the-book surgeries, she came to – and nearly beamed me into oblivion with that arm," he chuckled. "I finally calmed her down, caught her up, and convinced her to tell me her story."

"Fynn got me the papers," Lyra explained, "but he knew that a lone adult in a city like this, looking like I do, would attract attention. So he came up with a plan. We would pose as a married couple and set up shop, hiding as a pair in plain sight. And it worked."

V's heart leapt into her throat as the truth tumbled from Lyra's lips. Their marriage was a hoax, a show put on for the benefit of the Guards, a carefully constructed cover. The thought shouldn't have thrilled V like it did. She chided herself as a buzz suffused her veins, threatening to turn her giddy.

Fynn was still a liar, no matter his marital status. She could feel his gaze, so she schooled her features, refusing to let her emotions show. He didn't deserve her forgiveness – or anything else. If only her heart would stop hammering long enough to listen.

Lyra seemed ignorant of their silent struggle – or she just didn't give a damn.

"For the last two years, we've been slowly gaining access to the Senate, hoping to piece together what they're planning," she said with a frustrated sigh. "We've bugged rooms, hacked scryglasses, and tailed countless lackeys, but all we have to show for it is scraps."

V raised her eyebrows in a quiet request for more, and after a tense beat Lyra complied.

"A few senators have gone missing. We never lied to you about that. Your ship has an uncanny tendency to make its people disappear. What we conveniently failed to mention was why."

V shook her head, confused. "I thought the senators disagreed with someone powerful, so they had to die. Wasn't that the theory?"

"I'm not talking about the senators," Lyra corrected her. "I'm talking about everyone else, all the citizens who seem to be vanishing into thin air."

Lyra tossed the baton back to Fynn, unofficially anointing him as the bearer of bad news.

"The Echelon is running out of resources. Food, water, fuel, even power."

V's mind flicked back to the blackout, to her and Fynn stranded in the shadows, to him calling her important. The

sudden spark in her chest stung. Fynn had been right then –
and she had a horrible feeling he was right again.

"The senators know they don't have enough supplies to
support their citizens, and they can only get rid of so many
before society collapses," Fynn explained. "Unless they do
something soon, everyone aboard the Echelon will die."

"Something?" V asked, not liking the direction this dis-
cussion was taking. "What does that mean?"

"If our original informant was right and they're building
a weapon," Lyra said, "it can only mean one thing. The senators are preparing for war."

Chapter 23

Well, shit. Violet had known she was knee-deep in something serious, but a full-on war was more than she'd bargained for.

The ship seemed to shudder beneath her. V clutched at the desk, seeking a proxy for the strength that had seeped from her bones. Images of violence and the sound of screams bombarded her thoughts, prying her mouth open.

"War?" she parroted as she attempted to process the news. "Like actual, full-on battle? With who? When?" The questions came quicker than she could think, blending in her brain and conveying shocks of confusion.

"We've told you everything we know," Lyra stated, reverting to her normal hostility. "Now I believe you owe us an explanation."

V's offering felt paltry in comparison. They'd revealed a world outside the Echelon that she'd never imagined and a struggle inside it that could bring her very existence to an end. She had…fragments of memory and flimsy deductions. She couldn't help but think that she was getting the better end of the bargain.

Still, she shared what she knew, tracing the dotted lines of Apollo and Sky's alliance, how she'd given her memories freely, how it had all been part of some larger plan. Yet Fynn and Lyra's tale had thrust the details into a new light, and as she talked a glaring truth emerged.

"I think I knew about the war – and the weapon," she said, looking at no one and nothing as the pieces slotted into place. "We were searching for a solution, something to stop them. Yet I couldn't do it from inside their ranks. I needed a way out."

"There's another explanation," Lyra cut in. Inching closer, she studied V as she continued, "You keep assuming you're the good guys, on some quest to save the ship. But what if you're wrong?"

"What are you talking about, Lyra?" Fynn said, just as confused as V. "Stop beating around the bush and come out with it."

"It's just as likely that you were part of the problem. You are, after all, an Altair." There was no venom in Lyra's words, only logic.

"You're the product of generations of power and prosperity," she continued. "The Echelon is practically your birthright. You had as much interest as anyone in seeing it survive – no matter the cost. Perhaps you and Apollo developed this weapon, then killed the senators to keep it quiet. We've all seen how capable you are on that front. But when the backlash got too fierce, you were forced into hiding. Then, after a year, your pal Apollo finally deemed it safe to continue."

A wave of emotion crashed through V's body, battering her thoughts against the rocks. Sky couldn't have done that. It was insane. No version of V could have held such cruelty, such a simmering desire for destruction.

Then again, nothing she knew could contradict it. That was the most painful part, the possibility of truth. Of course, relinquishing her memories seemed an exorbitant cost for such a ruse, but it was feasible. The simple fact was that she had no proof to dissuade them – or herself.

"Maybe you're right," she said, surprising everyone. "Maybe Sky wasn't the saint I've built her up to be. But it doesn't matter because that girl is dead. Sky gave up her life for me, and she's never coming back."

It was the first time V had said those words out loud, but the truth of them rang in her bones. For a year, V had hunted for the person she'd been and the life she'd left behind. She'd viewed this version of herself as temporary, a weigh station between where she'd been and where she was meant to be. As she'd once told Fynn, she was the space between pages – and Sky was the story.

Slowly and suddenly, over the course of a second and a year, everything had changed. It had changed when she'd met Mouse and Riyah, Leo and Asher. When she'd found her voice and began to sing. When her world had tilted and spilled her into Fynn and Lyra's laps. And when she'd realized that her memories might never come back.

She'd started out thinking she was lost, but maybe V was the person she was destined to find. *This* was who she was meant to be – not some senator's daughter or some heir to the throne. This *badass*, who was not defined by her past but rather the power she held to shape the future.

Sky was gone. Even if her memories came streaming back, she'd never be the girl she was. Because V had taken hold. She'd formed a life out of nothing and a family out of friends. She'd become her own storyteller, and it was time for her to write the next chapter.

"I hope Sky wasn't that person. I honestly do," V told the pair. "But either way, it doesn't change a thing. Because I'm still here. I don't know what that weapon is, but if it really has the power to start a war, then I need to do something. I won't stand by and watch. That's not who I am."

Fynn and Lyra stayed silent for a long time. V waited patiently despite the fact that her bruises throbbed and her accumulated injuries ached. She looked back and forth between the pair, suddenly longing for the power to read their minds.

For once, Fynn broke out of Lyra's shadow to speak first. His tenacity almost impressed her.

"We need her," he said, stating a fact rather than asking for permission. "She is the closest we've come to cracking this thing."

Lyra thought about it for a minute, then exhaled an exaggerated sigh. "Well, we've already told you too much. At this point we either have to trust you or kill you – and I don't feel like cleaning blood off the floors. Again. So I guess we're doing this."

V smirked, a strange sort of vindication rolling through her system. Lyra was starting to like her. She could feel it.

"Now that we have that settled," V said, her tone

brightening, "where do we start?"

Lyra responded by leaving the room. It was an odd reaction, and V looked to Fynn in question. The man simply shrugged, as if to say, "Your guess is as good as mine."

Lyra returned a moment later, her plastene screen held between bionic fingers.

"I have a theory," she said, placing the screen on the desk and flipping through its pages. "And now that you live amongst the elite, we can finally test it."

V wasn't sure she liked the sound of that. Yet this was what she'd signed up for, so she crowded closer, peering at the map on the screen.

It was the scan she'd taken of Apollo's study, complete with the surprise secret passage. Lyra zoomed in on the tunnel until grainy green dots rimmed its edges.

"For the longest time, I couldn't figure out why this was here," Lyra said, an energized lilt to her tone. "It's clearly not new, but rather something built into the building from the start. And it wasn't just placed there for fun. It has to lead somewhere, right?"

A couple of unenthusiastic nods greeted her from V and Fynn's separate spheres, but their lack of passion didn't faze her. She continued on, her voice getting louder and quicker as she approached the point.

"What if this tunnel is just one of many, a single outlet in a network of passages that span the sector? Think about it. Senators are suspicious. They don't always want eyes on their affairs. They crave secrecy, so they create a series of routes across the area, connecting labs and offices and homes. Allowing them to operate outside of the public eye."

"And Apollo didn't know about it, this secret senatorial highway with an on-ramp in his study?" V inquired, taking the role of devil's advocate.

"Maybe not," Lyra said with a shrug. "His term was relatively short, in comparison with someone like Celeste. And, judging from the manner of his death, he wasn't universally liked. It's possible he never knew it was there – or never thought it would be used in that manner. Or maybe he believed no one could access it but him. But it's irrelevant anyway. What matters is that you now have the chance to prove me right."

"Back up," Fynn said, clearly puzzled by his partner's train of thought. "While I'm all for boosting your ego, how will this help us? It's not like we're going to find their weapon stashed in one of these secret hallways."

"You think too small, Fynnrar," Lyra chided him. His scowl deepened at the use of his full name, and she smirked at how easy it was to torment him. "We're after access, and if this exists, it would be the perfect way to get around unseen. Presuming that V's espionage skills have improved along with her knack for combat."

V flashed through what she knew of her training, scanning for any lessons in stealth. As per usual, nothing clambered to the surface. However, she could have sworn a spark of something caught on the idea, so she nodded, beckoning for Lyra to continue.

"I say that we find a way into the tunnels, then use them to investigate our remaining suspects. Senator Griffyn, Captain Arctura, Corvus Huxley, and of course Sky's mother. Hopefully one of them will hold the key to solving this."

Lyra tried to breeze past the last name on her list, as if the mention would escape V's attention. It didn't. Yet from all she'd learned, she couldn't disagree. Celeste might be her mother, but she still had a motive and a vested interest in keeping the Echelon aloft. So V let it pass, sparing nothing more than a tight expression at the words.

"How do you plan to get inside?" V asked instead, forcing herself to focus on the details. "Another trip to Apollo's won't work. Not after last time."

She tried to stop herself from glancing at Fynn, but her eyes acted of their own accord. His eyes found hers at the same time, and the look they shared pulled her back to a less complicated time. A time before deceit had curdled their conversations. A time when hiding together in the shadows or nearly touching on a train brought a torturous sort of thrill.

V broke away before he could, directing her gaze at Lyra, who had disappeared behind the desk. She resurfaced an instant later in an agile bob, a familiar gray sphere clutched in her polished silver fingers.

"I have a feeling we won't have to go that far to find an entrance," she stated smugly. "If I'm right, then there should be entry points across the sector. All we have to do is find one." She wiggled the ball back and forth between her fingers before lobbing it at V. "You're lucky I had a backup."

V caught the scanner with a nimbleness that still surprised her. She closed her hand around it, running a thumb over its cool surface before pocketing it in the folds of her deep blue pants.

An idea bubbled beneath the surface, and she snapped

her attention back to Lyra, eager to keep things moving.

"If we found the first one in a study, why not start there?" she asked.

Lyra looked relieved, like someone was finally operating on her level. "And would the study in question belong to a certain senator by the name of Altair?"

V shrugged in a show of nonchalance. "I'll have to investigate her sometime. Might as well get it out of the way. And if she just so happens to have her own secret door to the senatorial underworld, then why not use it?"

The idea of investigating her own mother threatened to turn her stomach sour. Celeste was, after all, a formidable woman who wouldn't take kindly to someone rummaging through her life. She was also the only concrete link V had to her past.

V steeled herself, pushing back the yearning for connection and the desire to be a daughter. That wasn't her life. It wasn't her destiny. It was a fairy tale, and she needed to come back down to earth.

"I'll start tonight," she declared, covering her nerves with feigned conviction. "I assume you two will be taking up your usual seats in the viewers' box?" she asked, gesturing ever-so-slightly toward her implant.

"We wouldn't miss it for the world," Lyra said, flashing her teeth in an unsettling grin.

Then she took off in a whirlwind, accumulating gadgets to outfit V for her mission. It felt akin to being equipped for battle, save for the fact that none of the contraptions were capable of doing any real damage. While they could aid her in sneaking into spaces unseen, none could inflict injury or render her rivals unconscious. That particular burden fell to V.

It wasn't lost on her that she was going into the unknown alone. While Fynn and Lyra would be watching, they wouldn't be able to help, and if she was caught, they wouldn't be able to save her. Not again. Apparently that fact wasn't lost on them, either.

"Good luck tonight," Fynn whispered as she gathered her things to go, having already spent too much time away from her newfound home. "And thank you. For coming back, I mean. And agreeing to help."

"I'm not doing this for you," V said curtly – and it was true. She had her own motives, her own scores to settle. For the moment, though, their paths had aligned.

"I know," Fynn said quickly. "But I'm still grateful. *We're* still grateful."

"Yeah," V replied awkwardly, not sure what to say. "Me too." She held his gaze for a second too long before ducking out onto the sunlit street.

It took a handful of seconds for her eyes to adjust, but she didn't wait, barely missing a passing stranger before regaining her bearings. V felt more than ever like she needed to run, to push away her racing thoughts as her legs pushed her forward, but she knew a sudden sprint would only draw attention. So she reigned herself in, forcing her feet into a measured rhythm as she wove through the crowds.

Exhaustion tore at her, forcing its leaden fingers into her mind and across the arc of her shoulders. She massaged her temples as the reality she'd built once again cracked, flaking away under the burden of facts. A skeletal framework remained, and V gradually layered it back up, adding everything she'd learned.

The Echelon wasn't alone. There were other ships, other species, other planets packed to the brim with people. The universe was teeming with life. The enormity of that fact dwarfed her, casting her adrift like a speck of dust in the boundless reaches of space.

Yet somehow, it also thrilled her. While V was small in the scheme of things, she was anything but insignificant. She had the power to protect this fragile peace – and perhaps save the souls aboard the Echelon in the process. She didn't know how yet, but the mere idea gave her purpose, and she stood a little straighter as she walked.

Little by little, V sensed a change in the air. The weight of surreptitious stares and outright glares mingled with the whoosh of whispers to stop her in her tracks. She glanced around, catching the edges of eyes as people tried to turn away.

Even without sprinting through the streets, V had managed to draw attention – and she didn't like it. In a matter of days, she'd achieved a minor amount of infamy, and despite her sudden pardon, she was still a pariah in these social waters.

A bubble of space drifted around her as she began to walk, as if she were a magnet set to repel. After days of being chased and tracked, plastered on screens and pursued by Guards, it was unnerving to stand in the open and be seen – and even worse to stand alone and be feared.

V breathed through the knot that had rooted in her chest. They'd branded her a villain, but she couldn't let that stop her. Nothing she could say would change their minds, and nothing she could do would dissuade them. So she continued on, putting her hood up and her head down as she pushed through the throng.

The Senatorial Sector promised a modicum of relief, with the crowds of onlookers thinned by the selective scanner. Still, eyes followed and murmurs swirled and spit mysteriously found its way onto her suit.

When the elevator finally arrived at Celeste's doorstep, she felt bruised, as if the words and glares had dented the barriers she'd erected against the world. V took a minute to compose herself, wiping the harsh lines of strain from her face. She couldn't quite manage a smile, but at least she no longer brandished a scowl.

None of it mattered. The moment she crossed the threshold, coming face-to-face with her mother, surprise stole every ounce of her composure.

"Celeste!" V exclaimed, her voice pitching up an octave. Her heart beat out a staccato melody, and she tried to calm it, taking deep breaths as she backed against the solid steel doors.

"Where have you been?" Celeste demanded, full of righteous indignation. Her arms were crossed over an expensive ensemble, part winged vest, part sleek fitted shirt, all a deep, luxurious purple.

"I...left you a scry," V explained weakly, hoping her evasion wasn't as blatant as it seemed.

"Yes. I am aware," Celeste retorted. "You were looking for memories – but you're not going to find them out there. Or am I wrong? Did everything suddenly come streaming back to you?"

Her mother's words were a slap in the face. V hadn't expected the sharp edge, nor the intensity. Not knowing what else to do, she shrugged.

"No, mother," she said dutifully. "They didn't come back."

"That's what I thought," Celeste sneered. "You're broken, and gallivanting around the Echelon isn't going to change that. This kind of damage requires a doctor, and I've called one to come look at you tomorrow morning."

"I don't need…"

"No," her mother said with a wave, cutting her off. "You've had a day to find yourself, and you've failed. Now it's time for my measures. I want my daughter back. Not this *girl* who sings silly songs, sleeps with unwashed bartenders, and gets herself thrown into prison for slaughtering Guards. I'm sure your life has been difficult these past few months, and you did what you had to to survive, but that's done. You don't need to be this person anymore. It's time for Sky to come home."

A ferocity clawed its way up V's throat, begging to be released, but she swallowed it down. This was not the time to fight, nor the sword she wished to die on. This was a mother desperately seeking her daughter, and V didn't have the heart to tell her that Sky was gone. No number of doctors could fix her because she wasn't broken. In fact, she was exactly who she needed to be.

V tamed her scowl into a straight line and nodded. "Of course, mother," she replied. "Whatever you say. Now if you'll excuse me, I've had a long day, and I'd like to get some rest."

She strode past Celeste and turned the corner toward

her room, breathing a sigh as the glare of the spotlight faded. She felt flattened and thin, a façade without form or substance. Celeste's words had reduced her to a husk, and the woman's disappointment burrowed its way to her core.

V would never be the girl Celeste had raised, and her future could never be the one she'd envisioned. V's choice to turn her back on Sky had cemented that in stone. Celeste had lost her daughter, yet she held onto hope like it would save her. The least V could do was play along.

Still, V didn't want some doctor poking around in her head. The last time someone had tinkered with her thoughts, things hadn't quite gone as planned. V needed to keep her wits about her and her remaining memories intact if she hoped to discover anything about the Senate.

The reminder of her mission was oddly calming. Despite the danger, it promised a reprieve from the stress of Celeste's gaze, and V found herself looking forward to it. She couldn't wait to test Lyra's theory, to poke and prod at the seams of this world until something gave. Except she couldn't exactly do it with Celeste stationed outside.

So V bided her time, taking scans of her space on the off chance that it held a secret – which it didn't. The walls were solid, the floors unyielding, and the door the only means of escape. It was a fortress, a stronghold, a cell.

V waited – past curfew sirens and calls for dinner, until the lights went out around the house. Then she waited some more, falling in and out of a fitful sleep as the Echelon drifted deeper into the night.

Two words woke her, branding themselves on her eyelids and beckoning her back to life: "It's time."

Chapter 24

Violet was out of bed before the Eos clan could type again. Their two-word wakeup call was a shock to the system, enough to rouse her from sleep and send her straight into spy mode. In less than a minute, she was dressed in the deepest black and perched by the door, listening for any hint of movement. But the world was silent.

She crept into the hall with the lightest steps, aided by soft black shoes that seemed designed to muffle the sound. V had found them in her closet alongside the garb, conveniently placed there for such a purpose, as if her wardrobe could predict her wishes.

Naturally, the door to Celeste's study was locked. The woman didn't seem the type to trust, even when it came to her own daughter. V wouldn't be surprised if the front door was locked, as well, secured by some secret code or biometric key to hold her captive.

V fished the number pad from her pocket and affixed it

near the handle, pressing the green button with more force than she'd intended. The contraption did its thing, thinking for a beat before bypassing the door's defenses. V pocketed the pad with the ease of a thief, this time intending to keep it.

She squeezed inside, guided by specks of blue light from the hall, only to find herself shut in suffocating darkness. She felt along the walls until she found the panel, swiping the lights to life and bringing the brightness to just above a glow.

A desk floated in the center of the space, held aloft by air and a magnetic sort of magic. Around her, a set of glossy screens ringed the room, running from the wooden floors to the flat black ceiling. The tech was clean and stark, the type that could transform the space and transport the user in the blink of an eye. With it, Celeste could be anywhere, with anyone, plotting anything.

Incriminating evidence, however, was thin on the ground. There were no logs or journals or documents to describe her affairs, only a sleek plastene screen. It sat in the center of the desk, but as V tried to turn it on, she found her efforts thwarted. Its data was cloaked by encryption, hidden by an algorithm which V could never crack. Even with Lyra's prowess and detailed commands, it would take far too long to topple.

Sighing, V pulled the orb from her pocket and set it on the desk, activating its core. Just like before, the green light roamed around the room, its tentacles probing every crack and crevice. The scanner seemed to take its time, the seconds spanning eons as it searched. Then all at once, its embers died, leaving a suffocating stillness.

It felt quieter than before, although nothing had

changed. V prowled around the room, waiting for the findings, using motion to quell her doubts. It didn't work. Soon enough, though, a message appeared, scattering her worries to the wind.

"I told you so."

Lyra's smug voice screamed from behind the words as V read them once, then again. The tension that had gripped her chest and held her airways captive began to loosen, and she took a steady, centering breath as she waited for more. This time, it didn't take long.

Instead of words, a picture painted in green consumed her vision, overlaid on the world like a second skin. As V moved, it moved with her, the millisecond of delay making it strangely unsettling. She stumbled, colliding with the desk before course correcting and inching toward the wall, hands outstretched.

V didn't know what she was looking for, with the space before her laid out like a gallery of crisscrossed lines. She wanted to ask, to admit defeat and beg for help, but Lyra was already on it.

"To your left," came the command. Followed quickly by, "It's not on the ceiling. Look down."

V trained her vision on the spot Lyra had indicated, just managing to make out the lines of a hallway hidden behind a solid wall. The moment she spotted it – and uttered an unintentional "aha!" – the emerald overlay vanished, flattening the world back to its familiar form.

With the scan gone, V could see no way through and no sign that a passage even existed. Her hands naturally gravitated toward the wall, scanning the screen for anomalies. Yet the surface was smooth and static, unyielding and unwilling to give up its secrets.

"I could use some help," V muttered beneath her breath, spinning around slowly in search of a clue. "Is there a code word or a key? What am I missing?"

Lyra thought for a beat, no doubt processing V's scan and parsing through its details. V imagined Fynn beside her, pointing out every blip in a bid to be helpful, and her chest constricted.

A moment later, the words "Check by the desk" appeared in her eyes, and she obeyed, turning around to examine the suspended surface. She bent low as her hands roamed its plain, sweeping across its shell before dipping over the edge. Her fingertips snagged on a notch hidden just out of sight, and elation mingled with excitement as she pressed it.

At first, nothing happened. The world stood still and the room remained quiet as V stood, not daring to move or breathe or speak. Then all at once a grinding sound grew from the silence as the wall beside her sprang to life. One of the lofty screens shuddered, then began to slide, rotating to grant her access to a tunnel.

All V could see was stairs, dropping downward into the darkness where they petered out of sight. V craned her neck to peer inside, but the shadows hid its secrets, concealing any Guards or traps that protected the passage.

"What are you waiting for?" It was the same question V was asking herself, but Lyra was the first to voice it.

"Don't rush me," V muttered beneath her breath, ever the contrarian. "Just do your job and steer me toward the target."

Lyra readily complied, delivering her first set of directions. "Straight. Down. Go."

V took a deep breath, bracing herself, before setting off into the shaft. As soon as she was safely ensconced, the screen swung shut behind her, trapping her in the tunnel. Just as the thought of retreating swelled in her mind, a series of lights sputtered to life, illuminating a few feet of the passage. Taking a tentative step, then another, she watched as the lights responded, brightening the path before her while extinguishing the trail behind.

Slowly, V crept down the stairs, which descended several stories before leveling off. With Lyra's guidance, aided by a map of the city, she navigated a set of sharp turns and stick-straight corridors before stopping outside a blank steel door. If the coordinates in her head were right – and Lyra assured her they were – this was the home of their first mark: Senator Rigel Griffyn.

The man had held his seat since before any of them were born. He knew the people aboard the Echelon, the political landscape, the ins and outs of the Policies. Surely he had to know what the Senate was planning. Surely he had to be a part of it.

V used Lyra's lock pick to steal her way inside, listening at the crack before slipping through. As if on cue, the door closed, sealing her into the senator's space.

Once again, it was an office. And once again, most of the walls were appointed with sprawling screens. Most, but not all.

On one side of the room, a bookshelf soared, stocked to the brim with promising pages. Without waiting for her cue,

V dove at the stacks, ripping out a tome and plunging in.

Unfortunately, it was less secrets than sums. Strings of numbers, tabulated and calculated, met her eyes – before quickly sending them crossing. V fetched another book, then another, her disappointment mounting with each volume.

"There's nothing here!" she hissed to her colleagues through the comms. "It's just numbers. No weapon designs or meeting notes or plans. Just pointless numbers!"

"Numbers are never pointless," Lyra typed, clearly of a different mind. "Take your time. Catalog everything. This could come in handy."

V seriously doubted that. Yet she did as she was told, grumbling all the while. For what felt like hours, she pored over pages and ledgers, looking but not seeing. When she finally closed the last cover, she was tired and aching, her limbs stiff from spending so long on the hard ground. And she was pissed. She leveraged herself up and cast her sights around, hunting for her next mark.

Except there was nothing left to discover, save for a familiar plastene screen. V had half a mind to rip it from its housing and run, to claim the only thing that promised clues, consequences be damned. But her handlers promptly dissuaded her with a dose of common sense.

"We'll come back once we have a key to break their encryption," Lyra wrote in a poor attempt to placate her. "It'll take some time. For now, though, you have to go. It's almost morning, and I think Celeste will notice if you're gone."

V hated to admit defeat. Leaving felt like letting them win. She yearned to stay and search, to scour this room and the tunnels beyond it, but she knew Lyra was right.

Angrily, she found the lever beneath the desk and freed the door, stalking back into the passage. She could see her future in these halls, and it stoked the frustration that burned in her heart. By day, she'd be poked and prodded like a lab rat, and by night she would playact the vigilante who couldn't catch a break. Night after night, she'd find herself here, alone with the voices in her head. Until, of course, she was caught – or ran out of time.

"This was a shit strategy," she whispered to the empty air, which responded with quiet echoes. "We're not getting anywhere. We need a better plan."

"Stop spiraling," came the command, which felt like Fynn's doing. "It's only our first night. I know you're impatient, but uncovering what the Senate is up to is going to take some time."

Clearly. Fynn and Lyra had been at it for years without success. Maybe their foes were simply smarter. Maybe they'd left no trail to follow, just a maze with a multitude of dead ends.

Just as that terrible idea surfaced, the sound of footsteps began to echo from behind her, bringing her thoughts to a halt. She froze, glancing up and down the passage for an escape that didn't exist. All she could see were walls, which felt like they were closing in by the second.

She could try to run, but in such a place any sound would be a siren, revealing her presence. So V crept along as quickly as she dared, imploring her feet to stay silent and the walls to keep her secret.

"Why are you being so weird?" The words popped before her eyes in an instant, nearly startling her into a sound. She could feel Lyra behind her gaze, watching without the benefit of surround sound.

"I'm not alone," she breathed into the darkness. "There's someone else here. I'm trying to disappear."

Lyra's response was immediate. "DON'T."

"What?!" V hissed in surprise, but Lyra was already typing.

"Stay where you are and find a way to follow them. Maybe they'll lead us to a *better plan*."

Her own words came back to bite her in the ass. V should have expected that.

"How am I supposed to do that?" she asked, a hint of panic rising in her chest. It drove her heart to recklessness, releasing a symphony of drums beneath her ribs.

"You're the expert," said Lyra, passing the burden back to V. "But might I suggest not killing anyone this time?"

"I hate you," V reminded them with her last available whisper before noise became too precious to spare.

"I know," read the goading reply, sending V's ribs rumbling with a growl.

V stopped her spy-like shuffle and took stock of the passage. It was achingly bare, so narrow it felt constricting and dim to the point that she could barely make out the ceiling. Meanwhile, the figure kept coming, drawing nearer by the second with measured steps.

V's body took control before her mind could catch up. Putting the pieces together, it landed on a solution, then sprang into action. Before V knew it, she was hurtling forward, her quick steps tapping in the quiet passage. Then she was in the air, using the light wells as leverage as she began to scale the walls.

She capitalized on the constricted space, switching her weight from one side to the next as she rose. Soon, the ceiling came within view, and V crawled inside its curve, bringing her legs up to straddle the space. Her core stiffened as she fixed her arms and legs to the walls and pushed, drawing power from their stability.

"OK, that was cool," Lyra admitted, clearly impressed.

Her outright ogling gave V a small sliver of satisfaction. Unfortunately, she had precious little time to enjoy it. The lights, which had dropped into darkness at her departure, sprang to life once more, bringing her new companion into stark relief.

Even from above, she recognized his short-cropped salt-and-pepper hair, the proud set of his shoulders, and his official gray robes. It was Senator Rigel Griffyn.

V's abs began to buckle, and she muffled a groan, struggling to keep hold of her perch. Thankfully, the senator seemed preoccupied, striding forward like a man on a mission. He didn't look up or around, confident that no one could possibly break into his bubble and spy on him from above.

V, on the other hand, was doing just that, ignoring the ache in her core as she strained to stay put. She watched as Rigel passed beneath her, fading once more into the dying light. Then she dropped, barely managing to break her fall by bouncing awkwardly off the walls.

She was surprised when no lights turned on – and no senators came scurrying at the sound. But, she supposed, they both had better things to do. As did she. Picking herself up and dusting herself off, V followed in the senator's footsteps, hanging far enough back to stay out of sight.

The man wheezed as he walked, clearly winded, yet he plodded through the corridors with ease. Each twist and turn was thoughtless, a matter of memory rather than choice. He knew where he was going, and he knew what he would find when he got there.

In contrast, V was a jumbled ball of adrenaline and anxiety, rolling along in his wake. Her heartbeat roared in her ears as she crept, and she clung to the sinister silence. Deeper and deeper they dove, until all sense of direction disappeared, casting her adrift in this endless sea with a single point of light.

V lost track of Rigel as the turns grew quicker, forcing her closer. The danger intensified until it sang, sweet and intoxicating in her veins.

Her prey slipped around a corner, then another, vanishing from view. When V finally caught up, she found him stationary, pressed against a wall with his hand outstretched. Yet there was no door, no knob, and no trace of anything other than a dead end.

Suddenly, a ghostly specter appeared in midair, a keypad composed of mist and light. V blinked, unsure what she was seeing and uncertain of its purpose. Yet Rigel knew what to do. With startling swiftness, he typed in a sequence, inputting some secret code.

The apparition vanished, revealing a doorway that hadn't been there a second before. Rigel stepped through it and V moved to follow, but it slammed shut in her face with a muted rumble. She cursed at the air, at the wall, at the floor, searching for a way through.

"Just do what the senator did," came Lyra's condescending words, amplifying V's annoyance until it hummed.

"I didn't see what he did. If I had, don't you think I'd have done it by now?"

V could almost feel Lyra sigh as she read the woman's reply. "Of course you saw. You just weren't paying attention."

V had no words, only a growl and a grimace, but it was enough to get her point across.

"Your retinal implant recorded it," Lyra clarified – likely with some help from Fynn. "Just give us a second to replay it."

V didn't have to wait long. After less than a minute, the commands came through, directing her to the proper place to push. The spectral pad sprang up at her touch, inviting her to play. With steady hands, she typed in the code, freeing the door from its prison and watching it fold open before her.

V found herself standing atop steel, looking down into the darkness. There was no sign of Rigel, only a thin walkway framed by railings and crowned by a mess of pipes and cables. It felt industrial, like the entrance to a factory, only V couldn't tell what they were making.

A few feet ahead, the catwalk changed to stairs, leading her down. There were lights below and the echo of voices, but they faded as she approached, drifting into the distance and leaving her alone to take in the scene.

Except she wasn't alone. In fact, she was far from the only person present.

Windows lined the walls, looking out into crowded rooms, each cradling the impossible: children. More children than she had ever seen in one place.

Without conscious thought, she gravitated forward, fingers splayed against the glass. Inside, teenagers sat in rows, confined to desks. Yet this classroom held no teachers, only screens, which blasted images to blank eyes. The sight made V's skin crawl.

The next cube was just as cruel. Preteens sat beside weapons, their hands a blur as they assembled guns against the clock. Their fresh faces were empty as they created and destroyed, practicing ad nauseam for some deadly game.

Next door, 10-year-olds trained with sticks that were sharpened like knives, dealing bruises and bloodshed as men with white coats watched. Beyond that, toddlers practiced puzzles as wires monitored their minds, tracking patterns and trends.

And on and on and on. The rooms disappeared into the distance, with no end in sight. They must have held thousands, from birth through adolescence, all trapped inside this endless trance.

"What the hell are we looking at?" Lyra typed, tearing V's attention away.

V knew. She desperately didn't want to, but she knew.

"It's the weapon," she whispered.

"How can you be sure? This doesn't look like any weapon we've seen."

V scanned the row of windows, feeling the stick in her palm, the gun in her grasp, the screen and its messages in her mind.

"Because I'm one of them," she confessed.

Chapter 25

"Violet, talk to us. Tell us what you know."

Only she couldn't. Because the world was collapsing around her, and she had to get out.

Air eluded her grasp, leaving her lungs to burn, and each gasp sent her deeper into the spiral. The floor rose up to meet her as she tried to move, with splinters of memory confusing her thoughts and clouding her vision.

Flashes of childhood raced across her mind, looking eerily similar to the scene before her. The only difference was that she was alone, forced to endure the trials and training as a lone soldier instead of a squadron. The memories were thick and viscous, like a sticky sludge trying to hold her back from the truth, but she pressed on, straining to see more.

From behind adolescent eyes, she looked down into small hands to see weapons, their tips sharp and their barrels loaded. She watched herself study the components, piece together the parts, and wield them with a mastery that no child should possess.

All the while, an audience looked on, inspecting her progress from afar. They took notes, measurements, even blood, their manner clinical and cold. She saw tubes snaking from her arms, electrodes plastered to her temples, shackles holding her down. She felt hands poke and prod, the stinging pain of syringes, and the unwelcome touch of someone else's thoughts being buried in her mind.

The Senate and their scientists had built her into a soldier and brainwashed her into compliance. They'd boosted her skills by tinkering with her cells, then twisted her mind until violence was all that she knew. She'd emerged as their perfect little weapon, smart enough to play the spy yet programmed to never ask questions.

Then they'd sent her out to do their bidding. When V looked down at Sky's hands again, she saw blood. The realization made her want to retch.

Sky was an assassin, a hit man. She had killed cleanly and quickly, before most of her targets even realized she was there. She'd claimed senators and civilians without a second thought. And when she was done, she'd returned to her masters, who'd wiped her mind and set her back to a clean slate. So no one could ever access the memories and so guilt would never mar her missions.

Except her programming had gone wrong. She'd started to remember – what she'd done, what she was – and she'd sought out Apollo to save her. And to stop her.

Only the man couldn't untangle who she was from what they'd made her, so he'd stolen it all, taking her memories and martial prowess in one fell swoop. It was the only way to ensure that they couldn't control her, he'd said, the only way to set her free.

Apollo had promised to return, to restore her past and proficiencies so they could shut down the Senate's plans. Yet first he'd needed to parse through the code in her mind and the cypher in her cells and extract the Senate's conditioning. Instead of the months he'd imagined, though, the work had taken a year. In the meantime, he'd left her empty, save for a new name and her nightmares.

V thought back to the demons that had haunted her sleep. She envisioned the faceless figures slicing her skin, the beautiful people dripping with blood, the devils who made her dance. Those nightmares weren't merely creations of her subconscious, but warnings, threats from the waking world that had wormed their way into her dreams. They were fragments of Sky straining to get through and warning her to stay away.

Yet V had ignored them. Night after night, she'd disregarded the darkness in search of herself, groping around obstacles she'd placed in her own path.

"They made me kill," V finally stammered, answering one of the ten questions that had scrolled before her eyes. "They used me to clean up the streets and dispose of anyone who disagreed with them."

Lyra was quick to ask for more. "Who's *they*?"

"The Senate. Celeste." The words and the pictures they produced slashed at the protective layer surrounding her heart, revealing questions she could never answer.

How could Celeste have done that to her own daughter? She'd trained Sky up not to take her place, but rather to take lives, to be a mindless weapon in a one-sided war. How could someone who was supposed to care be capable of such cruelty?

V's thoughts flew to Riyah, as they so often did, and her heart burned. Riyah's love was boundless, bottomless, fierce. Unlike Celeste, she would fight until her last breath to keep her children safe.

Except she didn't have a choice, not in this. None of them did – not the children in this place, the mothers robbed of their memories, or the families who would never be full. Families like Fynn's.

Was his sister here, trapped in this hell? Was Riyah?

V was on her feet before she could fully consider her plan. The words before her eyes were washed of meaning by a deluge of resolve, which drowned out all other thoughts. A clarity so pure that it transcended reason overtook her senses and drove her forward, with a single mission in her mind: to save Riyah and to stop this tyranny once and for all.

She stumbled into a run, her legs waking up as her brain shifted into gear. V didn't know where she was going, but she followed the curve of classrooms past countless more atrocities, praying it would lead her to the core. Each step fueled the fire that blazed in her chest, the wrath that demanded revenge.

Lights flickered on as night gave way to day, illuminating the evils taking place behind the glass. Children lay stock-still on tables, asleep or sedated, with needles in their arms and monitors beeping away. Others sat bleeding from accidents and injuries, their eyes dull from drugs and their screams swallowed.

"WHAT THE HELL ARE YOU DOING?" Lyra typed in all caps, tearing V's attention away. "You're going to get yourself killed."

"If that's what it takes, then so be it," V snarled through clenched teeth, never slowing. "Either way, this ends now."

She put on a burst of speed, rounding the corner into a room filled with blinking machines and a myriad of black-and-white screens. And several extremely startled people.

They looked up in unison at her entrance, all wide eyes and open mouths. V, too, stopped in her tracks, realizing in that instant that she was weaponless. Weaponless, but not powerless.

A split second later, she was in motion, hurling her body toward the nearest target. He was a round man, dressed in the garb of an Iridium Guard, with nonexistent eyebrows to match his nonexistent hair. V flung him to the ground with a single kick and watched as his body undulated with the impact. Easily evading his flailing arms, she brought her boot down on his neck, crushing his windpipe with a painful crack. Before anyone else could reach her, she scooped up his blade and set herself up for a fight.

With the lies of her life washed clean, V's movements flowed, fluid, precise, and deadly. She'd been built for this, conditioned for this, destined for this, and she was determined to use every ounce of her training to take these monsters down.

A dark-haired woman in a lab coat charged next, followed by an angry-looking fellow with too many teeth. The woman held a knife, while the man seemed intent on tackling her to the ground in a bear hug that held no warmth.

V side-stepped the man with impressive speed before twisting to the woman's side. A slash to the gut cut cleanly through her coat, drenching it in rough splashes of red. She cried out but kept her balance, retaliating with a sloppy thrust toward V's heart. V parried, expertly knocking the blade from her grasp.

To her credit, the woman didn't buckle. She merely growled, showing pink gums and pearly teeth, before lunging forward with her hands outstretched, hoping to choke V into submission. V reacted out of instinct, slamming her assailant's arms to her sides before plunging a knee into her stomach.

By then, the toothy man had recalculated, and he came at her from behind, wrapping his arms around her chest in another hug – clearly the only move he could think of. V's conditioning kicked in, and she dropped her weight down, straining his arms before kicking back toward his knee. She made contact, hearing a satisfying crunch as something gave. He teetered, then fell, freeing V from his grip and giving her time to spin. Her blade swiped cleanly across his neck, but his gurgle of pain was lost as V retrained her sights on her final foe.

The woman had managed to reclaim her blade, but the sight of her comrade crumpling to the ground temporarily stunned her. V didn't wait for the cogs to click back into place. She billowed forward, the dagger clutched so tightly that she could feel its outlines etching themselves on her palm. With a backhanded swing, she steered the knife toward the woman's chest, eager to end it.

Yet V's strike met with empty air as the woman stirred

at the last second, then pedaled into reverse. The sudden movement sent her off balance, however, and she screeched as the floor fell out from beneath her.

V was astride her before she'd even struck the ground. Despite its convenience, she discarded her blade, rocking forward to fasten her hands around the woman's throat. Something inside of her called for it, demanded it, like a voice she could almost hear.

When the woman had gone still, V released her and tottered toward the bank of screens. She had no clue where to start or how to make the strings of code obey her commands. Fortunately, she had someone on her side who did.

Unfortunately, it didn't look like she was going to get the chance to ask.

A squadron of Guards stormed in, their weapons trained on V. She should have expected it, should have known there would be more men standing in her way. She sighed and consigned herself to another round of bloodshed.

The first sonic blast tickled the hairs on her arm as she flung herself off the spot and somersaulted toward the crew. The next one missed her by a mile. By the time they realized that no man's aim was a match for V's momentum, she was already on them, the blade suddenly back in her hand.

Their armor was tough, but the men inside were much less sturdy. Once V found the soft spots skirting the edges of their breastplates and the curve of their groins, it was all too simple to slash and strike until the room ran red with blood. The men managed to scratch at her arms and bruise her body, but their blows were harmless, mere annoyances amidst the rush of adrenaline.

Then a familiar face appeared amongst the crowd. It brought V up short, allowing her attacker to affix his arm around her neck and pull her against him. V's body took control as her mind whirled, and she dropped low before bucking the man over her shoulders and onto his back. She kept hold of his arm and twisted, feeling it pop out of place as he groaned.

In her moment of reprieve, V glanced up, hunting for Celeste. The woman was there, stone-faced and silent, staring down at her daughter through a mess of bodies and blood. V yearned to make her talk, to force her to answer for her crimes. Yet Celeste had other plans.

With a stiff movement, she nodded at someone stationed behind V, giving them a signal she couldn't read. V spun, regarding the soldiers with unease. But instead of guns, they met her with syringes. Then she heard Celeste's voice, loud and clear through the commotion.

"There's no use fighting, my dear. You can't win. You may as well surrender."

"Go to hell!" V gritted out, aware that it wasn't overtly clever yet unable to summon a wittier retort.

Celeste ignored her. "I might as well thank you, though. You saved us the trouble of dragging you down here. I was going to let the doctor do it when he stopped by, but you stumbled upon it all on your own. Such a good little girl. Now drop the dagger and come quietly. We'd hate to have to damage government property."

The words went over V's head, then circled back around to bury themselves in her brain.

"Property? That's all I am to you people? Property?!"

"No, of course not," Celeste said with a snicker. "You're very valuable property. One of a kind, in fact. That's why we're so delighted to have you back."

V saw red – beyond the slicks of blood that drenched her hands. She was no one's possession, no one's weapon, and she would die before she let them control her.

This time when she leapt, her brain and her body worked in tandem to take her opponents down. She dropped and spun and sliced through the air, evading hands and bodies and needles. Her sights were set on Celeste, and she ached to make the woman pay.

Before she could sink her claws into Celeste's chest, however, she felt a shallow prick break the skin of her back. A handful of heartbeats was all it took for her limbs to go numb. V dropped to the floor in a heap of fury and desolation, watching the world gradually fade to black.

Chapter 26

There were no nightmares lurking in the spaces between consciousness. Lyra would say that it was due to the poison they'd plunged into her system, but V knew better. She knew that nightmares couldn't come for you when you were already in one.

The first thing she knew was pain. The second was paralysis. Although this time it wasn't in her bones but in the bonds secured across her body, holding her down. She could move her fingers, her lips, her eyelids, yet her body remained trapped against the table, stubbornly incapable of fight or flight.

V peeked through squinted eyes to see a room shrouded in shadow and peppered with vague shapes, all inorganic and ominously medical. The entire space radiated a quiet menace, as if it might come alive at any second and eat her whole. Yet for the moment it waited, biding its time and feeding on her tension.

V peeled her eyes open the rest of the way, scanning for threats. Except everything was still – the machines, the medical instruments lined up perfectly in rows, the mirrors ringing the room. She was alone, imprisoned in a sterile cell somewhere inside the Senatorial Sector.

V writhed and strained, testing the strength of the straps that held her until they groaned, yet they didn't give. Her body ached from the effort, while her head pounded out the seconds in perfect time. As her attention rose from her body to her brain, she noticed the wires attached along her scalp, silently monitoring her mind. V whipped her head back and forth, attempting to dislodge them, but they held tight, staunchly refusing to budge.

She couldn't tell how long she'd been there, lying like a corpse on a slab. There was no light and no line separating night from day, only darkness, which devoured seconds and swallowed hours whole. In the absence of anything, V was left to contend with her thoughts.

She had failed. It was glaringly apparent. Her efforts to sabotage the Senate and save Riyah had come to nothing, and she had only herself to blame. She'd wound up right where she'd started, a puppet back in the hands of its masters, and they'd happily seized control of her strings. They would kill her or wipe her memories and set her back to a default state. Either way, this was the end.

At least Fynn and Lyra had their answers. At least they knew the truth. They could take what they'd learned to the Alasia and claim the credit. And what would their leaders do? Declare war? Wait to see if the Echelon struck while amassing their armies? Kill these children and their creators in hopes of advancing peace?

There was no ending where everyone lived. This story had no happily ever after. There would be bloodshed and casualties and chaos aboard the Echelon – but at least V wouldn't have to watch it burn. There was a small kind of solace in that.

The hiss of a door met V's ears, and she tensed, her muscles turning rigid as she braced for the end. She expected Guards, doctors, the entire Senate to storm in. Instead, she got Celeste, smiling sweetly down at her daughter.

"I'm sorry it's come to this," she said, motioning at V's restraints. "But soon you'll be back to your old self, and this will all be some distant dream."

So they didn't plan to kill her after all. They planned to steal her memories and brainwash her back into the assassin she'd been. The thought made V's stomach lurch.

Celeste continued, her voice light and upbeat. "Of course, we hoped that your programming would reassert itself without the need for...intervention. But Sky is clearly not coming back to us on her own. So here we are. Don't worry, though. You're in good hands."

"Why?" V breathed, barely above a whisper. She took a breath and said, stronger, "Why are you doing this? Me, those children – what's the point?"

Celeste scoffed, brushing off the query. "Don't concern yourself with such things. It's not a weapon's place to comprehend war."

V bristled but bit her tongue, saving her strength for the questions that mattered. If Fynn and Lyra still had access to her implant, perhaps she could do one more bit of good before she was gone.

"Was this the point of the Policies all along?" she tried. "To build the Echelon an army?"

"Sadly, no," Celeste said breezily. "It was only a few years before you arrived that the Senate began to see the potential. Our ancestors just didn't have the vision. They were wasteful. Children are, after all, our future. And these children are going to help us secure ours."

V was getting somewhere, but she still couldn't see the big picture. So she tried a different tactic.

"I know you're running out of resources. Energy, food, fuel. We have, what, a few months left? A few years if you keep killing off the *dead weight*?"

Celeste was surprised, and the arch of her eyebrows gave V a sick sort of satisfaction.

"The little lackey has a brain!" she declared with mock amusement. "How did you figure it all out? Did Apollo help you connect the dots?"

V's train of thought derailed at the mention of the man. Celeste knew about her alliance with Apollo – and, most likely, she knew that he had helped Sky escape.

"You killed Apollo." It wasn't a question, and V didn't need her answer. If Celeste hadn't stabbed him herself, then she certainly knew who had, and that fact alone made her guilty in V's eyes.

"I never trusted that man," Celeste continued, unfazed by the accusation. "But he was harmless enough. Just another old man with his head in a book. Then you went missing and everything changed." Celeste picked up a scalpel and began fingering the blade.

"I have to hand it to you. You did a wonderful job of disrupting our plans. We had no idea where you'd gone or how you'd done it. You just disappeared, like magic."

Celeste circled around toward V's head, looking down at her with an inscrutable expression.

"Apollo changed after that. He disappeared, too, hiding himself away for weeks at a time. The Senate barely saw him, but that was no great loss. We kept an eye on him, though, and when he re-emerged – and suddenly began planning a party – we knew something was up."

V ached to voice the questions that consumed her mind, but she couldn't bear to break the flow of Celeste's story, so she kept her mouth shut.

"Naturally, there was no evidence linking the two of you, so we found some. We sent Guards to inspect his study while he was out at some club. They only found scraps – a few shots of you on his surveillance cam, a drop of your blood on a slide – but it was enough to place the two of you together. Then his colleague, Sabine, kindly helped confirm our suspicions."

The small upturn of Celeste's lips gave V chills. She didn't want to hear the rest, even as she hungered to know more.

"We'd had plenty of practice disposing of senators by that point, so it wasn't hard. Although you typically did the dirty work," Celeste chuckled. "This one was a little different. We wanted it to be public. We wanted to flush you out. I volunteered to do the honors."

So Celeste had been there that night, in the room with Apollo and V. She had been so close to Sky and she hadn't even known it.

305

"Why?" V asked again. "Why go through all that trouble for me? You already have an entire army of kids under your command."

"Because you were the first. The first one to live, at least, and not succumb to madness. You are our masterpiece. And inside your little head lies the key to turning those children into champions."

V's eyebrows acted of their own accord, furrowing down her face and tugging at the wires on her forehead. Celeste saw the question in her eyes and sighed.

"The Anomalies that survive make fine minions. They do what they're told, and they can hold their own in combat, but they're basically bots made of blood and bone. They don't have that creativity, that spark, that *killer* instinct. You do. You have the power to make people believe you, follow you, want you."

V thought about the love letter in her room, the one she'd found beneath the floorboards. The man behind it had been yet one more mark, just a mission she'd been programmed to lead. Her mind fluttered to the child's wrist cuff, and the implications made her shudder.

"We were so close to teasing out the parts that made you unique when you pulled your little stunt. We continued without you as best we could, using old scans and samples, but they were no match for the real thing. We needed you here, in the flesh, to forge our way forward."

V's thoughts started then stopped, stuttering in their attempt to process her words. She was the key, just like Fynn had said. She was the template on which their entire army was based. And without her, they were ruined. A beam of light streaked through the mist of her mind, and a tenuous hope took root.

"I hate to break it to you, *mom*," V said with a smirk, "but it's gone. All your programming and code. Whatever you planted inside my head. Apollo stripped it from my mind and erased it."

Celeste remained stubbornly unperturbed. "Silly girl. Apollo could never remove it completely. It's in your cells. It isn't just a part of you; it's who you are, your very essence. You are a creature of violence and vengeance, and nothing will ever change that."

V yearned to believe that wasn't true, that Sky and Violet were separate creatures who just happened to share the same soul, but she wasn't certain. There was a hunger in her even now, a desire for destruction that defied reason. Was that her or what they'd made her?

While V was parsing through her muddled thoughts, Celeste walked over to the mirrored wall and nodded. A moment later, the door swung open, ushering in a stream of strangers in lab coats.

"It may take some time to reboot you, but it's certainly not impossible. Unfortunately, though, it will be painful." Celeste didn't seem upset. In fact, she almost seemed pleased.

"You're a monster," V said, unable to stop herself. "How could you do this to your own daughter?"

"My daughter?" Celeste laughed, sounding surprised and painfully amused. "You are not my daughter. That was just your cover, a way to hide you in plain sight while we perfected you."

Celeste paused for a second to let her words sink in.

They settled in V's stomach like a leaden weight, pulling her down. V couldn't believe she hadn't seen it, hadn't realized the ruse. Now it seemed all too clear, stoking the embers in her chest until they sparked into an outright blaze.

"You are no one, nothing," Celeste continued, enunciating every word. "We found you in the gutter, dirty and starving, and gave you a purpose. We saved you. And now you're going to return the favor."

Hands descended on her from around the table, pinning her down. She writhed, reacting instinctively, but they held on tight, keeping her limbs flat and her neck straight. They could have dosed her, knocking her out with a drug, but they gave her nothing, content to see her suffer.

The sound of a saw sprang to life, buzzing too close to her ear. V couldn't see it, but she could feel the vibrations as it tore apart the air, slowly advancing.

She wanted to scream, to call for help, to beg, but all that came out was a whimper. She couldn't lose herself, not when she'd finally started to figure out who she was. She was Violet. She was strong and loyal and brave. She was a fighter. And she would hold onto that knowledge until they tore it from her body.

The first bite of the blade touched right above her eyebrow, ripping a scream from her throat. The pain was sharp and fierce, and blood trickled down her temples to saturate her hair. She could smell its metallic scent and feel the warmth of it running down her face, even as they mopped it from her brow.

In a matter of seconds, the saw struck bone and began its descent, slowing ever so slightly as the density changed.

Pinpricks of blackness poked holes in the scene, but V held on, struggling to keep herself together even as they tore her apart.

A sudden sound from the hall brought everyone to a screeching halt. A series of thuds shook the space, and confusion settled across their faces in familiar lines. Ever the general, Celeste was the first to react.

"Don't just stand there," she barked. "Go out and check!"

The lackeys in lab coats did as they were told, leaving V's side to investigate. Another round of noises ensued, landing somewhere between a racket and a clamor. The room seemed to shudder in response.

Celeste was clearly unhappy. She was about to send another set of surgeons into the hall when she was saved the trouble. V heard the door to the room tear open with a blast, ushering in a billow of grayish-black smoke.

From her inconvenient vantage point, V couldn't see who it was. She could, however, sense the confusion that radiated from the group as they processed the threat. Those precious seconds of inaction were all the assailant needed. A series of short, sharp blasts rocked the room and downed its occupants in rapid succession. Even Celeste fell, hitting the ground with a gratifying thud.

A second of silence lapsed as the smoke cleared. When the figure finally ventured around the table and entered V's vision, she balked, staring at the last person she'd ever expected to save her.

"Mouse?!"

Chapter 27

V was half afraid to blink lest Mouse disappear, like a dream conjured by her mind and sent to distract her from the pain. Except the subject wasn't exactly one she would have selected to star in her fantasies.

"What the hell are you doing here, Mouse?" she cried, failing to hide the note of scorn. She hadn't forgotten their last encounter – or what he'd done to her friend.

"I'm here to save you," he said like a white knight, all pompous swagger and showmanship. He shouldered his sonic blaster and waited for her thanks, but V was fresh out of gratitude.

"Forgive me, but that seems unlikely," she blurted, her tongue freed by the pain and adrenaline fighting for control of her brain.

"I understand you may be suffering from some blood loss," Mouse countered, "but I fail to see why this is so confusing. I'm here. I have a gun. The bad men are unconscious.

You're welcome."

"There are a few gaps in your story," V spat back, "but perhaps we could discuss them while you GET ME OUT OF HERE!"

"Of course, your majesty," Mouse said with a bow, his tone syrupy sweet.

He quickly cut through the band constricting V's chest, then considered the metal shackles around her wrists. There was no noticeable clasp or keyhole, so he wedged his fingers beneath one and began to pull. The effort produced no discernible effect, only a thin line of sweat that dotted his brow and a scowl that contorted his features.

"It doesn't look like your *muscles* are a match for this one, Mouse," V said, flicking her eyes across his scrawny form. "Perhaps a key fob would be more useful."

Mouse muttered unintelligibly but managed to extricate himself from the manacles before beginning his search. Naturally, he gravitated toward the Guards, rifling through their many pockets but finding nothing.

"Try the woman," V advised, inclining her head toward Celeste – then instantly regretting it. The move made her head pound, and a fresh wave of blood trickled over one eye, impairing her vision.

Mouse extracted a thin silver card from Celeste's breast pocket and brought it up to rest on the cuff. It released without a sound, and V relished the freedom, flexing her fingers before reaching up to touch her forehead. Her hand came away covered in blood, and the sight of it made her feel faintly sick.

"You're gonna have to stitch me up," V said, hating the

idea of needing his help but knowing it had to be done.

"I'm not the best with blood," Mouse replied with a grimace, refusing to look up as he freed the last of her limbs.

V groaned, rubbing her wrists. "You're terrible at this whole *rescuing* thing," she snarled, reaching up to remove the electrodes from along her hairline.

"Hey!" Mouse shouted. "I'm doing what I can. It's not like I volunteered for this mission!"

"Then why the hell are you here?" V asked, still confounded by his presence.

"It's kind of a quid pro quo situation," Mouse countered with his usual opacity. "Your friends made an offer I couldn't refuse."

V made a move to dismount from the table, but her head wasn't having it. Shadows swam at the edges of her vision, and her legs buckled beneath her.

"Damn it, woman!" Mouse growled, rushing to prop her up before pushing her back onto the table. "Can't you stay still for one second?"

"We have to go. We have to get out of here." The words were slurred as V's dwindling energy was diverted to keeping the lights on and her eyes open.

"Astute observation," Mouse bit back, "but we won't be going anywhere if you're unconscious. So just sit there and shut up, will you?"

V obeyed. It wasn't because she wanted to, but rather because her body wouldn't allow her to do anything else.

Mouse skittered away, then returned a moment later with a stitcher. Cringing, he dabbed at the wound with a wad of gauze, then fired up the wand.

Sticking his tongue between his teeth, he began to stitch her forehead back together. It was nothing like Fynn's gentle touch. This was jagged and clumsy – and would almost certainly leave a scar. Yet it did the trick, stemming the flow of blood to a trickle.

V's thoughts didn't clear completely, but the fog abated enough for her to form the semblance of a plan. She lowered herself to the ground, managing to remain upright, then scoured the bodies for key cards and weapons, confiscating both before shuffling toward the door. She looked back to find Mouse still standing by the slab.

"Come on!" she said, tilting her head. "We have to leave before that lot wakes up."

Mouse shrugged and reshouldered his weapon, pocketing the stitcher. Knowing their luck, V thought, the device could prove useful – although she wasn't about to commend his foresight. She still had too many questions.

"How did you escape from that cell?" she asked, checking the hall for company before easing out. With Mouse's help, she dragged the remaining Guards into the room and locked the door, hoping it would buy them some time.

"In the most dastardly, unthinkable way possible," Mouse said while they worked, his voice steeped in sarcasm. "They let me go."

V raised an eyebrow, turning around just long enough to get her question across. Then she set off, with Mouse tagging along in her wake.

"Once your *situation* cleared up, they had nothing to hold me on," he summarized. "They let me off with a warning and told me to go."

"That doesn't explain how you ended up *here*," V countered, gesturing around at their unfamiliar surroundings. She assumed it was part of the passages she'd discovered, but she had no way to know for sure. There were no lines of text from her cam, no helpful hints from Lyra to guide her back home.

V's confusion was cut short as Mouse seized command, guiding her through the stark white halls like he knew what he was doing. V followed warily, still puzzled by his presence but slowly piecing together the clues he'd dropped along the way.

Her friends. Quid pro quo.

"Fynn and Lyra sent you!" she all but shouted, clapping her hand over her mouth when Mouse turned around to stare.

"You finally figured it out, did ya? Took you a while," he sneered.

V felt a sudden surge of warmth as she realized what the pair had done. Yet something still didn't sit right.

"But why would they come to you? I mean, they know what kind of man you are." Even if V hadn't spelled it out for them, they'd seen it on her cam, witnessing his deception in real time.

"And what kind of man am I?" Mouse demanded, spinning around to face her. "The kind who would do anything for family? The kind who rescued you from the streets, gave you a place to live, then risked his life to save you? I might be the villain in your story, but did you ever stop to think that maybe you're the villain in mine?"

"What do you mean?" V asked, taken aback by his intensity. "What have I ever done to you?"

Mouse laughed a mirthless laugh. "You are so self-centered! You don't care about anyone other than yourself – your drama, your memories, your past. If you did, maybe you would remember that I wasn't the only one they took that night. I was, however, the only one they released."

A cold wave engulfed her as she processed the words. "Solamine," V whispered, appalled.

Mouse nodded. "They have him, and they plan to kill him. But thankfully, you're going to help me save him. Quid pro quo, remember?"

V had walked out of one fire and straight into another. "That seems like a lot to ask of a girl whose skull was exposed a minute ago," she grumbled. "Why did Fynn and Lyra even come to you in the first place? Why couldn't they do this themselves?"

"Because they needed my connections. They needed weapons. And it just so happened that I could hook them up."

"I still don't understand why you're here and they're not," V replied as they took off once more, rounding two corners before ducking behind a third.

"They're a little busy securing our way out of here," Mouse said, speaking slowly so she wouldn't miss it. "They're our way off this ship."

"What?!" V exclaimed, her too-loud voice echoing off the too-white walls.

A hand sprang up to cover her mouth, and suddenly Mouse was far too close. "Keep the hysterics in check," he commanded. "You didn't think we'd all just hide out on the Echelon like two-bit criminals, waiting for the Guards to find us, did you? Because if we stay here, there will be no safe place to hide. They will find us, and they will finish us off."

V knew he was right. As long as she was aboard the Echelon, she would never be safe – and neither would the people around her. There would always be Celeste, the Senate, the Guards. There would always be someone on her trail. She needed to disappear.

But first there was something she had to do, someone she had to save.

"Fine," she said, pushing Mouse's hand away. "I'm in. Where do we start?"

Mouse looked suitably relieved to hear her say it. He was, after all, not the fighting type. He'd gotten lucky in the lab, but from here on out he would need her – and he knew it.

"Now? Now it's time to do some damage."

"Then I certainly hope you've brought more weapons," V retorted, eying his lone blaster.

Mouse smiled, then opened up his coat to reveal a small arsenal. "Will this do?"

Chapter 28

It turned out that Mouse's plan was strangely similar to V's own. Find the hub, locate Solamine within the system, then blow some shit up. Hopefully in that order.

The first part was simple. The interconnected tunnels led them in a loop, which brought them back to central command – with only one or two *minor* obstacles along the way. V took care of them swiftly, falling back into the swing of things with ease, despite her injuries.

When they came to the core, V felt a swell of déjà vu, but she hardened herself, taking solace from the weapons and their strength. The now-familiar hunger hummed in her veins as they perched on the precipice, taking stock of the station and its crew.

V counted six souls inside – more than before but still not enough to stop them. Someone had cleaned up the blood and bodies and reset the scene, as if nothing traumatic had happened. As if nothing like that could possibly happen again. V would be happy to show them just how wrong they were. With a silent nod and a smile, the unlikely duo turned the corner and began to fire.

V took down two of their targets before the rest had time to react. Mouse downed an additional sentinel with startling accuracy before being driven back by a return volley. V, on the other hand, surged forward, easily evading the waves of force that shook the room.

Dodging a close-range blast, V dropped to the floor and slid forward, knocking the shooter's legs from beneath him. He fell hard and fast, landing beside V with a thud. She made her play, drawing a dagger from her belt and slipping it inside his ribcage like a sheath. His resistance came too late. By the time her hilt reached bone, blood drenched her hand and his eyes had started to lose their sheen. She didn't wait to see the rest.

V sprang to her feet just as a boot came down where her head had been. An accompanying snarl from her other side alerted her to a second assailant, who had come to surround her with a show of force.

Both men were pure muscle, easily outweighing V by a hundred pounds. They could have been twins, save for the hair, which one man had grown long and the other had shaved to the skull. They circled her in unison, as if they were of one mind with one motive: to kill her as quickly as they could.

They moved at the same moment, surging in more swiftly than V had expected. The bald one captured her arms while the other reared to strike, letting loose a series of blows that left her breathless.

A sudden wave of force shocked her long-haired assailant out of his trance, sending him staggering. V seized the chance, smashing her head back into the other man's skull and spinning out of his grasp.

Blood spurted from his broken nose, but all it did was make the bald man more menacing. He looked like a carnivore straight from a kill, with red dye painting his teeth and dripping from his chin. He bared blood-drenched fangs and tore a blade from his belt, intent on finishing the fight.

With a growl, he barreled forward like a bull, fire in his eyes and his arms flapping. V sidestepped at the last second, meeting his aggression with agility. He attempted to turn but found himself surrounded by a puddle of blood, which slicked his steps. He stumbled, then slipped, dropping to the ground in an utterly ungraceful flop.

V appeared beside him with an easy slide and slashed cleanly across his neck, adding another surge of blood to the river at her feet.

The sole remaining Guard let loose a guttural roar. V spun, surprised to see the long-haired man still standing, albeit with his right arm hanging uselessly at his side.

She clocked the gun in his grasp right before it erupted. The blast should have struck her straight on, killing her instantly, but it didn't. Instead, the off-handed blow missed her by mere inches, shoving V back but leaving her body intact.

The Guard knew it was over the instant their eyes connected. V was across the space in the span of two heartbeats, ripping the gun from his hand. At point blank range, she pulled the trigger, bracing herself for impact as the body before her fractured and tore.

The sudden silence was heavy, but true to form, Mouse broke it with his easy banter.

"That was savage," he said with a whistle, skimming over the destruction. "Your talents were wasted as a singer."

"You sound like my mother," V said without thinking, immediately regretting the statement. Celeste had never been her mother, only her captor. That realization filled her with a white-hot rage, which took a conscious effort to corral.

Mouse zeroed in on the bank of screens, his hands flying across the switchboard. V mirrored his movements, accessing the station's records with the help of their pilfered keys.

"I found him," Mouse declared after a minute. "He's still alive. We just have to...wait, what are you doing?" Mouse's mouth finally stopped as he focused in on V.

"I'm changing the arrangement," V informed him. "I'll help you save your grandfather *after* we fix the damage you've caused." She watched his face fall as he processed her plan.

"Riyah?" Mouse squeaked like his namesake creature, all anxiety and tension.

"Yes, Riyah," V confirmed, delighted to see that her words had made an impact. He deserved that weight on his shoulders, that guilt that burrowed into his soul. "Sound like a deal?"

The question was purely rhetorical, yet Mouse nodded anyway, swallowing his resistance and accepting his fate.

"Good," V barked like a leader in battle. "Then we better get going."

Without another word, they did just that, although not without leaving a few tokens of their regard, courtesy of Mouse's cache. The small explosives, placed artfully around the room and set to detonate upon entry, were sure to wreak havoc on the senators and their Guards – while hopefully destroying some rather important data in the process.

With their land mines set, the duo departed in search of Riyah. This time, V took the lead.

The halls were impossibly still and insufferably quiet, as if they hadn't heard the war being waged just beyond their reach. V expected enemies around every corner, an army at every door, but they remained alone, their path unhindered by obstacles.

By the time they reached Riyah's room, V was all but buzzing with suspicion. It was too easy, too calm. V didn't trust it. One look through the window, though, and V's mind was wiped clean.

"Oh," was all she could think to say, the dread in her veins solidifying into shock. "Fuck."

Rows upon rows of beds were laid out in a grid, stretching across the room and continuing into the next. Each was occupied, with a woman draped in white lying stationary on its surface and a monitor beeping merrily beside her. It was a lifeless infirmary, a deathless morgue, an in-between place that was made to be forgotten.

V shook herself from the numbness and back into feeling. She let the rage consume her, let it drive her through the door and across the rows until she found her. Riyah. Her friend's red hair acted like a beacon, reeling V in until she stood at Riyah's side, gazing at her frozen form.

She was peaceful and pale, and for some reason V couldn't bear to touch her, to drag her from dreams and back into this nightmare. Mouse, however, had no such qualms.

With a firm hand, he tugged the tubes from her arms and squatted down to stare. When she didn't immediately stir, he began to shake her.

"What are you doing?" V asked in a horrified whisper, pulling him back from the bed.

"I'm speeding this along," he said. "We don't have all day. Now help me sit her up so I can slap her."

V's appalled expression turned anxious when she caught a hint of movement from beneath the covers. She watched as Riyah's hand twitched, then her arm, then her eyelids. Suddenly, they flew open and she sat upright, grabbing Mouse by the collar.

"Whoa!" he shouted. "We've got a live one. Maybe you could put me down so we could finish saving you?"

A familiar fog rolled across Riyah's eyes then dissipated as she studied her surroundings. V could see the questions forming even before she asked them.

"Mouse? V? Where...where am I? What happened? Wait – Leo and Asher! Are they alright?"

"They're fine," V assured her. "And so are you. Don't worry. We're going to get you out of here."

Riyah brought her eyes up to rest on V's face, with relief and concern vying for control of her features. She looked so small in this place, so helpless, and V's heart couldn't help but break. She yearned to tear it all down, to uncage the demon in her veins and let it decimate everyone who had dared to hurt her friend.

As if sensing her thoughts, Riyah reached out, clasping V's hand in her own. "Are *you* alright?" she asked, her concern clear in the tilt of her head and the thin line of her lips.

V let out a huff of breath halfway between a laugh and a sob. "No," she said truthfully, squeezing Riyah's hand. "But I'm a hell of a lot better now."

"I hate to break up this tender reunion," Mouse interjected, sounding anything but sorry, "but I should remind you that once your friends find a ship, they won't wait forever."

"Ship?" Riyah repeated, not entirely following the plot.

V sighed and started to explain, condensing the drama of the last few days into a rough outline. That V was a weapon and her mother a monster. That the Senate had built a brainwashed army of Anomalies. That the Echelon wasn't the only one of Earth's starfaring vessels to survive. And that her newfound friends were securing a ship to fly them all to safety.

"Unless I want to end up leading an army of second children into battle," V concluded, "it's in my best interest to leave. All of our best interests, really. There's no place for us here – not anymore. Come on. We have to hurry."

V helped her friend up, and the two stood face to face, each with wildly different expressions. It wasn't until that instant that it struck her, but she should have known it all along. The look on Riyah's face said it all.

"I can't go with you," she said in the smallest voice. The words cracked V's heart straight through the center.

"But…it's too dangerous," V pleaded. "The Senate will see you as a threat. You know too much now. You'd be safer with us, away from it all."

"I know," her friend replied, pulling V into a soft, familiar hug. "But it doesn't change a thing. My place is here, with my family. You, on the other hand, were always meant for

323

something bigger. So go. Find your destiny. Be free."

V wanted to protest, to say a million things, but not a single word came to mind.

Instead, Riyah said it for her. "I love you and I always will. You're my sister – by choice if not by blood – and I'll never be able to thank you enough for what you've done."

V nodded, swallowing all but the most insistent words. "I love you, too."

As if to emphasize the emotion, the ground beneath their feet began to rumble and the sound of distant explosions drifted to their ears. An eerie silence descended before the alarms blared to life and all hell broke loose.

"Shit!" Mouse shouted. "They've set off our traps. Our time is up. Say your goodbyes and let's get out of here."

"Are you strong enough?" V asked, shelving the sentiment and guiding Riyah to the door. "Because if you're gonna go, now's your chance. They're after us, not you. And with their systems down, they won't be able to spot you. If you head away from us, along the outskirts, you should be able to make it out of here unseen."

"Don't you dare underestimate me, V," Riyah responded with a hint of her usual fire. "I've got this."

"I'm sure you do," V said with a smile. "But just in case, take this." She handed Riyah her gun, with the safety off and the setting turned well beyond stun. The woman took it with surprising strength.

"Take care," V whispered, letting her heart out in that whoosh of breath.

"We will," she promised. "Although we'll always be waiting for you. Come back to us if you can."

"I will," V promised in return.

Lyra chose that moment to crash back onto her cam, startling V out of the saccharine moment.

"We've got a ship and we're ready to go. I've sent you the coordinates. The countdown is set for 15 minutes. Get your assess on board or we're leaving without you."

By the time V finished scanning the message, Riyah was gone and she was alone with Mouse once more. She didn't have time to dwell on the sudden sadness.

"Let's get Solamine," she said, gesturing for Mouse to lead the way. "We've got a ship to catch."

Mouse didn't need to be told twice. Before V even had time to draw her blade, he'd taken off, gun raised and eyes on guard.

It wasn't far, but the halls and corridors were filling by the second, pulsing with an ever-present threat. V took down two Guards without trouble – and a third who put up a fight – but the sounds of their struggles were drowned by the sirens. Mouse set more mines to slow their foes, hoping to scrounge enough time to get Solamine and go.

When they arrived outside the designated door, Mouse waved his card before it, but it didn't take the bait. V repeated the movement only to find that their access had been blocked, adding one more obstacle to their uphill climb.

With a manic laugh – half panic, half glee – Mouse hefted the gun, trained it on the handle, and fired. The close-range blast knocked him back, laying him flat out on the floor, but it did the trick. The door shattered, bursting into splinters that V cleared in a matter of seconds.

Unlike the last room, this one was small, more a solitary

cell than a storeroom. Its lone inhabitant sat in a corner, hugging his knees to his chest. When he saw V, however, his whole countenance changed.

"Ora?" he asked again, sounding so young. "Ora, what's happening?"

"Just go along with it," Mouse pleaded, suddenly by her side. "Help me get him out of here."

It pulled at V's heartstrings to nod, to say the words and watch the old man's face transform.

"Don't worry, Dad. I'm here. I've come to take you home."

The man rose without help and tottered to her side, placing one gnarled hand on her cheek. The move was so tender, so different from Celeste's calculated displays, that it brought a tear to V's eye.

"My darling daughter. How I've missed you."

The words whipped up a swell of emotion that threatened to capsize her heart and leave it in a puddle at her feet. She wanted to swim in that moment, to float forever on that feeling, but she knew they didn't have the time. So she gently grasped the man's hand and brought it to her side, leading him toward the door.

"It'll be alright, gramps," Mouse said as they stepped out. "We're almost there. Just a few more minutes and we'll finally be free."

Solamine turned his head toward the sound, his gaze meeting Mouse's. Then he smiled, with recognition crinkling the skin around his soft brown eyes.

"Mouse," he whispered tenderly, cupping his grandson's cheek. "It's you."

Mouse's mouth opened and closed as he choked on

emotion, unsure if he should laugh or cry.

"Yeah, grandpa," he finally said, placing one hand atop Solamine's. "It's me."

The heartwarming sight was broken in an instant as Celeste careened around the corner, gun at the ready. Seconds ticked by as if trapped in syrup, unfolding in slow motion.

A shouted protest. A shot. An old man stepping, arms outstretched, to shield the others.

The gun was set to stun, but the sound his head made as it cracked against the tiles left no room for doubt. Solamine was dead.

Chapter 29

"N<small>OOOO!</small>"

The sound that tore from Mouse's throat could only be described as anguish. It was a million heartbreaks crammed into the space of a second and given a voice. It was torture – and V couldn't take it.

As Mouse crouched to cup his grandfather's head, V charged, like a bull seeing nothing but red. Celeste dodged the unfocused attack, spinning to knock V's head back with the butt of her gun. V crumpled as color drained from the world, its edges turning gray.

"Why are you resisting this?" Celeste screamed as she dealt a kick to V's stomach, stealing the air from her lungs. "You can never outrun your fate. You were built to save us, to put an end to our struggles and set us free!"

"I was built to kill," V cried as she tried to stand. "You created me to start a war."

"So what?" Celeste asked, stunning her with another

swipe of the gun. "War is what we do, what we've always done. It's in our nature to fight, to survive. It's a human imperative."

"It's a death sentence," V spat back, spitting blood in the process. "You'll send those kids to be slaughtered and destroy the Echelon in the process. Yet you're all too happy to set it on fire and watch as it burns."

"You think you've got it all figured out, that you're some kind of savior?" Celeste countered, grabbing a fistful of hair and jerking V's head back. "Let me fill you in on a secret. This ship is failing. Those kids will die either way. You're not saving anyone. You're damning us all. Do you really want that? Do you?!"

V couldn't answer. For the first time since she'd found out what she was, she couldn't see a clear path forward. All routes were marred by death and muddled with blood. Their world was set to explode, and she was the catalyst.

"Seven minutes and counting!" a sudden message read, scrolling across her cam. "Would you hurry up and hit her already?!"

Lyra was tactful as always, but it did the trick, snapping V out of her moral dilemmas and dropping her back into combat. At least this was something she could do.

V reached up to where her mother's hand was tangled in her hair. Targeting the woman's pinkie, she twisted, feeling a snap as her grip gave way. Celeste let loose a high-pitched scream – part pain, part fury – dropping the gun in her panic.

With the bond between them broken, V sprang to her feet, ignoring the sudden tilt as the floor spun. She surged forward, her hands seeking Celeste's neck and her knee thrusting toward her gut.

V squeezed the woman's throat, her fingertips sinking into skin as she let the fire consume her. V yearned to let it burn away her burdens, to let it singe her stinging nerves until nothing could hurt her. Except that wasn't who she was. It was who they wanted her to be.

V loosened her grip ever so slightly, giving Celeste the cue she needed to bring her arms up and break free. V blocked a blow to the face but was caught with a kick in the gut that sent her reeling. She collided with the wall but never stopped, using its surface as a springboard to launch herself back into the fray.

She came at Celeste with a swipe across the chest, suddenly holding her dagger. V couldn't remember drawing it, but it nestled against her palm as if it had always been there. The strike met its target but tore uselessly at cloth, exposing a tactical vest beneath.

Celeste took her turn, seizing on V's second of surprise to lunge for the gun. V's arm acted of its own accord, swinging toward the small of the woman's back. This time, no armor stood between the dagger and its mark, and it slashed through skin with satisfying ease.

Celeste cried out and collapsed, falling forward. V grabbed the gun and aimed, with Celeste's head clearly in her sights, but for some reason she couldn't bring herself to shoot. An invisible hand warred with her own, forcing it off the trigger and pulling her back from the brink.

V longed to kill this woman, to bring an end to her games, but what good would that do? Another senator would just take her place, continuing the campaign, and V would be

330

left with the lingering guilt of taking another life.

When Celeste realized that she wasn't about to die, she smiled – then started to laugh.

"You can't do it, can you?" she asked, almost taunting. "It's because you're weak. You've always been weak. It's what made you the perfect little lab rat, so easy to control. Your mind is soft and malleable. You were made to obey. You are *ours,* and nothing will ever change that."

That was the wrong thing to say. While V had her qualms about killing the woman, she wasn't against causing a little pain. V returned her finger to the trigger, and this time nothing stopped her.

The wave of force shattered Celeste's leg, and the woman's screams broke the scene into jagged shards.

"You will pay for this!" she shouted through howls of pain. "Believe me: We will make you pay!"

"You took the words right out of my mouth, *mom,*" V said evenly. With a smirk, she slammed the butt of the gun into Celeste's head, rendering the woman unconscious.

V turned to find Mouse seated on the ground beside Solamine, cradling the man in his arms. He was pleading to any god who would listen, but the man remained immobile. V could barely bring herself to interrupt, but the countdown in her head was insistent.

"Come on, Mouse," she pleaded, tugging on his shoulder. "We have to go."

Mouse looked up with shining eyes, staring at V. She watched as the grief in his gaze hardened, curdling into rage. With a cry, he sprang to his feet and hurled himself forward, pinning her against the wall.

"This is your fault!" he shouted, the anguish stealing the edge off his words. "This is all your fault. None of this would have happened without you."

"I know," was all V could think to say. "I'm sorry."

And she was. She was sorry for every heartache that had trailed in her wake, every life that had crumbled because of her quest. She felt them burrow beneath her chest, making a home in her soul, and she knew that she could never shake them. Still, she had to keep moving.

"I hate you," Mouse said without malice – but meaning it nonetheless.

"I know," V said again, "but we have to go."

A series of low explosions punctuated her words and emphasized the urgency. The mines were their cue to move, their hint that someone was on their trail. Or, more likely, a small army of someones.

Mouse's scowl didn't change, but he relaxed his grip, letting V off the wall. Then he nodded, turning his back on her as he began to run.

"Four minutes!"

V's muttered "shit" barely registered above the blaring alarms. They weren't going to make it. Lyra's directions led them out of the Senate's tunnels, then into the maze that lurked beneath the streets. They would need to skirt the engines and sneak into the docking bays, all without being seen – or shot. And they didn't have the time.

V's legs worked faster than she knew they could, and her side ached with the effort. A set of doors loomed within view, and V raised her gun, blasting them off their hinges.

Somehow, they surfaced at street level, breaking free

from their enemy's den. V breathed in her first full breath in hours, raking in the cool night air. Mouse didn't pause, barreling toward the entrance that would take them to the Echelon's core, but V stopped on a dime, an idea emerging through the surge of adrenaline.

"What the hell are you doing?" Mouse shouted back, enraged at her general existence.

V summoned the words but couldn't get them out, so she simply showed him. Darting to a nearby bike, she flipped the cover and pushed aside the wires, inputting the proper pattern. Its velvety purr was delicious, seeping into V's soul as she jumped astride it. She toggled the controls, bringing it to a hover, and motioned for Mouse to join her.

"You're out of your mind," Mouse muttered, shaking his head – but hopping on behind her, nonetheless.

Together, they careened toward the sturdy iron gate that stood between them and the tunnels, crashing through with a dissonant bang. The impact was jarring, forcing them forward, but they both managed to keep their hold.

The stairs beyond were a different matter, but V wasn't stopping. The bike beneath them shook as they plunged down the steps, diving deeper and deeper. By the time they reached solid ground, they were bruised and shaking, unable to scream or even speak but unwilling to slow.

Mouse held on for dear life, constricting her core until her breaths came out in shallow puffs. The bike's gentle hum turned savage as V slammed into high gear, pushing their speed well past reckless. Tears streamed down her face as she strained to see, steering into every curve of the treacherous track.

Footsteps and shouts emerged from the tunnels as Guards sprang from the woodwork to strike. Waves of force chased them as shots were fired, but V swerved, expertly dodging the blasts. The ceiling crumbled and walls collapsed as errant blows claimed chunks of concrete, but it only spurred V on.

"1 minute."

The reminder was unhelpful. In fact, it stole a slice of V's focus, nearly sending her into a wall. She course-corrected at the last second, turning a corner so tightly that the bike nearly toppled. Skittering to a halt, she took in the scene before her.

They were close – but not close enough.

A line of Guards stood between them and the docking bay, guns raised. Beyond them was a ship, gleaming and silver and surrounded by soldiers. They pelted its skin with rays of force, but its shields were up, blocking their attempts to break through.

There was no way V could make it. They were outnumbered, outgunned, outmatched. They were sitting ducks.

"Trust us," Lyra typed.

Those two words asked far too much.

V didn't think. If she had, she would have stopped, would have turned around and fled, but instead she revved the engine, released the brake, and raced toward the wall of men.

Their surprise was evident. Some faltered, some looked toward their leader, some raised their guns and fired.

V felt the sting of force bite one arm, ripping it out of its socket. She grunted as it fell to her lap, lifeless from the shoulder down, but she still didn't slow. Steering with one hand, she tore through the tunnel, steadily increasing her speed.

The line of soldiers stood their ground, daring her to do it. So she did.

At the last second, the string of Guards snapped, peeling apart to reveal a gap just big enough for a bike. V thundered through, the roar of the engine mingling with the purr of the ship to encase the chamber in sound.

There was still no ramp, no door or entrance, but V did as she was told and trusted. Mouse, however, squeaked his displeasure and tightened his grip on her waist. Together, they hurtled forward, heading straight for a silver wall.

Just when V started to think that her trust had been misplaced, a crack appeared in the hull, rapidly widening to a ramp. V took a breath, compressed herself against the bike, and flew up the incline, barely clearing her head through the narrow gap, which quickly closed behind her.

She braked instantly, spilling forward into a pile at Fynn's feet. The bike continued on, crashing into a set of seats near the front of the ship and lodging itself between them. Mouse, meanwhile, tucked into a ball and rolled off to one side, screaming through it all.

"Prepare for takeoff!" Lyra commanded, already at the controls.

With the flick of a switch, the ship shuddered then rose into the air. V felt a strange pull as the ship's pressure stabilized and her ears popped. The sound of gunfire intensified as the thrusters sprang to life, growling in pleasure as they prepared for the launch.

Without another word, Lyra flicked a second switch,

propelling the vessel forward. The force of it sent Fynn flying, and he landed with a thump on top of V.

The momentum rendered V mute, and she tried to stop her insides from spinning. Fynn's weight atop her was firm but not unpleasant. His scent was in her nostrils – and his head buried in her neck – threatening to pull her back in time. She clung to him as he clung to her, each waiting for their worlds to settle.

As soon as her stomach caught up with the rest of her body, V leapt to her feet and rushed to the rear of the ship. Two small windows bordered the sealed ramp, looking back toward the Echelon. V plastered herself against one, her nose nearly touching the glass as she strained to see into the quickly shrinking ship.

Aside from static pictures, V had never seen the Echelon from outside. Its magnitude was astounding. Its domed crown glittered in the light of a thousand stars, and the ship itself stretched back farther than she could see. Buildings grew and branched from its surface like silver trees, and streets crisscrossed its landscape like ugly black scars. The ship's dark belly blended into the surrounding sky, dipping low and disappearing out of sight.

V trained her attention on the docking bay, tracing the outlines of tiny figures as they rushed to board their ships. Unease hardened in her chest as they abandoned their guns and prepared to set off in pursuit.

"Hey Lyra?" she said, her voice unsteady. "Can this thing go any faster? I think we're about to have company."

Lyra looked back from her position at the helm, giving V an exasperating smirk. "Don't worry," she stated, all confidence and conviction. "I took care of it."

Unsurprisingly, V's unease didn't dissipate. "What do you mean you took care of it? What, exactly, did you do?"

Lyra turned back around to concentrate on setting their course. "I infected the bay with a little bug," she shouted. "They'll find their way through it in time, but for now, they won't be following us. And they won't be tracking us, either. Consider it a clean getaway."

They were safe. The relief was sudden and strong, sweeping through V in a rush that cooled her heated skin. The adrenaline pounding through her heart eased, allowing her to rake in a full, deep breath. The air around her was stale and recycled, yet it was still the sweetest thing she'd ever tasted.

She allowed her eyes to drift closed, blocking out the world. A gentle sigh escaped her lips, releasing the tension that curled around her muscles in tight knots and the anxiety that consumed her mind. For the moment, she was free, and the bittersweet beauty of it settled over her in a blanket of calm.

"I'm glad you made it," came a deep voice beside her, causing her to turn.

"So am I," V replied, looking up at Fynn. "Thanks for getting me out of there."

Fynn shrugged. He was about to speak when Mouse popped up and interjected.

"They did nothing! I'm the one who saved your sorry ass. But you can keep your thanks and shove it."

"Shut up, Mouse," they said in unison, then smiled a tentative smile. It was a shy thing, a new thing, a brave thing. It was the first step into an unknown future.

V felt light, almost buoyant – then she looked down to see her feet floating several inches above the ground.

"Uh…Lyra?" she said with some concern as her body began tilting toward the ceiling.

"Sorry!" the woman shouted before flipping on the gravity and pulling V back down. "These Echelon ships are old-school. It might take a minute to get used to. It seems sturdy enough, though, so we should make it to the Alasia in one piece."

The mention of their sister ship was sobering, centering V in the here and now. The reality of her situation – and the pain in her arm – grounded her like a rock tied around her ankle, holding her down. She was hurtling through space with relative strangers at her side, hoping their future held something better than what they'd left behind. The past hour imprinted itself on her soul, branding her with questions.

Who was she, beyond what they'd made her? What was she capable of? And what would happen to the Echelon without her?

V thought about Riyah, Solamine, Celeste, about everything she'd lost and found. About everything she'd done – and everything still left to do. Her heart ached in a thousand different ways, but she couldn't deny the hope blossoming beneath it. The future swirled around her, intangible and unpredictable yet full of possibilities.

V shuffled to the front of the ship, settling herself in the seat beside Lyra and finally raising her gaze. The sight outside left her breathless.

The boundless vista of space fanned out in every direction. V had never seen it so clearly. Stars dusted the sky in a smattering of cosmic freckles, while brilliant swirls of violet danced around them. Planets floated beside moons and meteors, held aloft by invisible hands. In the distance, nebulae pulsed and galaxies spun and constellations conveyed stories through their stars.

The beauty of it all brought to mind a snippet of song, and V smiled.

When this world passes soundlessly
Without a thought of destiny
A shadow on a waveless sea
You'll sail away with me
Sail away with me, my love, come sail away with me
Sail away, sail away, for tonight we'll all be free

AUTHOR'S NOTE
& Acknowledgments

Thank you for taking a chance on *Violet Skies*, for letting this book and these characters into your hearts and lives. For me, they aren't just words on a page. They're a part of me, and I feel lucky to be able to share that part with you.

I have to admit that being an indie author isn't easy. In fact, it's grueling, expensive, and emotionally taxing. It's also the best thing I've ever done.

It's a daily struggle to convince someone to take a chance on a book like this. Most people only read what they see on store shelves and bestseller lists, the books which publishers can afford to put millions behind. It may come as a shock, but I do not have millions. What I do have is a passion for words and a talent for putting them together.

Thank you for supporting my work in your own small way. Every new reader, every paperback sale or page read on Kindle brightens my day and makes this work feel worthwhile.

Thank you to my husband, Robert, for being my perpetual alpha reader and for answering my never-ending questions on computers, robotics, and words I can't seem to remember. (And a shoutout to Google for answering everything else!)

My gratitude also goes out to my beta readers – Kayla Suhm, Steve Johnson, Kinnon Schreiber, and Greg Poppy. Your feedback, suggestions, and support have been invaluable and have helped shape this book into something I'm proud to publish. Finally, thank you to Wes Cathon (Instagram @wessuri) for the amazing cover artwork!

If you're looking for an easy (and free!) way to support your new favorite indie author, consider leaving a star rating or a review on Amazon or Goodreads. Your words and opinions can help countless more readers discover the magic inside these pages.

If you've loved *Violet Skies*, then good news! The adventure will continue over the course of two more books. In the meantime, why not travel to a different dystopian world – and discover some equally colorful characters – in my *Burn this City* trilogy.

Looking to show your love in a different way? We've got Glass Fish Publishing and book-related merch available for purchase at *glassfishpublishing.com*. You can also follow us on Instagram and TikTok or like us on Facebook for all the latest news, including updates on the next book in the *Violet Skies* series!

ABOUT THE AUTHOR

Brenda Poppy has spent more than a decade writing and editing for publications across the country, as well as lending her writing and graphic design talents to companies to help them craft their brands. With a degree in journalism and sociology from Marquette University, she loves to seek out unique stories and capture them for others to enjoy. When not writing, the Milwaukee native can be found acting in local theater, spending time with her adorable corgi, Darcy, or traveling around the world with her husband in search of craft cocktails, good food, and inspiration for her next novel.

Connect with Glass Fish Publishing on Instagram, TikTok, and Facebook!

glassfishpublishing.com